GREAT AGAIN

BILL DAY

Library of Congress Cataloging-in-Publication Data has been applied for.

ISBNs: 979-8-9907824-0-2 (paperback),

979-8-9907824-1-9 (ebook)

Printed in the United States of America

For Sweet Caroline

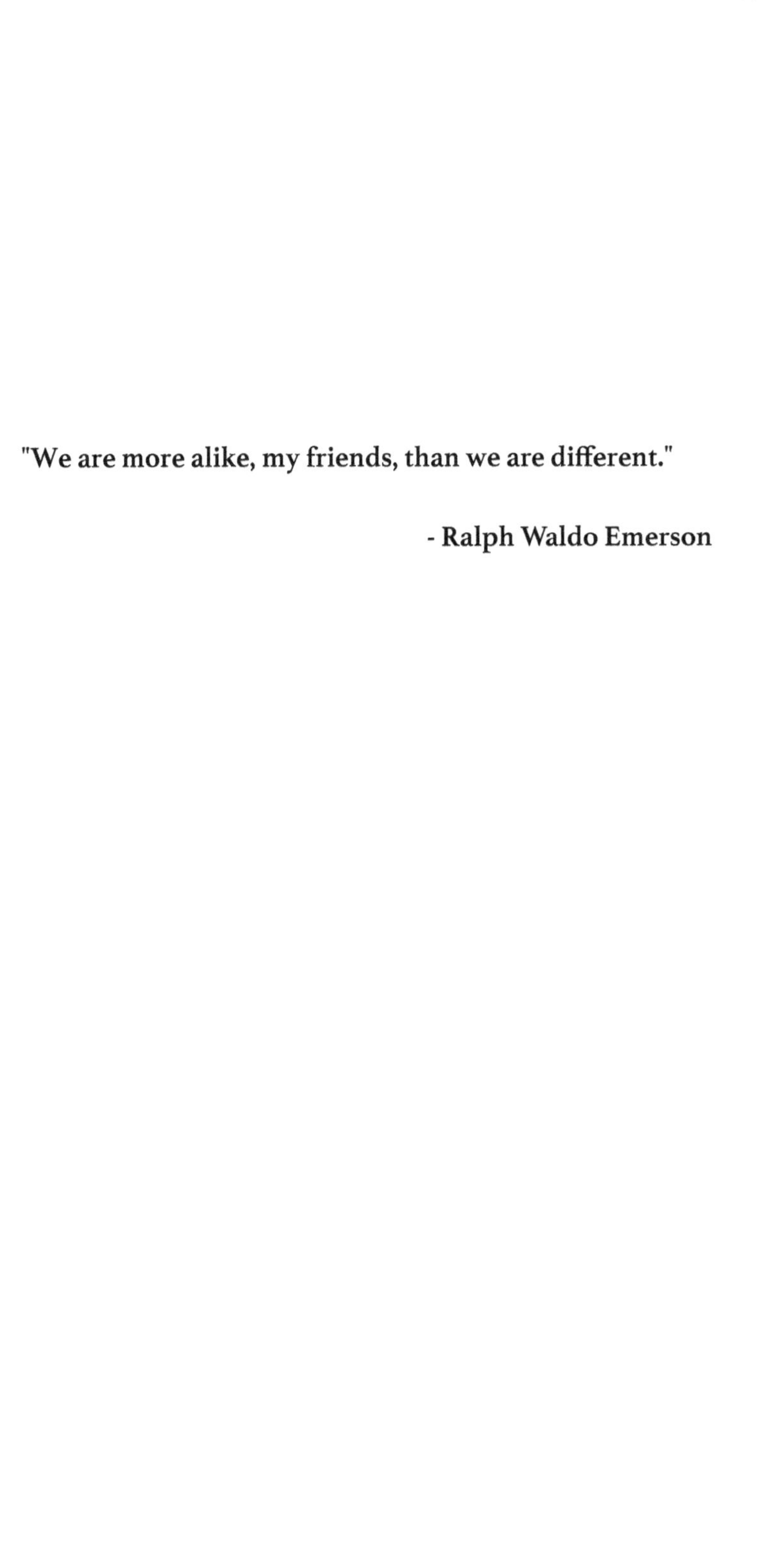

"We are more alike, my friends, than we are different."

- Ralph Waldo Emerson

PART I

1

JACK IN A HOLE

"Everybody's gangster until they run out of money," Fitzy says with a wry Irish smile from behind his desk.

From the client seat, Jack O'Mally stares back at him with anger. "What the hell does that mean?"

Fitzy realizes his mistake. For a moment, he forgot who he was talking to. Even when Jack was the "Irish Bulldog" on the wrestling team in high school, he didn't have much cool. He was a straight arrow who worked as a lifeguard in the summer and shoveled snow in the winter. Unlike most other kids back then, Jack was more attracted to military programs like the ROTC than growing his hair and starting a band. And when it came to appreciating slang, he had a blind spot the size of the Empire State Building. Now, on the doorstep of his golden years, Jack is still Jack. Twenty years in the Marines couldn't change that.

"It is just an expression my kids use," Fitzy smiles. "The point I'm trying to make is that this accident has put you in a place where you have to make some serious changes."

Jack looks around the office. The high-end furnishings,

expensive artwork, and personal photos from exotic fishing trips make clear his money man has done well—maybe too well. "How about we start by lowering your financial advice fees?"

Fitzy smiles like an old friend. "Good one. Now, let's talk about the house. If we sell that and you find a nice, comfy condo somewhere, you could come out with an affordable place to live and a bag of cash. You could even keep your boat."

Jack doesn't like the sound of that. "What do you say we just hold tight until I get back to work."

Fitzy groans with frustration. "Jack, c'mon. You know that isn't happening. They eliminated your position. And who else is going to hire you at your age? Unless you want to be a school crossing guard."

Jack shakes his head. "Bastards. I brought in over a half-billion dollars worth of business, and the second I'm a liability, knife right in my back."

"Yeah, I know," Fitzy says softly. "But your old job isn't going to fix what you've got going on here. You've been living beyond your means for a long time, and well, the chickens have finally come home to roost. It's time to move on. Now look, you're living in a four-bedroom house by yourself."

"Four bedrooms and a guest house," Jack responds sharply.

Fitzy moves on to his next point. "Camille remarried long ago, so she isn't coming back. When was the last time you talked to your daughter?"

"Last Christmas."

"You sure that wasn't Christmas two years ago?"

Jack looks at the floor. "Maybe."

Fitzy suddenly feels like he is getting through to Jack. "At this point, I think it would be safe to say you don't need the space. And if you want to know the truth, the place is starting to look like it's seen better days. But, on the other hand, the market is up right now, so take the money and run."

Jack looks at the floor. It's hard to imagine leaving his home. How did it come to this? "Freak'n illegals," he murmurs.

Fitzy frowns. Here comes the blame game. "Yeah, I know what you mean, but they didn't make you get up on the roof and try to clean the gutters yourself. That was a mistake."

"It's not that I didn't try to find somebody to do it," Jack says. But all these outfits are the same. White guys show up to do the estimate, but when it comes to doing the work, some guy named Jose shows up with a bunch of guys that don't speak two words of English between them."

Fitzy reaches into his desk for a card. "I know, but hey, it isn't like these businesses don't try to find Americans to do the job. They can't find anybody."

"Bull shit," Jack barks. "They just don't want to pay. So they pick up these illegals for nothing and make out like bandits. If the politicians would stop playing games and get serious about stopping illegals at the border, we wouldn't have this problem."

"Maybe," Fitzy absently says as he searches the desk drawer. He's seen Jack up on this soapbox before. No big deal.

"Dumb asses in Washington don't seem to understand," Jack rambles on. "If you don't have a border, you don't have a country!"

Fitzy finds the card and pushes it across the table. "This is an excellent real estate agent I know. Give her a call and see what she says. That is all I'm asking."

"I'm not sure you have my best interest in mind here," Jack grunts as he slowly stands up using a cane. In the tumble he took off the roof, he broke his back. Doctors fuzed his broken vertebrae as best they could, but Jack has a long way to go before he can play golf again. "You collecting a kickback from this gal?"

A question like that would end any other relationship. But anyone who knows Jack well, as Fitzy does, knows there is a good heart underneath all that Patton-like bravado. The old bulldog also possesses an independent mind, capable of momentary bouts of wisdom. Fitzy leans back in his chair and looks Jack in the eye. He could laugh it off, but he knows that isn't how it's played with the old jarhead. "Hey Jack, screw you."

Jack seems satisfied. "First real thing you've said since I got here. Same to you and your real estate girlfriend."

"Hey, you lost the crutches finally," Fitzy says.

"Yep. My physical therapy is up, but I got a good trainer over at the health club."

"Don't try to go too fast," Fitzy says with genuine concern.

"That's what she said," Jack jokes as he heads for the door.

Fitzy stands up. "Get any real estate agent you want, but do it, Jack. You're in a hole here. You remember the first rule of holes in the military, don't you? If you're in one, don't keep digging."

Jack seems offended. "Hey, I taught you that."

It's a sunny day for Jack's drive back home. Despite being less than 40 minutes south of New York City, this area of New Jersey has a rural feel to it. The roads are thin two-lane affairs that wind through tall Red Oak, Maple, Dogwoods, and Spruce. Lining the asphalt are big, expensive homes, some with enough ground for horses. The way sunlight sparkles through the trees and illuminates the roads with patterns of light makes the whole place feel like something removed, protected, and special—especially now with the orange and reddish colors of fall.

Normally, Jack enjoys this drive, like he has for most of his life—but not today. Today, he is overwhelmed with a sinking feeling that his money man, Fitzy, is right. This retired Lieutenant Colonel is out of options, and it is time to move on. But what Fitzy doesn't understand is this isn't just a case of putting up a for sale sign and walking away with a pile of money. The house Fitzy wants him to sell is the cornerstone of three generations of Jack's family. And what makes the situation worse is knowing how hard he worked to preserve it. He did everything in his power to keep the place as it was when his father gave it to him, but no matter how much he tried, it was just one thing after another that dented his life and his home. With each passing year, the modern diversifying world kept pressing in on him — kind of like the aggressive delivery van in his rearview mirror.

The black delivery driver can't pass Jack because of the double yellow centerline, so he closes in with a clear message, "Hurry up!" When Jack feels the driver has crossed the line into rudeness, he lets off the accelerator and slows down. "Read the bumper sticker," he yells into the mirror. On the back of Jack's Caddy is a sticker with large print. "THE CLOSER YOU GET, THE SLOWER I GO."

The van closes in. Jack ducks his head a bit to see the driver better. "Okay, have it your way, bro!" Jack cuts his speed even more. The van driver starts honking and flashing his high beams, but Jack slows to an absolute crawl. It pushes the van driver over the edge. The van crosses the double yellow and passes Jack with his horn blaring. "You're breaking the law, dumbass," Jack scolds.

Once the van clears Jack's car, it swings hard back to the right but doesn't keep going. Instead, the driver slams the brakes and forces Jack to stop behind him. The driver jumps out, looking very angry. Jack responds by reaching for his police security nightstick in the door's side pocket. He also produces a pro-level walkie-talkie from the center console storage box and pushes the button to transmit. "Any unit," he says professionally. "Code red, Barnesdale Road in front of Sutton Stables. Any unit. Code red."

The black driver heads for Jack's car, already yelling. "What is your problem, man? What is your problem?"

Jack lowers his window with one hand while gripping the nightstick with the other. The driver gets close.

"Oh, a grandpa," the driver says upon seeing his fellow road-rager is a senior. "You want to mess with me, Pops? Really?"

Jack isn't the kind of guy who can be intimidated regardless of age or medical condition. "You like crawling up people's asses? Because you sure seem interested in crawling up mine."

"Who the hell are you to tell me how to drive?"

"I'm captain of the neighborhood watch. We put signs on the side of the road that read '35 means 35.' Did you happen to notice them?"

"What kind of bullshit is that, man? You see *that* sign? It says, 'share' the damn road!"

"That's for bicycles." Jack moves the nightstick to make it more visible.

The driver lets out a sarcastic snort when he sees the nightstick. "Is that what you want? Huh? Bring it on!"

Without hesitation, Jack opens the driver's door and starts to get out. But with just one foot on the pavement, a sudden sharp pain in the back freezes him in place. "Shit. Damn it!"

The van driver suddenly realizes how feeble Jack is. "Man, are you kidding me?"

"I'm stuck!" Jack grimaces.

"Man, get back in the car. What the hell do you think you are doing?"

"Lift that leg up," Jack commands.

"What?"

"I can't get back in unless you lift that leg."

The driver shakes his head. "Shit. I don't believe this."

The driver dips down and tries to get Jack's leg up, and Jack suddenly cries bloody murder. "Stop!" The driver stops but doesn't let go. He doesn't know what to do.

Out of the blue, a late-model pickup truck with a big American flag sticking up from the middle of the cargo bed slides to a halt behind Jack's car. Frank, an old but huge white guy with a smashed nose and a red baseball cap, is behind the wheel. Seeing the black guy holding Jack, he grabs his nightstick and jumps out of the car. "Hey!" he yells as he charges toward Jack's car.

Seeing this huge guy charging forward with a baton, the van driver lets go of Jack and backs away quickly. "Hold on, man! Hold on!"

"You hold on!" Frank yells at the driver. "Jack, you alright? This guy robbing you or what?"

"No, no. He was tailgating me. Now I've got my back twisted."

Frank looks at the driver and then at the delivery van. "When are you assholes gonna learn this isn't a NASCAR race track through here?"

"Look man," the van driver says. "I wasn't going fast. This dude was just messing with me."

Frank's weathered face turns deep red with anger. "You think that gives you the right to drive like an idiot?"

"Okay," the driver says, sounding intimidated, "I'm sorry for the mix-up, but I got priority packages that need deliver'n. I have to get going."

"You're not going anywhere till I get some ID."

"What? You ain't the police."

"Nope, but I'm part of the Neighborhood Watch. Trust me. You don't want to mess with us. Voted number one in the nation, thanks to Jack here."

"They vote for that shit?"

"Uh-huh." Frank then pulls out a notepad and writes down the van's license plate. "Let me see your driver's license."

"No, you got no right!"

Frank starts to move in on the driver.

"It's alright, Frank. Let him go," Jack says, still trying to get his leg back in the car. "I think he gets the point. Help me with this leg."

Frank slowly backs down according to Jack's orders. The van driver turns back to his van and angrily mumbles to himself as he gets into his seat. "They ain't no neighborhood watch. They're white militia dudes. Brother can get his ass shot just for driving through here."

Back at the car, Frank helps Jack get his leg back in. "You wanna call this one in to the police?" Frank asks.

"Nah," Jack grunts. "I don't want them to see me like this. I'm not ready for prime time yet."

"You've come a long way from a few months ago," Frank says seriously, then smiles and giggles. "You're still the most badass road rager in town!"

Jack shakes his head. "Not easy, this getting back on your feet thing."

Frank feels sorry for his old friend and tries to cheer him up. "Don't worry, ole buddy. You're still as sharp as the day they canned you."

Jack grins. "I wish it were true, but I'm not feeling it today."

Frank nods, still trying to cheer Jack up. "We may be old and white, but it's still our world, right Jack?"

Jack smiles. "So you say."

"The only thing getting replaced around here," Frank says, "are my old steel belted radials at forty thousand miles, and they haven't even hit twenty yet."

When Jack is out traveling and people ask where he lives, he first tells them the name of his town, Atlantic Highlands. Then, when they inevitably shake their heads, having never heard of this place, Jack follows up with "Northern tip of the Jersey Shore." That usually brings a smile to their faces but for the wrong reasons. In their minds, they are thinking of TV shows like *Jersey Shore*, so Jack paints a bigger picture to get their mental maps better situated.

When the cruise ships leave New York City, they head south down the Hudson River into Upper New York Bay, where they cruise past Ellis Island, the Statue of Liberty, and Governors Island. Then, they pass under the Verrazano Narrows Bridge into Lower New York Bay and turn left in front of Coney Island before slipping into the Atlantic Ocean. But if the ship doesn't make that left and proceeds straight, it will pass into Raritan Bay and eventually hit land just about where the township of Atlantic Highlands is located.

The downtown area is pretty straightforward for this part of New Jersey. It's unpretentious and has just one main commercial street with a few decent restaurants. However, the harbor marina is well developed, with an annual fireworks show on the Fourth of July. The surrounding upscale homes are up off the water on a series of hills that offer the highest elevations along the Eastern Seaboard south of Maine. For those lucky enough to be in the first row of homes, the view of the New York City skyline is nothing short of spectacular. Being this close to the Big Apple in a town with less than five thousand people is the best of both worlds. The residents are almost exclusively white.

The colonial house with plantation shutters that Jack calls home is behind the row of homes with New York City views. Nevertheless, it boasts a favorable angle of the bay and, with a keen eye, the Statue of Liberty and Ellis Island. The property encompasses approximately an acre of land, featuring a flagpole proudly displaying the stars and stripes. The driveway is connected to an indoor two-car garage with a workbench and well-organized utility cabinets.

While the front yard is suitable by community standards, the trees and shrubs have lost their once-meticulously trimmed appearance. The house bears signs of neglect and could be aptly described as "outdated." The paint, once vibrant, has dulled and exhibits signs of peeling. The crown of the roof is littered with fallen branches. The once-proud shutters are now stained with a tint of green mold. The backyard showcases a pool situated in front of a small guest house, which also mirrors the declining state of the front yard.

Inside, the house has four bedrooms and four and a half bathrooms. It has a large living room with a stand-alone dining room separated by a traditionally large kitchen.

Descending into the main house's basement, one discovers a game room from a bygone era. An antiquated and dusty card table stands in the middle, with well-worn chairs still surrounding it. In this room, Jack can almost hear the echoes of his grandfather and the old man's Irish friends, their voices and laughter as they played dominoes and sang drinking songs like "The Old Dun Cow."

And there was Brown, upside down
Lapping up the whiskey off the floor
"Booze, booze," the firemen cried
As they came knocking at the door
Don't let them in till it's all mopped up!
And we all got blue-blind drunk
when the Old Dun Cow caught fire.

Jack's grandfather, James O'Mally, built this house. Old "Pop," as Jack learned to call him, was the first person in his family to move to America from Ireland. Like many Irish, he ended up in the tenements of New York and struggled just to survive. But James was a tough and highly energetic young man straight out of the pages of a "rags to riches" Horatio Algier story. Through hard work and perseverance, he made enough money to escape the city's crime-filled, gang-controlled streets in the 1920s for the sanctuary of Atlantic Highlands, a quaint little retreat town built and dominated by Methodists. Here, he started a successful ice business and used that to propel him into home construction. He built many of the homes in the area, including the one where both his son, Sean, and grandson, Jack, were born. The same one that Jack still lives in today —alone.

Jack's favorite place in the house has always been his study, which has always been his man cave and his retreat. No place feels like home more than this room. He likes to call it his "home home." On one side is a bookshelf filled beyond capacity with fiction and nonfiction on a wide range of topics. Next to that is an enormous mahogany desk that serves as HQ for his Neighborhood Watch operation. There is a tall schedule board and a bulletin board filled with incident reports. On the desk are extra walkie-talkie handsets standing in their chargers. The other side of the room is dominated by an old stuffed chair that looks like it came with the original house. It's big with fat arms—fat enough to rest a dinner plate or a book on, depending on the mood or the time of day. The chair faces a wall filled with military memorabilia, including pictures of famous American generals like Patton, MacArthur, and Schwarzkopf. There are crossed swords, weapons, photos from the battlefield, and honor plaques, including a purple heart. In the center of it all is a headshot of George Washington, peering out quietly with a serene and wise expression. Below Washington is a table occupied by a family photo collection. They include his grandparents, parents, siblings, and two children. The one with his son James "J.J" is old and faded, but the one with his bright-eyed daughter Beth is newer. There is, of course, no picture of his ex-wife. At one end of the table is a picture of

Jack with his dad aboard the family boat, a big white cabin cruiser.

Hoping to forget the troubling events of the day, Jack falls into his evening routine. He works himself into his favorite chair with a hot microwave dinner, a glass of red wine, and a chunk of toasted French bread. He places the meal on the arm of the chair while taking a sip of wine with one hand and picking up the television remote with the other. He clicks on his favorite conservative news station. A reporter stands in front of a battalion of firefighting equipment and speaks excitedly. "Huge plumes of smoke cover the skies of Denver and Boulder as these latest grass fires explode near Kipling. Over 170 homes have already vanished in the blaze. John Carlyle and his wife Cindy just learned their family home of 37 years burned to the ground." In the video, Mr. Carlyle is doing everything he can to hold back the tears as he stares at the burned ruins of what used to be his home. "It just took away everything," he says. "Our whole life is gone. I feel like I lost myself."

Jack turns away from the TV and looks out the window. He recalls sitting in the backyard with his father when the old man was getting on in years. His father said, "Life gives to the young and takes from the old." Jack never thought much about it, but now he wonders if he has reached that stage of life. He does a quick mental inventory of the things life has taken from him over the last few years. First, two molar teeth went bad and had to be removed. Next, lots of hair turned gray or just vanished into thin air. Then there was his balance. That just went to hell like his golf game. Same with holding his liquor. Then he noticed the younger people at work stopped taking him seriously, and women no longer smiled back at him. He could no longer hear well in noisy restaurants, and money started going out faster than it was coming in. Then there was his family. They, too, went away. But that was more of a "house divided" kind of thing. He remembers his daughter Beth having a

Jamaican boyfriend when she was 17. "Dad, can Ziggy stay with me upstairs for a while?"

"What in God's name makes you think you can even ask me a question like that?"

"Mom said it's okay."

And that was *the* problem, as far as Jack was concerned. Everything was always *okay* with Mom.

Until now, Jack had been able to background all his losses like it was just another lousy day in the stock market. Down today, back up tomorrow. But the thought of losing his home is a blow that tips the ledger so far into the red it can no longer be ignored. With a sigh, Jack turns back to the TV and tries another news channel. This time, the video shows undocumented dark-skinned migrants wading across the Rio Grande into the United States, carrying knapsacks filled with all their worldly possessions above their heads.

"There is little doubt," a chalky white talk show host yells from her bully pulpit on the television screen, "the situation at the border is worse than it has ever been. The current administration boasts about the new legislation to crack down on illegal immigration, yet thousands and thousands of undocumented aliens continue to slip in and remain in this country with only a handful of deportations."

Usually, Jack would just shake his head at the spectacle and voice his agreement with the host. But tonight, he reacts a little differently. The angry voice of the announcer fades away as the images of homeless immigrants fill his belly with a tingle of fear. When he loses his home, where will he go? What will he do? What will become of him? He doesn't know.

2

SOFIA'S SONG

flock of Canada geese honks as they fly over a tiny house in the Latino section of Red Bank, a New Jersey township across the river from Jack's neighborhood. Unlike Atlantic Highlands, which has no Latinos, Red Bank is a "sanctuary" town, with laws forbidding law enforcement from checking the immigration status of its residents. As a result, over a third of the population is now Hispanic. The majority are from Mexico, but there are also many people from El Salvador, including 16-year-old Sofia Rivera. Her family came to the area to escape gang persecution and search for a safer, better life.

Sofia doesn't think about the gangs back home too much. She was too young to understand the serious danger they posed to her family. She just stands at the bathroom window of the tiny house, watching the Canada geese. The birds are already migrating from Canada for the winter, but unlike her, the geese can fly back home when warmer weather returns. She's not going anywhere. She's stuck in a tiny house with an extended family of eight people in a cold, ugly part of town. The seasons will come and go, but not her. The best she can hope for is a few minutes of peace in the only private spot in the house. It's a small, three-foot by three-foot space between the toilet and the sink.

Sofia sits in her little cubby hole with her phone and checks her social media. She can't find anyone she knows posting from El Salvador. What used to be a stream of recognizable faces is now just a parade of strangers with even younger faces. She gives up and switches on her camera for a selfie. She shakes her dark hair to add some fluff. She pulls on a small patch of hair dyed blue to make it more prominent and then holds up an open pill bottle to her mouth as if she is about to swallow all the pills and kill herself—but not really. With the other hand, she lowers the phone a bit, then pushes the shutter button with her thumb.

There is a sudden knock at the door. *"Tengo que ir al baño.* I have to pee," a young boy calls out, mixing Spanish and English.

"Saldré en un segundo, Ricki," Sofia responds in both languages. "Two more seconds."

Sofia moves the picture into the phone's photo editor. She tries different filters to add a touch of style to her selfie. The "vivid" filter doesn't give her a look to match her mood, so she tries the "dramatic" filter instead.

Outside the bathroom, Sofia's 10-year-old nephew, Ricardo "Ricki" Hernandez, stares at the bathroom door with a strange, distant look. He is rocking back and forth on his feet with his mouth open, wheezing a bit as he breathes. Then, grabbing tighter at his crotch, he lets his head fall on the door, making a thumping sound. He then repeats the move as only an autistic child would.

"Okay, just a few more seconds," Sofia says. She rejects the dramatic filter and moves on to the monochromatic filters. "Silvertone" might do it, but then again, maybe "Noir" would add the touch of dark angst she is looking for.

"I need to go pee," Ricki yells with anger.

The situation draws eight-year-old Angelica to the bathroom door. Angelica is Ricki's younger sister and a true angel. She produces a small cheap phone. "You want your phone?"

Ricki sees the phone, but his biological needs far outstrip his video game pursuits. "I have to pee—I have to PEE!"

Inside the bathroom, Sofia finally gives up on the suicide selfie. She quickly deletes the picture, stands up, and takes a picture of the birds outside. She then types, "I wish I was a bird" and hits share.

Sofia fake flushes the toilet and opens the door to the bathroom. There to greet her is Ricki, young Angelica, and their Mom, Roberta. Ricki jumps past Sofia and starts to do his business right away. "Sorry, Ricki," Sofia says without much conviction. Roberta, a tall, rotund woman, is Sofia's older step-sister. She pulls the door closed as Sofia clears it.

"What is this?" Roberta asks. She grabs the blue part of Sofia's hair.

Sofia smiles without protest. "You like it?"

Roberta smiles and replies, "You never cease to amaze me, little sister. Mom seen it yet?"

"Not yet."

Down in the tiny basement is a cramped living space with a microwave and mini-refrigerator. There is a small table to eat at, a couple of chairs, and two beds. Matching figurines of Jesus and Mary stand on top of the dresser.

Sofia's grandmother, Estella, is sitting on one of the beds, whimpering. Next to her is Sofia's mother, Ana. Ana is a small but pleasant-looking Salvadoran in her early 50s. Her soft-spoken Spanish is gentle but strong at the same time. "Mama, nobody is left there. We're all here now. Who would stay with you?"

Estella wipes away a tear. "My friend Clara will help me."

Ana sighs as if this is an often repeated topic of discussion. Estella has been showing early signs of dementia for almost a year, but now it seems to be getting worse. "Mama, Clara is no longer with us, remember?"

Estella thinks about this just as Sofia comes down the stairs and interrupts the conversation. Estella turns toward Sofia. "Sofia will take me, won't you, my love?"

Sofia knows the conversation all too well. She smiles and sits next to her grandmother. If there is one person Sofia gets along with, it's her grandmother, her "Abbi." "Yes, I will take you," Sofia says warmly.

Estella wipes a tear away. "I don't want to die here. I want to die in my own country. In my own home."

Sofia puts her arm around Estella. "I want to go home too."

Ana watches all this with her usual displeasure. "Sofia, come here," Ana says, ordering Sofia to the other side of the room. Sofia doesn't move at first, but then Estella nudges her to go. With a huff, she stands, walks to the other side of the room, and sits on her mother's bed.

"How many times have I told you not to play with Abbi like that?" Ana asks in a low, angry whisper. "You know she can't go back. And if she did go and pass away there, none of us could go to her funeral."

"Why not?" Sofia asks defiantly.

"Stop acting dumb, you know why. We would not be able to come back. We are not here legally yet."

"Then maybe we should just stay there," Sofia responds defiantly. "Abbi didn't ask to come here, and I didn't ask to come here. You just decided for us all to come here without even asking. You even made Roberta lie to my teacher about where I was going!"

"I am your mother, and yes, I will make decisions for you. I'm sorry you can't respect that. You have no idea the danger you were in. The danger all of us were in. It just takes time to adapt to life here."

Sofia shakes her head, unpersuaded. "You've been here over five years and don't even speak English," she says.

Ana frowns at Sofia with determination. "Abbi is not going back, so stop giving her false hope."

"I am right here," Estella calls out from the other side of the room. "I can hear you, you know."

Anna looks past Sofia for a second and is about to say something but then notices something under Sofia's sleeveless shirt. She grabs the material and pulls it back just enough to reveal a small bird tattoo just above her daughter's breast.

"Oh my god! What did you do!?"

"I got a little tattoo."

"Why? Why would you do that?"

Before Sofia can answer, her stepdad Juan bounds down the stairs. Juan is a pleasant man in his early fifties. He has a solid build with a warm smile. Despite the fact that he is dressed in a work uniform from the Gulfstream Health and Fitness Club, he carries himself with dignity. Yes, he is just a cleaner of exercise machines, but solid work makes him one of the main bread-winners in the house. "What's going on here?" Juan asks when he sees that Ana is upset.

Ana pulls back Sofia's shirt angrily and points to the tattoo. Sofia pulls away from her and covers it back up. Juan frowns. "Sofia, why would you do that?"

Sofia is more defiant than ever. "Because I wanted to."

Ana is still in shock. "It makes it look like you are with a gang!"

Sofia snorts sarcastically. "A bird? Seriously?"

"Where did you get the money to pay for that?" Ana asks.

"Memo paid for it. We both got one."

"Memo? Where did he get the money?"

"He has two jobs, Mama! He works at a restaurant and also a catering company."

"Memo is crazy. Stay away from him."

"He's not crazy!

"He's full of crazy ideas! That's why everybody calls him '*Memo Loco!*'"

"I like him. He's different."

Juan steps in, trying his best to be fatherly. "Sofia, you are too young for all this. It scares us. You are not getting involved with any gangs, are you?"

"I said no! It's my body, and you are not my father!"

Ana frowns when she hears this. "Don't talk to Juan like that."

"Well, then he needs to stop talking to me like that!"

And with that, Sofia bolts out of the room and up the stairs. Ana yells, "Don't leave! "I need your help in the upstairs kitchen."

A rarely used railroad track crosses the street near Sofia's house and runs into a maintenance yard for the New Jersey Transit trains. The sides of the tracks are covered in weeds, and the yard is filled with strange-looking contraptions used to perform various maintenance jobs up and down the rail line.

Sofia walks down the tracks along a chain-link fence with her phone in hand. She spots her boyfriend, Guillermo "Memo" Gonzales, on an electric delivery bicycle approaching on the other side of the fence. He's only 19 years old, but he has a look about him like he has big plans for where he is going in life. His eyes are bright and filled with hope. His smile tells you he is a force of positivity and a good guy all around. He's tall for a Latino. His build is thin. He has longish dark hair and dark eyes. His smile is warm and likable. He wears a Star Wars t-shirt displaying an image of Yoda peeking out over the top of a dirty white apron.

"*¿Qué pasó?* Memo asks as he walks his bike on the other side of the fence.

"My mother found the tattoo."

Memo realizes this is a big deal for Sofia. "Oh, *mierda, hombre*. Did she get mad?"

Sofia stops, a bit angry. "I told you she was going to think it was gang ink."

Memo stops and leans his bike up against the fence. "It's just a bird, flying free, like in a dream."

Sofia puts her hand on the fence. Memo tries to wrap his hand around hers from the other side, but Sofia pulls hers away. "I just want to move out."

"Move in with me. I will make you a *casita* so beautiful you will never leave. It will be a castle with tall towers, surrounded by a moat filled with giant alligators."

"Alligators?" Sofia asks with a look of mocking fear.

"Yes, to protect you from ICE!"

Sofia giggles at Memo's crazy description but then gets serious. "I want to take my Abbi back to El Salvador."

"I know, you told me. But you're coming back, right?"

"I don't think so."

"What? *¿Por qué?*"

"I told you. I just don't feel at home here, and besides, they lied to me."

"They lie to you? Like what?"

"They said El Salvador is too dangerous, and we will be safer here. That's a lie. You can't go to school here or even the mall without worrying about someone shooting you."

"But that is just random. Back home, you have no chance. You know the gangs are going to get you one way or another."

Sofia stands her ground. "The new president has locked up most of the *pandilleros*. It's better now!"

Memo frowns. "Yeah, as long as he is president. But what happens when he is gone? Besides, there is no work back there for us—just selling pupusas on the street for six dollars a day but paying the same prices at the store as they pay here. Here, if you work hard, you can make real money and buy what you want."

Memo turns and plays some rap music on his phone. He lip-syncs along with the song and pretends he is singing it to Sofia.

American Dream, ain't a single definition
From concrete cracks to open skies,
chase that fire in your eyes
Rewrite the narrative, own your truth,
rise and take the prize!

Sofia puts her hand back up on the fence. This time she lets Memo lock hands with her. "But my Abbi doesn't want to die here. She cries all the time about it."

Memo looks back at her seriously. "*Pero*, I have big plans for us *aquí*. A place of our own."

"Oh yeah, how are you going to do that?"

"Come with me for a quick ride. I want to show you something."

"I can't," Sofia asks. "I have to get back and help my mom."

"It'll only take a minute."

"I can't."

"I'll ride you back home."

"Don't you have to go back to work?"

"My shift just ended," Memo says as he walks his bike toward a break in the fence. Sofia follows on her side of the fence until they meet at the opening. Then, she slips onto the bike just in front of Memo and rides side-saddle.

Memo cruises through the streets, thrilled to have Sofia with him. He turns down an alley behind some shops and then pulls into a small parking lot under an apartment building.

"Where are you taking me?" Sofia asks with a confused look on her face.

"Right here," Memo says. He stops the bike in front of a parking space being used to store what looks like construction materials.

"You know what that is?" Memo proudly asks Sofia.

Sofia looks at the mess with little interest. "Uh, no."

"That, *querida*, is a million-dollar business."

Sofia laughs. "Who's parking space is this?"

"*Mi Tía*, Auntie Paloma. She lives upstairs but doesn't have a car."

Memo leads Sofia past a small cement mixer, metal rods, wood, and finally, to something covered by a tarp. "Are you ready for something special?"

Sofia is curious now. "Yeah, sure."

"Something very new?"

"What is it?"

Memo waves his arms. "Something so cool, people will pay anything to buy it?"

Sofia gets frustrated. "Okay, okay. Let's see it!"

With the flair of a true showman, Memo rips the tarp from its resting place and reveals an oddly but artistically shaped bench made out of cement.

Sofia isn't sure what she is looking at. "What is that?"

Memo runs his hand over it proudly. "It's the first bench for my outdoor cement furniture company."

Sofia looks harder. The bench looks more like a tiny bridge than a bench. Its top is smooth concrete, about six feet long and three feet wide, supported by two triangular shapes. The overall impression is "artsy," even avant-garde, but cool in its own way.

"Well, what do you think?" Memo asks.

Sofia nods her head apprehensively. "This is really a bench?"

"Yeah, I got the idea doing deliveries. Sometimes, I go to these rich people's homes. I notice they buy all these expensive furnitures for their patios, but it's always covered up because it can't take the outdoors. My furniture solves that problem. You never have to cover this bench."

Sofia looks back at the bench, reaches out, and touches it. She nods her head again, but this time with approval. "I like the way it looks. It's cool."

Memo moves closer to Sofia with a look of pride on his face. "When I'm not thinking about you, I'm thinking about all the furnitures I could make—tables, chairs, lounge chairs. Sometimes I think my head is going to explode!"

Sofia giggles.

"I call this one *La Sofia*."

Memo reaches out to Sofia. She smiles at him, and they embrace. But then she pulls away with a sad look on her face.

"What's the matter?" Memo asks.

Sofia puts her head in her hands. "I'm leaving."

Memo grabs her again. She doesn't resist. "Mommy, you're trying to go backwards to something that went to outer space and got sucked into a big black hole. You can't hold a river in your hand, *mi corazón*. You can't rewind the shifting sand! You can't ride a bike backward to go forward. When I say I can make a home for us here, I'm no kidding. I can do it. Just give me a chance!"

Sofia looks at the bench, all the junk surrounding it, and the dirty parking area. It's not exactly her idea of a dream come true. She looks back at Memo and starts to say something, but Memo puts a finger over her mouth.

"Just close your eyes for a second."

Sofia goes along with his wish. She closes her eyes.

"Just let yourself dream."

"Dream?"

"Yeah, just dream. About the big house we will live in and all that kinda stuff."

Sofia keeps her eyes closed and lets her mind go, but nothing particular appears. While she does this, Memo looks at her adoringly. He leans in and kisses her. Sofia responds warmly for a moment but then suddenly pulls away.

"What?" Memo asks.

Sofia is suddenly frightened by Memo. "What are you doing to me?"

"I'm just kissing you with some sunshine," Memo half-jokes. "It's a good thing."

Sofia shakes her head as if she is shaking off his spell. She really likes this crazy guy and the way he feels about her. But she just can't trust it. It can all go away so quickly. Just like her life in El Salvador. All her friends, the farm animals, and most of her things just vanished.

3

NO PLACE FOR HIPPIES

"I'm not sure about these," Mia, the realtor, says, staring at the militaristic wall of trophies in Jack's den. "I would have said yes a few years ago, but the demographic is changing. We're seeing more progressive types priced out of the New York boroughs and moving down here."

"That's what I am afraid of," Jack says sourly.

Mia looks like she is in her forties but is really in her fifties. She's a fast-talking Jersey girl and she is well put together. Jack was pleasantly surprised when he opened his door and saw her for the first time, but from the moment she opened her mouth, things went south. Hearing her discuss his treasured wall of honor so offhandedly has him pissed off. "Well, how about they just f-off if they don't like them? They won't be here when they move in."

Mia realizes she has hit a sore spot. Jack's finance guy, Fitzy, warned her it was a forced sale. She knows passive-aggressive behavior comes with the territory. Jack points out the window and says, "Hopefully, they will notice a Navy ship or two at the end of the Naval Weapons pier in the bay. This area is the weapons depot for the Atlantic Fleet. It's a high-priority target in a nuclear war."

Mia opens her eyes wide with a sarcastic look. "I'll make sure that little factoid is boldly pointed out in the listing. That will really draw them in."

Jack becomes stern. "What I'm getting at is this isn't a place for hippies."

Mia gets a curious look on her face. "I'm not sure hippies still exist—oh wait, I have a friend who's kind of a hippy. So yeah, I get ya."

"I was born in this house," Jack says with an edge of irritation in his voice.

Mia is honestly surprised by this. "Really?"

"True."

"That's rare these days," Mia replies, staring intently at Jack. "And you lived here your whole life?"

"Almost. My sister lived here after the folks died. I was off in the military and got married—raised a couple of military brats as we moved around and eventually ended up in Florida. But then my sister moved to Greece, and I moved my family here."

"You and your wife still together?"

"Naw, she didn't feel as much at home here as I did, so she moved back to Florida."

"And your kids? Boys? Girls?"

"Boy and a girl. Lost my son, though.

"Oh, I'm sorry to hear that. And your daughter?"

"Moved to the left coast—Los Angeles. Hooked up with a musician."

"And what are they doing?

"Monkey business—I mean, music business."

Mia decides she doesn't want to go much further than this on the personal front. She takes another look around the room. From what she has seen, the house needs some serious updating. To her, the whole place has a stale and musty feeling to it.

It happens when people age and don't move on from their homes. The home becomes frozen, rusty, and stagnant without fresh blood. The kitchen looks like something out of the 70s, complete with drop-down ceilings and fluorescent lighting. The countertop has a thin layer of grease—or is that dust? Who knows? The living room has the same dusty feel to it. The furniture is hopelessly unappealing and poorly arranged. The bedrooms are like Egyptian tombs, best aired out before entering.

Mia sighs. "Jack," she says, "this house could be great with some work. But if we want to sell fast, we will have to stage it."

Jack frowns, "What does that mean?"

"It means we take your furniture out and put it in storage. We then place rented furniture here."

"Rented?"

"Yes, for a place like this, I think we could stage it for around $7500."

"Are you really a real estate person, or did Fitzy send over a crazy for fun?"

Mia has pretty tough skin, but Jack is starting to irritate her. "Fitzy tells me you need to sell. So I'm giving you my best advice on accomplishing that quickly."

"Well, maybe Fitzy is in more of a hurry than I am. No way I'm paying for rental furniture. This is still a good house. It will sell on its own."

Mia sighs with frustration. "Okay, well, you know what they say. There's a bone for every dog. But at a bare minimum, you need to do some serious cleaning around here."

Jack looks around the living room. "Where are we talking about?"

Mia switches to wrap-up mode. "Uh, well, how about everywhere."

Jack frowns.

4

THE GODS OF STEAM

lthough Jack won't admit it, the Gulfstream Health and Fitness Club is the center of his social life. It's not a cheap place, but the clientele is older, more affluent, and, well, more white. The trainers are knowledgeable and capable of providing physical therapy. And the superior amenities are the best in town. It has a pool, steam rooms, saunas, hot tubs, showers, lockers, and even a snack bar. In addition, there is free shaving gear, blow dryers, and towels. But one thing Jack doesn't like about the club is the cleaning staff. It is exclusively Latino, and none seem capable of speaking English. Every time Jack has a question about getting more soap for the shower or something out of lost and found, it is always a struggle. He's complained to the front desk numerous times but always gets the same response: "I will let the manager know."

For revenge, Jack now tells the staff to speak English whenever he hears them speaking Spanish. And this particular evening is no different. When he enters the locker room after his physical therapy, he comes across Robert Mathews, an older but boyish-looking gentleman with a close-cropped beard and glasses. Robert is speaking Spanish with Juan, one of the staff members. *"¿Cómo está Sofia, su hija?"* {How is your daughter, Sofia?}

Juan smiles. *"Mi hija está bien. Pero estamos enojados con ella por hacerse un tatuaje."* {My daughter is fine. But we are angry with her for getting a tattoo.}

"Speak English!" Jack interrupts loudly. Suddenly, the room grows quiet. Some other guys near the lockers stop what they are doing to see what will happen.

Robert reacts to Jack's flagrant behavior like it's nothing new. "Hi Jack," Robert says with a friendly wink.

Jack doesn't respond with a hello to Robert. Instead, he just launches into a script that always goes the same. "If he wants to live in this country, he should learn to speak English!"

"Okay, Jack," Robert says calmly. "I understand what you are saying, but truth be told, he is helping me practice Spanish for my trip to his country. I mean, by your logic, if I visit his country, I should speak Spanish, right?"

"Why would you want to go to Mexico?"

"El Salvador, actually. Juan is from El Salvador."

Jack turns and heads for his locker wondering why he ever befriended Robert. Robert just showed up in the club one day like somebody visiting from out of town, but he never went away. Then, one day, Jack ended up on a recumbent bike next to Robert, and they started talking. It started with Robert saying, "You know, I just want to tell you, you're a real inspiration."

Jack was thrown off by the statement. He wasn't used to receiving compliments from strangers. "Oh yeah?" Jack responded suspiciously. "Why's that?"

"Can I be honest with you?" Robert asked.

"Be my guest."

"Well, tell me to shut up if I get too personal, but you know, the first time I saw you in here, you were walking, bent over at what, a 45-degree angle? I thought you wouldn't last two days. But then I sat here and watched you stick with your trainer and your routine day after day. And I could see it was painful for you. But man, you never gave up, and now, I can see how much better you are walking. It's inspiring to see that. Unusual."

Robert, it turned out, was a transplant from California, which should have nixed any further conversations with Jack. But Jack liked being appreciated, and when he found out Robert had some Irish blood, well that sealed the deal. Jack no longer cared if Robert was a liberal or a journalist or married to a Japanese woman who works at the United Nations. He was a compatriot who could help Jack hold the line against all the Italians that dominated the club. Especially in the steam room.

After dumping his workout clothes in a locker, Jack wraps himself in one of the white towels provided by the facility to join the nightly session of what somebody once called "The Gods of Steam." It's a collection of mostly bare-chested olive-skinned guys who sit around night after night complaining about the world and providing god-like advice on how to fix it. The would-be godfather of the room is a half-Sicilian who is known as Big Lou. He's a menacing fellow of nefarious means who is always accompanied by his cockeyed son, Roberto, aka "Bobby Brown Sheets." The other Italians, like Tomasso, the jeweler, and Vic G, the supposed real estate guy, come and go, but Vlad, the Russian computer geek, is always there and works hard to be one of the guys.

Jack pulls open the door to the steam room, or *quarto de vapor,*" as Juan likes to call it. A wave of steam escapes into the locker room as Jack enters and grabs his usual seat on the slippery tile bench, second row from the top, just below Big Lou.

"You know what I'd say if anybody talks Spanish to me around here?" Bobby Brown Sheets asks no one in particular as the steam vent hisses. "I'd say, 'No hablo fucktardo' straight to their face."

Bobby's dad, Big Lou, snickers a bit, then turns to Jack. "Jackie Boy, you must be feeling your old self. We missed our man telling it like it is—'If you want to live here, speak English.' Good for you."

Jack chuckles to himself a bit. Then, without looking up, he says, "First, we get rid of the Mexicans, then all the Wops and Dagos."

Bobby Brown Sheets takes offense to this. "Hey, my dad was paying you a compliment. Why you insulting us?"

"Bobby, relax," Lou says with a wave of his hand. "It's just his way of saying we're friends. Right, Bulldog?"

"Haven't heard that name in a while," Jack scoffs.

Lou leans into Bobby. "That is what they called Jack when we were on the wrestling team together. He was tough like a bulldog."

Bobby gets curious. "When was that?"

"High school," Lou says with a nostalgic smile. "We were killers, weren't we, Jack?"

Jack wipes some sweat off his face without looking at Lou. "Yeah. You still are."

Bobby looks at his dad as if to ask, why are you putting up with this shit? But Lou laughs it off. He's got higher priorities on his mind. "So Jack, you ready to get back to our project yet?"

"What project is that?" Jack asks.

"You know, the project," Lou says with a raised voice. "The thing."

Jack looks curious. "The thing? What thing?"

"The thing," Lou says with a nod.

Just then, the door swings open, and Robert Mathews enters the room. "Hey guys," Robert says.

Lou sighs with disappointment. Everyone else just nods. Robert takes a seat and remains quiet.

"The neighborhood illegal watch thing," Lou says,

returning to Jack. That thing. Remember that? We were talking about it before your accident."

"Oh that," Jack says. "That was like a year ago, wasn't it?"

"Yeah," Lou says, with sweat dripping from his chin. "But the more I think about it, the more I like your idea. In my old age, I'm developing more of a social conscience kind of thing, know what I mean? I feel like I have a higher purpose to fulfill, like becoming more of a community activist, you know? And you are the one who got me started."

Jack leans back a bit. "Somebody told me Red Bank is over 30% Mexican now. Is that true?"

"Something like that," Lou responds. "Can you freak'n believe it? Those rednecks down in Texas are ship'n dem in. We're being taken over!"

Vlad jumps into the conversation with a heavy Russian accent. "You think it's true there will be no more natural blondes in 200 years?"

Vic G shakes his head. "The way things are going, it might be 20 years."

Lou nods. "I know, right? These illegals come in here and start soaking up all our social services for nothing while we taxpayers foot the bill.

"Except that isn't totally true," Robert ventures.

"Oh shit, here we go," Lou moans. "Commiefornia is in the room."

"From what I know, undocumented immigrants trying to get 'asylum' avoid social services because they think it hurts their chances of gaining legal status."

Lou scoffs, "I don't know who told you that, but it's total B.S. Just go to the fuck'n grocery store and watch them using those food stamp cards. It's ridiculous!"

Robert shrugs. "Those people might already have asylum status, green cards, or even be citizens."

Bobby gets a sour look on his face. Yeah well that's just it, right? We don't know who these people are. They all came from prisons and mental institutions!"

"That's just fake news," Robert smirks. "There is no solid evidence to support that - at all. In fact, it's the opposite for the vast majority of immigrants. They are on the run from criminal gangs and human rights abuses."

Bobby realizes he is out of his league. "How do you know so much about this shit?"

"I worked as a reporter in Central America," Robert says. "Back during the Iran–Contra days.

"When was that?" Bobby asks.

"Long time ago," Robert says.

"Yeah," Jack says sarcastically. "Back when Laurel was president, and Hardy was vice president. You remember that, don't you, Bobby?"

Bobby gets defensive. "What? You think I don't know?"

At this point, Tomasso, the jeweler, stands up to leave. "Okay, I think I have had enough of this. Time for a cold shower." As he passes Robert, he hesitates just a bit. "Robert, just so you know, not all Italians in this town are like this."

Before anyone else can say anything, Vlad, the Russian, suddenly speaks up. "I saw a bumper sticker on car. It says Press 1 for English, Press 2 to learn English - Press 3 for ICE. What means 'Press 3 for ICE?'"

Robert smiles at the joke. "ICE stands for Immigration and Customs Enforcement."

Lou adds, "Those are the people who can grab illegals and throw them out of the fuck'n country." Then, turning to Jack, he says, "Your trainer, Midge. I think her husband works for ICE."

Jack frowns, "She's married?"

Vlad laughs. "Uh oh, you buy engagement ring already?"

Jack rubs some more perspiration off his face. "If anybody here catches me buying an engagement ring, shoot me."

"Next time you work with Midge," Lou suggests, "ask her. Maybe she can hook us up, and we can get this thing going."

Robert can't control his curiosity. "Can I ask what this 'thing' you are talking about is?"

"No," Brown Sheets says bluntly. "You're not part of this."

"Hey," Jack says. "Who are you to talk to him like that? Lou, teach your kid some manners."

Bobby tries to get tough with Jack. "What, you friends with this guy now?"

Jack gets red in the face. "He's Irish. You got a problem with that? Why don't you tell him why they call you Brown Sheets."

Bobby starts to stand up, but Lou pushes him back down. "Bobby, shut it already. Sorry Jack, my son is part moron. The only thing he knows is Bitcoin."

"Dad!"

Lou gets angry. "Shut it before you get your ass kicked. And if he doesn't do it, I will."

Bobby finally sits down in a huff.

"Seriously," Lou says, turning back to Jack. "We need to do something. Know what I am talking about?"

Jack shakes his head. "Yeah, but I have a lot of other things on my mind right now."

Lou looks disappointed but refuses to give up. "Jackie boy, c'mon. I'm asking for a little favor here."

Jack nods as if he agrees. "Okay, okay. Next time I see her, I'll ask."

As is customary for the gods of steam, they stay until the club closes, and then they all head out to the parking lot around 10 PM. This evening, Jack walks with Robert out the door. Robert isn't sure why.

"Jack," Robert says, "I appreciate you standing up for me in there, but you know I've only got a small amount of Irish blood in me."

"What's the rest?" Jack asks.

"Pretty boring. Mostly English and German."

"Well, nobody's perfect. Just don't tell those guineas that."

"Mum's the word."

"You know, Italians weren't even considered white until Sinatra came along."

Robert is caught off guard by the blatant racism but smiles anyway. Jack is his only friend at the club besides Juan, so he's hesitant to criticize. Besides, there is something so outrageous about how Jack throws out these lines; it's almost funny.

"But to be honest, I have an ulterior motive," Jack adds.

"Yeah?"

"I've got a ceiling light in the kitchen that went out. No way am I ready to get up on a ladder. I thought maybe a fellow 'Irishman' might have a little time to stop by."

Robert is a little surprised by the request. For a guy like Jack to ask for help must be challenging. He's not the kind of guy that likes to appear vulnerable. It also exposes the fact that he probably lives alone. "Sure, no problem. When do you want to do it?"

Jack doesn't hesitate. "Why don't you just follow me."

"Now?" Robert asks, looking surprised.

When Robert pulls into the driveway behind Jack and sees Jack's house for the first time, he is impressed. "Beautiful home," he tells Jack as they head inside. But once the door opens, he is caught, like many others, by the stillness of the place and how it looks like a time capsule from an earlier era.

"Okay, it's that one right there," Jack says, pointing to the light fixture on the kitchen ceiling. "This is the replacement bulb."

Robert takes the bulb from Jack and climbs up a small ladder. The fixture itself is pretty much standard equipment. It's a glass bowl flush mount held to the ceiling by a screw cap attached to a central threaded hollow rod. Robert quickly discovers the screw cap doesn't want to come loose. "Well, this isn't good."

"What's wrong," Jack asks.

"The whole thing looks like it's rusted," Robert says. "It's frozen."

Jack frowns. "Yeah, well, it's been there a long time. Want some WD-40?"

"No, no. I'm good. Okay, let's try this again." When Robert finally removes the glass bowl, he can see the rust following the hollow rod up into the ceiling. "Oh, wow."

"What?"

"I don't know about this, Jack. I think you need to replace the hardware up here. It's all rusted."

Jack clearly doesn't want to get into repairs. "Yeah, probably. But can you make it work for now?"

"I'll give it a try," Robert says without looking down. "Or we can just put the bulb in and leave the cover off until you get some new parts."

"Don't want to do that," Jack says, "I'm going to be selling the place soon."

Robert is surprised by the news. "You're selling?"

"Yeah. Unfortunately."

"Unfortunately?"

Jack suddenly becomes defensive. He doesn't want to explain. "Yeah, time to downsize."

Robert takes the old bulb out and screws in the new one. "Okay, hit the switch."

Jack flips the switch on the wall, and the light comes to life. "That's better," he says.

After they return the ladder to the garage, Jack walks Robert out to his car. "Thanks for that," Jack says. "I owe you a beer."

"No worries," Robert says, looking at the house. "Such a great place. It must be hard to let her go."

"It's time," Jack says.

Robert looks at Jack curiously. "You know where you are going?"

"Not yet."

"You selling soon?"

"Yeah, as soon as I can get a cleaning crew up here and spiff the place up, it's going on the market."

Robert briefly considers this and then says, "I can hook you up with Juan's wife, Ana. She cleans our house."

Jack gets suspicious right away. "Juan, your Mexican buddy at the club?"

"Salvadoran," Robert says, "but yeah, Juan. His wife, Ana— she's good and trustworthy."

"She legal?" Jack asks.

Robert smiles, "She's working on it."

Jack shakes his head. "No thanks. I have the name of a cleaning service I'm going to call."

Robert smirks a bit. "And who do you think they will send over, Martha Stewart?"

Jack thinks about this for a second and realizes Robert is probably right. And in the back of his head, he knows his attempt at circumventing "gray labor" is how he hurt himself before. He doesn't want to do that again.

"With a cleaning service, you don't know who you're going to get," Robert says. "With Ana, you know you have somebody you can trust."

Jack thinks for a moment. Then, he looks around the street

to see if any neighbors are within earshot. "How much does she charge?"

"A hell of a lot less than the cleaning service," Robert responds.

"Hmmmm." Jack thinks.

Robert doesn't wait for Jack's answer. "Let me give her a call for you. Really, she's awesome."

Jack looks around the area again before ducking his head. "Okay."

5

CHECKED OUT

Canada geese fill the sky over Sofia's house as the fall migration continues. But today, Sofia is not hanging out next to the bathroom window to watch. Instead, she's in bed, willfully blinded to where she is. Covering her eyes is a black sleep mask with an airline logo and the words "Checked out" printed boldly across the front. She picked it up at a clothing giveaway in the parking lot of Holy Family Church, which caters to the local immigrant community. Ana didn't see a problem with her keeping it, but once she saw how Sofia took to wearing it all the time, she regretted it. Instead of being a quickly forgotten novelty, it became a tool of rebellion. Anytime Sofia is unhappy about something or doesn't want to do something, she puts on the mask.

Today, Sofia is improvising. With the sleep mask on, she takes a selfie of herself as Memo sends dozens of text messages. "*Quiero verte.*" {"*I want to see you.*"}

"Let's make love, not war."

"I dreamt about you last night?"

"I'm so in love with you."

"*¡Qué emoción!.*" {*I'm on fire!*}

"Don't break my heart."

"I have good news!"

"I have a gift for you!

"¡*Por favor!*"

And for all this, all he gets back from Sofia is a picture of her with a sleep mask. "I don't want to see you!"

Between Memo's texts, Sofia rests her head on the pillow, guiding her thoughts back to a happier place. It is warm and tropical. There is a river. Sofia and her young friends giggle as they run barefoot through the fruit trees. She can feel the warm sand of the river bank on her feet. The cool rush of water. The heat of the sun. They are certainly pleasant thoughts, but they come with a price. Once she opens the door to her lost paradise, she can't stop what happens next. Her older sister's husband, Arnell, appears and takes her away from her friends. He returns her to the house where Roberta is waiting. Roberta has a big smile on her face. "Your mother has called for you! You are going north to live with her! It will be fun!" Then there is a bus station and an unfamiliar couple who take Sofia from Roberta and Arnell. That's when the world turns dark. There are cars and buses and strange rooms. Sofia is in a dark space with unseen, hot, smelly people all around her. She can't move. She can't escape. It's like a nightmare.

A tug on the sleep mask brings Sofia back to reality. She squints and sees her mother standing over her. "What are you doing in bed?"

"I'm tired."

"Did you forget you are helping me clean a house today?"

"What?"

"My new house. You are coming with me. "

Sofia gathers her thoughts. She looks past her mother and sees Estella staring back at her with a strange smile on her face. She then tries to pull the sleep mask back over her eyes. "No, not today."

"Yes, today," Ana insists as she rips Sofia's sleep mask off.

"Mama, no. Please."

"Sofia, stop. We're already behind on our part of the rent. Unless you want to give up the money from your *quinceañera*, you're doing this."

At the mention of the "*quinceañera*" money, both Sofia and Estella share a knowing look. The secret plot between them to use that money for a return to El Salvador has just been put in jeopardy. Estella silently urges Sofia to do as Ana says.

Anna pulls on Sofia. "We have to get going. Get up!" Sofia rolls over in a huff just as another text message from Memo arrives. "I will be under the bridge tonight at 7:00. If you do not meet there, I am throwing myself in the water and will welcome all sharks to devour my rejected and broken heart with all my skin and bones!"

"Will we be home by 7:00?" Sofia asks.

6

NORTH MEETS SOUTH

At 8:55 a.m., Jack crosses the Navesink River in his Cadillac Crossover and proceeds down Central Avenue towards the train station. He catches the red light in front of the Minimart, where Latino day laborers wait by the curb, hoping to pick up work. Some of the men check out Jack's car to see if Jack is buying. But Jack keeps his head forward, looking irritated and uncomfortable.

A shiny white pickup truck stops at the curb in front of Jack. The men gather at the passenger window. Behind the wheel is a white guy who negotiates a price for the day. It's probably the same guy who would have brought over a crew to clean Jack's gutters. It makes Jack think about how he could have saved himself a lot of pain and agony if he had just accepted this system. And who knows, it might have rescued him from the situation he is in now—forced to hire his own illegals just so he can sell his home. It's a maddening situation made worse by Robert smooth-talking him into being a goddamn chauffeur for the cleaning crew. How did he do that?

"There are going to be two of them," Robert told Jack as

they sat on exercise bikes at the club a few days earlier. "Ana and her daughter Sofia."

Jack thought about that for a moment. "They both work, and the price is the same?"

"Yep. Two cleaners for the price of one. The only thing is Ana doesn't speak much English, but Sofia is fluent and can translate."

Jack looked at Robert, clearly unhappy with that tiny bit of information. "You didn't tell me that."

"What? It's not a problem. You tell Sofia what you want to be done. She will respond to you in perfect English and then tell her Mom."

"Okay, but I don't want them speaking Spanish in my house. That isn't what I signed up for."

"Ana doesn't even talk. Once she starts working, you won't even know she is there."

Jack suspiciously agreed. "Anything else you want to tell me?"

Robert swallowed hard, knowing the next piece was going to be difficult. "Yes, I have to give you Ana's address."

"What for? She just needs my address, right?"

Robert couldn't look Jack in the eye for this one. He looked away like something else had caught his attention and casually said, "You'll need her address when you pick her up."

"'Pick her up?' You're kidding, right?"

"Hey, that's how it works. I pick Ana up when she cleans my house."

"She doesn't have a car?"

"Why would she have a car?" She doesn't know how to drive.

"What about the daughter?"

"She just turned 16 and hasn't put much effort into learning. And getting a license for either one of them is, well, let's just say difficult."

"Well, they can take the goddamned bus then. I'm not a limousine service."

"Jack, you know there is no real bus service out to where we live. It would take hours and hours for them to get there."

"Okay, Uber then!"

"You need a credit card for that. They don't have credit cards."

"Taxi!"

"That will cost more than you pay them."

Jack glared forward as he let it all sink in. Robert was expecting him to cancel the whole thing, but for some reason, he didn't. Instead, he just said, "God damn it," in a way that meant he was still on board, just not happy.

At 9:00 a.m., Jack turns onto Cherry Tree Avenue and enters the unfamiliar world of the barrio. A wooden pallet painted to look like a Mexican flag proudly leans against a tree, marking the transition to the vibrant Latino section of town. Young men on bikes with backward-facing baseball caps are peddling off to their jobs while young women with preschoolers walk to the grocery store. Latino music filters out from the run-down, classic working-class homes whose yards are filled with cheap plastic toys that all seem to be pink, yellow, or red. Neighbors yell at each other from one porch to the next, and some silently make note of the out-of-place late model Cadillac SUV that slowly glides down the street.

When Jack finds the address he is looking for, he sees two women who look like mother and daughter waiting on the front porch. Jack pulls up to the curb and rolls down his window. "Ana?" Ana nods her head affirmatively with a timid smile. The assumed daughter, Sofia, stares at Jack with suspicion.

Ana opens the back door and points to the front door for her daughter. Sofia refuses to get in the front and takes the back seat on the opposite side of the car.

Jack can't turn around because of his physical issues. So he just looks in the mirror and says, "Good morning."

Ana almost says, *"Buenos días,"* but stops herself. She's been warned not to speak Spanish in front of Jack. So instead, she nudges Sofia until Sofia says, "Good Morning."

Jack looks at her in the mirror. "You're the one that speaks English?"

Sofia nods with a forced smile.

Jack nods. "Can one of you sit up front?"

Sofia looks at him. "What?"

"Can one of you ride up front? I'm not a limo service, you know."

Ana isn't sure what is going on, so Sofia explains in Spanish. "He wants one of us to ride up front."

Ana nudges her daughter toward the front seat, but Sofia refuses. "No, you go."

The behavior angers Ana. "No, you go, you are the one that speaks English."

Sofia fights back. "No, you are the one who works for him, not me."

Jack is already frustrated. "Ladies, the deal I made is we are all supposed to speak English."

Ana has reached her limit with Sofia. She gets a look on her face that lets Sofia know the argument is over. She pushes Sofia once more, and Sofia finally gives in with a loud sigh. Sofia opens the back door, gets out, and enters the front seat. She glances back at her mother angrily, then turns forward without looking at Jack. Jack looks over at Sofia. "Thank you. Much better." Sofia glances over at Jack and gets her first close-up look. Jack looks back at her stiffly. "I'm Jack." Sofia nods and turns away, but Jack just sits there. He's waiting for her name. "Sofia," she says finally.

The ride to Jack's house takes them back across the river that separates Red Bank from Atlantic Highlands. The dense urban area where Sofia and Ana live gives way to a semi-rural landscape dotted with big homes and country clubs. Jack follows a hilly road that hugs the side of the river. Through the greenery, the river glistens in the distance. The traffic is very light, and it is an enjoyable crisp day.

Too nervous to speak, Sofia and Ana take in the scenery like they are in another world. The greenery seems to lift their spirits. At one point, Sofia cracks her window to smell the fresh air.

Jack looks over with a frown. "Don't do that, please."

Sofia looks back at him, surprised by his stern attitude. "What?"

Jack points at his center console. "I've got the heat on." He then reaches for the window controls on his side and closes the window without any further discussion.

Sofia glances at her mother, then turns and gazes out the window again in silence. Her eyes take in the beautiful river and big homes going by, but then a large bird leaving its perch in a pine tree catches her attention. She gets excited. "*Halcón*," she says, pointing to the sky and glancing back at her mother. Ana stretches to see if she can see it.

Jack glances up and recognizes it immediately. "Hawk."

Sofia speaks excellent English, but it isn't perfect. She hasn't heard the English word for this bird before. "I know, I know," she says. "Hought."

Jack scoffs at her pronunciation. "No, not 'haught'—HAWK. H - A - W - K. Hawk."

"Hawk," Sofia says, with irritation in her voice. She twists all the way around to see the bird pass behind the car and then up into another tree.

Jack looks at her coldly but becomes curious about her extreme interest in the hawk. "You like birds?"

"Yes," Sofia says without looking at him.

Jack turns back to the road ahead, reminding himself to keep his distance from these illegals, but up close like this, he finds it hard to see them as the "enemy" presented on TV. In person like this, they don't look like criminals. Nor do they look like terrorists or poisoners of American blood. They just look like regular people. After a few more seconds of silence, he caves into his own interest in birds. "That hawk we saw was a red-tail."

Sofia turns to Jack. "They have more than one kind here?"

Jack nods. "Yeah. There are lots of different species here. This whole area is one of the premier birding locations on the East Coast."

Sofia isn't exactly sure what that means but nods as if she appreciates the information.

"We have cardinals, song sparrows, common yellowthroats, and even some gray catbirds," Jack says, showing off his knowledge with an imperious voice. "There are ospreys closer to the beach and a few eagles too."

Sofia is overwhelmed by all the names, but she seems impressed.

Forgetting himself, Jack turns to Sofia proudly. "Teddy Roosevelt once stopped to check out the birds in this area when passing through."

Sofia gets a curious look on her face, making it clear she has no idea who that is.

Jack slowly repeats the name. "Teddy? Roosevelt? 26th president of the United States?

Sofia shakes her head. That isn't a name she recognizes.

Jack frowns at her. "George Washington?"

Sofia doesn't respond to Washington's name either.

"Gettysburg?"

This one sounds familiar to Sofia. "They sell hamburgers?"

Jack can only shake his head negatively, which makes Sofia feel like she is being judged. It irritates her, and she decides to retaliate. "Do you know Gabriela Triste?"

"No, who is that?"

"She's a singer from El Salvador on YouTube."

"Never heard of her," Jack frowns.

Sofia now mimics Jack, shaking her head negatively. Jack glances over at her feeling he is being mocked. He clearly isn't happy with the affront and decides to counter-attack. "Bon Jovi used to live on this road. Do you know who *that* is?"

"No," Sofia says, growing frustrated with this strange game. From the backseat, Ana senses the conflict with growing discomfort. Jack doesn't look like the kind of man who will put up with Sofia's antics. Ana worries about what will happen and whether it will cost her this much-needed job.

By American standards, Jack's house is relatively modest, but it looks big to Sofia. This is the first time she's been in a large American home. This is the America she has only seen on TV and in the movies. On the one hand, she is impressed. But on the other hand, it makes her feel poor, something less than Jack and all the other people who live in these big houses. It's a feeling that seems to dog her in America, and she hates it.

"How many people live here?" Sofia asks.

"Just one," Jack replies. "Me."

Sofia is shocked by this. "He lives here alone," she whispers to her mother.

Ana isn't surprised. This isn't the first big Americano house she has cleaned. But sniffing the air, she can tell it's dirty. "Lots of dust," she says under her breath.

Jack has never directed a cleaning crew before, so he is forced to fall back on what he knows, which means acting like a Marine commander. He soon has Ana and Sofia standing side by side in front of him in the kitchen. Jack pulls out a piece of paper with a long list of things to do. He explains the house is going up for sale and must be cleaned from top to bottom to make it ready for the market. Sofia is shocked that he is going to sell it. "You're going to sell this?"

"That is correct," Jack confirms.

Sofia turns to her mother and loudly announces in Spanish, "He said he is going to sell this house!".

Ana is shocked, too. "Oh yes?"

Jack suddenly puts the hammer down. "Ladies, once again. In this house, we speak English. No Spanish."

Ana slaps her daughter's arm as if to say, "Why are you speaking Spanish? You know the rules!"

Sofia pays little attention to her mother. Instead, she confronts Jack. "Why are you so against anyone speaking Spanish?" She asks.

"Because this is America, and we speak English here," Jack responds with an air of unyielding authority. "If you can't respect that, then you shouldn't be here."

"Okay," Sofia says, still unclear of the answer. "I thought maybe you had a Spanish wife or girlfriend who messed you up."

Jack is insulted by the full frontal disrespect in Sofia's remark. His eyes harden, and his nose flares. "It is not your place here to speculate on my personal life."

Undaunted, Sofia's anger rises. To add insult to injury, she asks, "Can you tell us why you are selling your house?"

Jack is pushed over the edge by Sofia's continued impertinence. "That is none of your business," he barks. "We will now proceed with the mission specifics."

Sofia doesn't turn away from Jack's angry gaze. Instead, she stares back at him and notices something in his eyes that tells her Jack is upset about leaving his home. She turns to her mother to see if she is picking up on the vibe, but she is staring awkwardly at the floor.

"Okay, our first and most important objective is to take 'Abu Ghraib' upstairs—the bedrooms and bathrooms. All surfaces must be wiped down, the windows cleaned, and the floors vacuumed. Sinks, toilets, and tubs must be scrubbed, and the bathroom floors mopped. You will also strip the beds and wash all the sheets and pillowcases. It's been a while."

Sofia leans toward her mother and whispers the translation so Jack can't hear it. As Ana listens, her eyes widen, realizing how big the job will be.

"Now, on the blinds in the windows. Don't just wipe them down. I want each one scrubbed. Understand?"

Ana whispers something to Sofia. Jack turns to Sofia for the translation. "She says she won't be able to get everything done in one day. This will take more times coming here."

Jack is disappointed. He looks like he is about to say something, but Ana interrupts. Sofia translates: "She wants to know if you have cleaning things like soaps and all that kind of stuff."

"You don't bring your own?"

"No, not really," Sofia says with a bratty tone. "I mean, you saw us get in the car. We weren't carrying anything."

"A detail I failed to notice," Jack says, slightly embarrassed. "That doesn't seem right to me. Is that normal?"

"It is for my mom," Sofia says defiantly.

Jack shakes his head with resignation and turns toward the sink. "Look under there and see if it has what you need."

Sofia stoops and opens the doors under the sink. Ana looks

inside and sees some all-purpose cleaner and a bottle of Pine-Sol and then complains to Sofia.

Jack turns to Sofia. "She said she has enough for today, but you will need to buy some things for next time. Also, she wants to know where the brooms and mops are. And a vacuum cleaner. And some rags."

"Anything else? Jack asks sarcastically.

Sofia translates quietly to Ana. Ana grabs her purse and opens it. From inside, she produces some wrapped-up food items and drinks. She hands the items to Sofia and tells her to put them in the refrigerator. Sofia, in turn, tries to hand them to Jack. "Can you put these in your refrigerator?"

"What is it?" Jack asks, not sure if they are overstepping their bounds with him.

"Just some *pupusas* and drinks for lunch."

Jack gets a twisted look on his face. "*Pupusas*? What is that?"

Sofia giggles at Jack's ignorance and whispers in her mother's ear. "This old man doesn't know what a pupusa is." Ana slaps her in the arm for being insulting toward their new client.

"On second thought," Jack says, feeling disrespected once again, "I don't want to know." He refuses to take the food in his own hand. Instead, he just opens the refrigerator door and uses his chin to tell her where to put them. "Just right there will be good."

Sofia isn't sure exactly where. "Here?"

"Right there, next to the apple pie," Jack says with a grouchy voice. He uses his cane to point to a place adjacent to a white cardboard container with a plastic window on top. Sofia places the bag of food next to it and closes the door.

"Okay, now, let's go to work," Jack says as if commanding a platoon of soldiers.

Sofia turns to her Mom but doesn't bother to whisper her translation. "He said it is time to go to work."

"Okay," Ana says forcefully, moving to get the cleaning supplies out from under the sink.

Jack's backyard is more developed than it looks from the street. A closer look reveals there isn't just a pool and guesthouse but also an abandoned pottery studio that now doubles as a tool shed. Off to one side is a large, half-built aviary that has fallen into disrepair. Corralling it all in is a black metal fence that was put there to keep the dogs that lived here long ago. They have long since died, but wooden crosses behind the guest house still mark where they are buried.

Jack appears from the kitchen's back door and tours the grounds with his to-do list. He walks around looking for things he can add, but it is hard for him to concentrate. Every square inch of the place is alive with memories. And for some odd reason, his strongest memories are the times he spent with his grandfather. When Jack was old enough to remember his time with Pop, the old man was already retired and focused on his elaborate garden next to the guest house.

One time, when Jack was less than 10, Pop took him into the garden. Pop had made a little winding path through the various plants. He designed it so the deeper you got into the garden, the taller the plants got. As you reached the rear of it, a dome of greenery hid you from the outside world. And that is where Pop kept his little canvas stool where he could hang out and smoke cigarettes. On this occasion, Pop had some small trowels with him. He gave one to Jack and told him to dig up some earth. Jack dug and soon had a large clump of moist soil in his hand. Pop leaned in and looked closely at the dirt. "What do you think we can grow in this?" Jack just shook his head, utterly vacant of an answer. Pop reached out and put his own hand in it. "Anything we want. It's ours," he laughed. "So you take good care of it when I am gone."

The ringer on Jack's mobile phone erupts with a bugle call. Jack checks the screen and sees the name Mia Russo—the sassy real estate agent.

"Hello, Mia, "Jack says.

"Hi, Jack. Just calling to see how things are going."

"The cleaning crew is here today," Jack says.

"Oh, you hired a cleaning crew! Excellent!"

Jack looks back at the house. In the window of his study, he can see Sofia, but she doesn't look like she is working. Instead, it seems more like she is snooping around. "Yeah, some real pros," he replies to Mia.

"When do you think the house will be ready? I may have a young family interested in taking a look."

"Uh," Jack hesitates with a tone of resistance. "This is going to take a little longer than I anticipated."

"How long do you think?"

"Uh, I'm not really sure at this point. We're just getting started. And I'm just starting to survey the yard. I'll know better in a couple of weeks."

Mia hesitates for a moment, then asks, "Weeks?"

"You're the one who told me to clean it. Now that I'm doing it, you want a half-assed job?"

Mia gives in with a sigh. "You're right. Well, call me when you know better."

"Roger that!"

Inside Jack's study, Sofia is indeed not working. Instead, she's just looking at all the military memorabilia on the wall and his desk. She fingers a few old pictures of him in his Marine uniform. One of them piqued her curiosity. It shows Jack in his late 40s looking super macho with a rifle in his hands and a cigar in his mouth. Sofia picks it up for a closer look.

"That was during the first Iraq war," Jack says as he enters the door, "Right after the Battle of Nasiriyah."

Sofia doesn't look over at Jack. She's not embarrassed that he caught her snooping. "Were you a general?"

Jack laughs. "Ha, I wish. I was a Lieutenant Colonel."

Sofia looks up from the picture. "Did you kill anybody?"

"In Vietnam, I killed a few, but by the time Iraq came along, I was doing logistics, so I was a little removed from direct combat."

"Did you get hurt?"

"Yeah, I almost got blown up by a grenade in Viet Nam once. He then points to his desk, where a frame holds a Purple Heart medal. "They gave me the Purple Heart for it."

Sofia takes another look at the picture and then puts it down. She looks around, searching for something else. Her eye lands on the large painting of George Washington. "Who is that?"

"That is George Washington, the man I asked you about in the car. He was a military officer and the first president of the United States. He was an amazing man—he presided over the drafting of the U.S. Constitution. If you are going to live in this country, you should know about him."

"Okay," Sofia says with no interest.

Jack reaches out to a bookcase where there are numerous volumes about Washington. He pulls one off the shelf and shows it to Sofia. "This one is easy to read."

Sofia's eyes have already moved on. She scans the personal pictures. "Do you have a family?"

Jack frowns at this question and answers sharply. "Yes."

"Where are they?" Sofia asks, looking around for more pictures.

"There," Jack grunts painfully.

Sofia studies the images of Jack's two kids. She's curious why there isn't a picture of his wife. She turns to ask, but Jack cuts her off. "I'm divorced."

"For a long time?"

Jack has reached the end of his rope with all this. "Are you here to work or ask a lot of questions?"

Sofia gets a funny look on her face like she has just been insulted. "I'm not here to work."

"What?"

"I'm just here to translate."

"Uh, I don't know who told you that, but that is not the deal I made."

Sofia shrugs her shoulders. "Sorry. I just translate as a favor to my mother."

"Nope. You got it wrong."

"No, I got it right. You got it wrong," Sofia says defiantly.

Jack hasn't liked this girl from the start and now it's confirmed. He looks at her thinking about all the young soldiers who tried to test his metal over the years. He got very good at breaking them like matchsticks. And this little illegal is about to find out how it is done.

"Alright," Jack says menacingly. "Why don't we start by getting the record straight." He pulls out his phone and says, "Call Robert Mathews."

Sofia shows no sign of fear as the computer voice on Jack's phone responds, "Calling Robert Mathews—mobile."

"Hey, Jack," Robert says through the phone speaker. "How's it going? Are the ladies there?"

"Yes," Jack says. "But there seems to be a little confusion about our cleaning arrangement."

"Oh yeah? What's the problem?"

"As I recall, it is for two cleaners, one of which is guaranteed to speak English."

"Yep, that's the deal."

Jack looks over at Sofia. Sofia looks back, showing the first signs of guilt on her face.

"Okay, thanks," Jack says into the phone.

"Is there a problem?" Robert asks.

"No, no problem. Just making sure we're all on the same page here. I'll talk to you later."

"You got it, Jack. See you then."

Jack hangs up and smiles at Sofia. "Now, what were you saying?"

Jack's authoritarian attitude angers Sofia. "I never agreed to that!"

"Of course you did. Otherwise, you wouldn't be here!"

Sofia just stares at Jack with anger in her eyes.

"Now, do you want to work, or should we get your mother and call the whole thing off?"

Sofia turns away from Jack and heads back to the kitchen. Jack follows her. "Where are you going?"

Once in the kitchen, Sofia grabs her purse and throws it over her shoulder. "Okay. I am ready to go."

Jack frowns, thinking, "What a little brat" to himself. "Okay, fine," he says. He turns, walks to the stairs, and calls, "Hey, Ana!"

"*Si,*" Ana responds from out of sight.

"Can you come down here?"

Ana appears at the top of the stairs.

Jack waves her down to the kitchen.

When Ana arrives in the kitchen and sees Sofia standing defiantly with purse in hand, she gets curious. "What's going on?"

Sofia looks at her mother sternly. "I want to go home."

Ana is confused. "Why?"

Sofia raises her voice in anger. "I don't like this house. I don't like this old man. I want to go home."

Ana sighs with frustration. "Sofia, don't do this."

Sofia crosses her arms, elevating her defiance. "I want to go home."

Ana becomes angry and realizes she can no longer remain polite in front of Jack. "No, you are not going home. You are staying right here until we finish our work!"

Sofia stares at her mother silently for a moment, then makes up her mind. She hops up on one of the high stools next to the center counter, reaches into her purse, and pulls out her sleep mask. She places the mask over her eyes, then leans back and crosses her arms resolutely.

Ana rushes to Sofia. "Oh my god. Take that off right now!"

Ana grabs at the mask. Sofia tries to hold it in place but loses the battle. She jumps up from the stool, grabs the mask back from her mother, and stuffs it in her purse. She then turns to Jack. "Can you take me home? I want to go home!"

"Sofia, please," Ana now pleads with her. "Please, don't ruin this."

Sofia ignores her and keeps her focus on Jack. "Can you drive me home?"

Jack assesses the situation. He senses Ana won't object if he applies a little pressure. He turns to Sofia sternly. "If you want to go home, you're walking home. We have work to do here."

Ana doesn't understand. "What did he say?"

"He told me to walk home." And with that, Sofia picks up her things, walks through the front door, and heads toward the street. Ana starts to chase after her, but Jack stops her. He holds up a hand to tell her to wait. Ana isn't sure what is going on. Jack points to his watch and then holds up five fingers to ask for five minutes. Ana looks worried but decides to go with Jack's plan. Jack slams the door shut with a loud thud.

Sofia gets to the end of the sidewalk and stops. She is surprised that her mother is not chasing after her. She turns quickly and walks away, lifting her phone to call Memo. No service. Not much farther, she encounters a Latina woman walking a white baby in an expensive carriage. Sofia asks. "Do you know the way to Red Bank?"

The Latina woman looks at her with surprise. "That's a long way from here."

Sofia looks around and then gives up her flight with a frustrated sigh.

Not much after 11:00, Sofia is with Jack in one of the bedrooms. They're standing next to a set of blinds that Sofia is attempting to clean with a duster. She moves the duster up and down over the top of the blinds with little enthusiasm.

"No, that is not how you do it," Jack says with a commanding voice.

Sofia closes her eyes in frustration. She is at the very end of her rope. Her anger has been shattered by a growing urge to cry. Without turning around, she offers the duster to Jack. "Okay, then show me how."

Jack can sense she is about to crack and prepares to push her over the edge as if she is a new recruit at boot camp. "Don't you try to hand that to me! Don't act like you are too high and mighty to do some honest work. Open the blinds."

Sofia starts to tear up. She silently obeys and opens the blinds.

"Run the duster sideways between each blind, starting at the top."

Sofia reaches up, but she's too short to reach the top one. "It's too high."

Jack snorts with extreme displeasure. "Please don't tell me you are more worthless and stupid than my old dog. He was deaf and blind but still knew how to steal food from the kitchen counter—which is more than I can say for you. Ever hear of a thing called a stool?"

Sofia finally cracks. With a sudden fit of sobbing, she crumbles to the ground. She holds a hand over her face and tries hiding the tears. Jack watches her silently for a moment but shows little sympathy. "Oh," he says sarcastically. "Is this what 'tough girl' looks like on the inside?"

Sofia says nothing.

"Is this how you act at home when your mom asks you to do something? Is this what you do when the teacher wants to see your homework at school?"

Sofia continues to hold her face, but some inner strength stirs. She feels her animal spirits rise. Her confidence returns. Without pulling her hands away, she coldly tells Jack, "I don't go to school."

The statement is so out of left field it throws Jack off his game. "What?"

Sofia slowly moves her hands away from her face. Her cheeks are still streaked with tears, but her eyes show no weakness. "I don't go to school. I quit."

"What do you mean, you quit?"

"Are you as deaf as your old dog? I said I quit. I dropped out!"

Jack is dumbfounded. He can't get his mind around it. "Wait a second," he says as he tries to grapple with the meaning of this. "Let me get this straight. You leave your country and go to all the trouble to come here. Then, despite the fact that you have no papers and no means of support, we let you into our schools, we teach you English, give you books, and we even feed you. Why would you want to come all the way up here just so you can thumb your nose at all that and drop out?

Sofia shakes her head at his ignorance. "Who said I wanted to come here?"

Jack just can't process all this. It's coming at him too quickly. "What?"

"I didn't want to come here," Sofia snarls. "I didn't want to leave my home, just like you don't want to leave your home. Can you understand that, old man?"

A few pieces of shrapnel have hit Jack during his military career, but he never took an enemy bullet. Today, he feels like he has just been hit by one in the gut. Somehow, this train wreck of a girl has blown past the perimeter and reached command and control. She has nailed him in the worst way. She has made him see something of himself in her. And in doing so, she has made him feel what no commander should ever feel in front of a new recruit—vulnerability.

"How do you know I don't want to leave my home?" Jack asks defensively.

"I can see it in your eyes," Sofia says.

It isn't part of Jack's code to cover up or lie about the truth, so he decides to confound the enemy with silence.

The drive back to Ana and Sofia's place is filled only with the sounds of Jack's Caddy as it travels down along the river toward Red Bank Sofia is sitting up front in the passenger seat, holding her hand out to shade her eyes from the afternoon sun. Ana sits in the back, fingering the beads on her rosary, while Jack stares straight at the road ahead of them. He pulls down the sunshade to protect his eyes from the sun, then looks over at Sofia. It reminds him of a similar situation with his own daughter, Beth, when she was about the same age as Sofia. Beth also preferred to use her hands instead of the sunshade. And like Sofia, Beth was rebel-headed. If he told her to use the sunshade, she would just refuse. Not because she didn't see the merit in it but because he, her father, suggested it. "I just don't want to use it," she would say with anger in her voice. At that point, Jack would give in and let Beth have her way, thinking it was just something she would mature out of. It was that way with a lot of issues, but considering how things turned out for Beth, he has often wondered if it was a mistake to let her have her way so much. The more he thought about it, the more he convinced himself that he should have been more strict. Without asking, Jack reaches over and pulls the passenger-side sunshade down for Sofia. Sofia glances over at Jack with suspicion but doesn't say anything and doesn't attempt to lift the sunshade back to where it was. Jack feels good about his successful move as if he has just redeemed himself from an old mistake. "You remind me of my daughter a little bit," Jack says without looking at Sofia.

Sofia doesn't look at Jack. She is still mad at him.

"She's strong-headed like you."

Sofia now glances over at Jack, interested.

"But here's the thing. Beth ended up living in a dump in the 'Hood' because she never used her strengths for anything worthwhile. I see the same thing in you, and well, you better be careful or you're going to end up like her, working at a fast food joint for dirt the rest of your life. Education is important."

Sofia turns away from Jack, pissed off by his lecture. She remains silent until Jack turns the corner and pulls up in front of the tiny house where they live. "I won't work at a fast food place because I'm going back to El Salvador."

Jack is once again befuddled by this girl and finds himself at a loss for words. Sofia opens the passenger door forcefully and quickly heads for the house. Jack turns back to Ana to say goodbye, but Ana doesn't move. She just sits there looking at him. "Ok, thank you," Jack says awkwardly. But still, Ana doesn't move. She just stares at him. Finally, she lifts her hand up where Jack can see it and blurts out the English word for what's on her mind. "Money."

Jack realizes his mistake and quickly grabs his wallet, looking embarrassed. He makes no further plans for them to clean his house. Anna exits without a smile, presuming the job is over.

7

A TRAIL OF TEARS

In the evening, Jack hits the health club like a torpedo in search of Robert, but from the moment he walks in the door, the Latino workers seem to take special notice of him. Mostly, they just smile, but one of the older ladies from the laundry room greets him verbally. "Hello, Meester Jack," she says with a big smile and an extreme accent. All this newfound attention from the staff unnerves Jack, who realizes they all know something about what just went on with Sofia and her mom. By the time he finds Robert sitting on an exercise bike, he is steaming.

"How did it go?" Robert asks innocently.

Jack looks around the exercise floor to see if anyone is within earshot. "I need a new cleaning crew. That's how it went. They were terrible. Useless!"

"Really? Ana does such a good job for us. I don't understand."

"She's okay," Jack barks. "But the daughter, Sofia. What the hell is wrong with that girl?"

"Oh, yeah," Robert confesses. "I heard you had a bit of a run-in with her."

"Oh, so you already know."

"Yeah, everybody keeps up to date on Sofia around here. She's kinda notorious. I guess I should have warned you she has a few issues."

"A few issues? She's a sorry excuse of a human being. Just sorry!"

Robert thinks for a moment, then asks, "You ever see that movie *Cool Hand Luke*?"

Jack seems to know it well. "Yeah, what's that got to do with it?"

"Remember when the warden at that prison beats Luke and says, 'What we have here is a failure to communicate?'"

"Yeah."

"Well, in Sofia's case it's, 'What we have here is a failure to assimilate.'"

Jack hesitates. "What does that mean?"

"Jack, you got to understand it can be traumatic for young kids to get ripped out of their homes and dropped into our culture. Some take it in stride and adapt quickly, but some don't. Sofia is definitely a 'some don't' kind of girl, and that is how we get a failure to assimilate. She isn't adapting to life here. She ain't buying it."

"Well," Jack says gruffly, "She didn't want to leave her home in the first place. Maybe they should have just left her where she was."

"You've got a point, but it just ain't that simple, unfortunately."

"Yeah, it is. She doesn't belong here. Her whole family doesn't belong here."

Robert hesitates for a moment, then asks. "Are you going to jump on a bike?"

"Why?"

"I got a story I want to tell you."

Jack gets suspicious. "What kind of story?"

"Well, you know, I spend a lot of time with Ana driving back and forth to my house, and we talk a lot. I know the whole story about what happened to Sofia. You should hear it."

Jack stares at Robert for a long moment, resentful that he can't stop himself from being sucked into this whirlpool of uncomfortable feelings he is experiencing. In the old days, he would have had the discipline to walk away, but his aging mind seems to come with an unexpected and unwanted weakness to hear people out.

Sofia's road to the States, according to Robert, really started before she was born. One day, while still pregnant with Sofia, Ana was coming out of a store when she was approached by a young gang banger from the notorious MS-13 gang. The young man with tattoos on his face just asked for her name and then stabbed her with a screwdriver in the abdomen. Luckily she was not seriously injured, even though the puncture was close to the baby. While she was recovering in a clinic, she made up her mind that it was too dangerous to stay in El Salvador.

Sofia's father had run off with another woman by that point, and Ana was living with her widowed mother, Estella, on a small farm not too far from the capital. Ana's older daughter Roberta was also living there with her man, Arnell. All in all, they weren't doing too badly as they had a mix of livestock and coffee that provided them with enough income to get by. The problem was the *"pandilleros"*—like MS-13—who had grown so powerful, they were a menace to everyone, always demanding money. Anyone who failed to cooperate, no matter if you were a taxi driver or policeman, would quickly end up dead. El Salvador had become the murder capital of the world.

Not long after Sofia was born, Ana's old childhood sweetheart Juan got in touch with her and struck up a long-distance conversation. He, too, had given up on El Salvador and was already living in New Jersey and had good, solid work at the health club, but he was very lonely. He asked her to come up, promising romance and employment opportunities. He also said he would raise the money for the trip north for both Ana and Sofia if she would come. Ana took a leap of faith and accepted Juan's invitation.

It took some time, but eventually, Juan did come up with some money, but it was only enough for one person. If Ana wanted to go to New Jersey, she would have to leave Sofia behind until they could raise more money. Ana was torn to tears, but Roberta pushed her mom to go. "Arnel and I can take care of Sofia," she said. "You can send for her if things work out. Otherwise, you can just come back. But you have to try. At some point, all of us will need to go."

Ana fretted about it for weeks, but in the end, she realized it was the best thing to do for herself and her daughters. It was a tearful goodbye at the bus station. Sofia cried for her mother, but Ana could only push her back into Roberta's arms and promise to send for her as soon as possible.

The loss of her mother was tough on Sofia, but over time she got used to living with Roberta and her husband as stand-in parents. She also became very close with her Abbi, Estella. She lived in blissful innocence, running free on the land with her animals and friends. She was too young to notice the growing corruption and gang violence surrounding her.

It took years, but Ana finally got enough money together to send for her daughter when Sofia was eight years old. At first, Sofia was pretty excited about going north. Everyone told her how great it was going to be and made the whole experience sound like a big, enjoyable adventure. But then the reality of the trip didn't turn out to be fun at all. Roberta and Arnell already had their son Ricki by then, and Roberta was pregnant with Angelica. They hoped Arnel could take Sofia, but there wasn't enough money for that, and Arnel didn't want to leave his wife while she was pregnant. Instead, they followed the common practice of placing Sofia into the hands of another couple going north who would pretend to be her parents. Roberta and Arnel knew the couple, but Sofia didn't.

The network moved Sofia's group up a series of back roads that avoided checkpoints on the borders of El Salvador, Honduras, Guatemala, and Mexico. There were occasional stops at stash houses, but for the most part, they were always on the move. When they got close to the U.S. border, things got scary. Sofia, her fake parents, and about 80 others were forced to crawl through a hole in the bottom of a cargo container lashed to the back of a semi-tractor-trailer truck. It was dark and smelled awful. There were only some apples to eat and very little water. There were no toilet facilities, only buckets for emergencies. The crew moving them handed out pills that would constipate them, saving them the embarrassment. It was dark, and it seemed like they were in there for days. People were moaning, crying, demanding to get out.

When the truck finally stopped and let them out, they were in the "middle of nowhere, Texas," close to the border. Before their eyes could adjust to the bright sun, the coyote guide had them marching across a long stretch of desert. It was an experience that Sofia remembers being worse than the dark cargo container. But somehow, they made it to a small town and were suddenly on an air-conditioned bus headed north.

Ana was at the bus station in Red Bank when Sofia finally arrived. Ana ran to her daughter with arms wide and her eyes filled with tears of joy, but Sofia was confused. She no longer recognized her mother and even wondered if this was another "fake" mother she would be traveling with. "I'm your real mother," Ana giggled. But Sofia didn't feel the connection.

Ana took Sofia to a run-down apartment in the downtown area of Red Bank. Almost immediately, Ana could tell that the migration experience had been very tough on Sofia. To make matters worse, Sofia arrived in New Jersey at the end of the fall. It was already cold, and a long gray winter was setting in. Sofia had never lived in cold weather and immediately disliked it.

Ana hoped that Sofia would feel better once she was in school and could make some friends, but that didn't work out either. For unknown reasons, the school staff mistook Sofia's culture shock for a serious learning disability and placed Sofia with the special needs kids. When she finally proved herself to be intelligent and capable, they placed her back in normal classes, but the damage was already done. This made it hard for her to have much interaction with the normal kids. Even the Latinos were put off by her and labeled her a "Tardo." It left Sofia demoralized, downtrodden, and angry.

Before long, Sofia started telling Ana and Juan how much she hated living in New Jersey. She told them she wanted to return to El Salvador and live with Roberta. Ana and Juan thought maybe this was something she would get over, but she never did. The drumbeat of demands to be sent back to El Salvador lasted for years. When she reached 12, they finally succumbed and, under the advice of more knowledgeable friends, pooled some money and bought her a plane ticket back to El Salvador. They were all amazed at how cheap and easy it was to leave the U.S.

Sofia was able to live in El Salvador for another three years and was very happy to do so. By this time, Roberta had both Ricki and Angelica, and they felt like siblings to Sofia. That, along with her ever-loving grandmother, made Sofia feel like she was home again. But all wasn't well in the *pueblo*. The gang problem had worsened, and the continual persecution of the family for money continued.

One day, when Sofia was about 14, two gang guys came to Roberta's door to discuss a new satellite TV dish they spotted on the roof of the house. It was a sure sign that the family was getting remittances from the States and that they could pay a monthly tax to the gangs. While they discussed the price, one of the gang guys spotted Sofia and became interested in her. He told Roberta that Sofia was the kind of girl he wanted to marry. He made it sound like a joke, but Roberta knew it was no joke. Other girls in the area had been dragged from their homes by *pandilleros*, and there was little to stop them.

Roberta called Ana to let her know Sofia was in danger, and they needed to get her out of there as quickly as possible. Roberta and Arnell understood it would be next to impossible to get her on a new bus headed north alone, so, in the end, they decided it was time for the whole family to go. Sofia and Estella were the holdouts against the move, but eventually, they won over Estella, and Sofia's fate was sealed.

"So then Sofia came back again?" Jack asked incredulously.

"Yep, that's about it," Robert replied.

"Unbelievable," Jack said, taking it all in.

Robert agrees, hoping he has elevated Jack's understanding of the situation. "I know, right?"

"They just come and go like it's a revolving door," Jack sighs. "Terrible."

Robert's expression falls, but he doesn't give up. "You know what is amazing is how we all focus on where these people are running to, but very few ask about what they are running from."

Jack doesn't respond. His thoughts are already steering back to his own predicament. "Being chased out of your home can be hell."

Robert senses a hint of sympathy in Jack's voice, but before he can say anything else, Juan passes them, pushing a mop and bucket. When Juan sees Robert and Jack, he stops with a big smile. "Hey," he says to Robert with the usual little-too-loud excitement in his voice. He then turns to Jack and awkwardly sticks out his hand for a shake. "How are you?" Juan asks in his thickly accented English. Jack hesitates, but then extends his hand for the shake. Juan doesn't have any other words he can say to Jack, so he just repeats the word, "Good, good," a few times and departs.

"What the hell is going on around here?" Jack asks in an irritated tone. "The staff are all over me today."

Robert smiles. "Well, they all heard you gave Sofia some 'tough love,' and well, I guess they have decided that is a good thing. You got some fans now."

Jack looks around the room to see what other staff might be around. He spots an older Latina woman rolling up small towels. She makes eye contact and smiles at him.

"So, what do you think?" Robert asks. "You want to give Sofia and Ana another shot so they can finish cleaning your house?" Jack just shakes his head, feeling the tug of that whirlpool of mixed emotions from which he can't escape.

8

NUNCA MÁS

"No! Never!" Sofia says, storming out the back door of the little house. She's just heard that the job with Jack is back on, and she must go up to his home again. "Find somebody else! I'm never going there again!"

"Increased resilience in the rejection of her circumstance" would probably be how Robert Mathews would describe Sofia's reaction to her encounter with Jack. It was her first time being around a white Americano for an extended period, and she hoped it would be her last. "It's not that I hate him for who he is," Sofia told Roberta, "but how he acts like he is so much better than me."

Ana comes to the back door but doesn't follow her daughter into the yard. "There is nobody else!" Sofia doesn't answer her. Instead, she walks up to where her grandmother Estella is feeding chickens in the backyard. Sofia says nothing. She just stands and stews.

How is our escape fund doing?" Estella asks without looking over. "You didn't spend your quinceanera money on that boy, did you?"

Sofia is caught slightly off guard by the question. "No, I still have it. But it isn't enough."

Estella turns to Sofia and asks, "Did your mother pay you for working at that man's house?"

"No!"

"Did you ask?"

"No."

"I'm sure she would if you asked her."

Sofia looks up at Estella, checking to see if the old woman has that distant look in her eye that appears from time to time. But Estella looks clear-eyed and in the moment. "It would help us get out of here faster."

Sofia can't argue with that logic. She turns and looks back at the house to see if her mother is still at the door. She is not.

"Just think what it will be like to be home again," Estella says. "Our real home."

Sofia turns back to Estella. She thinks about her Abbi's house where they all lived. It makes her feel better.

Estella smiles at Sofia wisely. "You are like me, child. You know we do not belong here. Maybe you should not look at cleaning the old Americano's house as something so horrible but as an opportunity to raise money."

Sofia looks into her grandmother's eyes. "You think Mama would give me some of the money?"

"Without you, there is no money," Estella says with a wise smile. "So, I'm sure she will if you are nice about it."

Estella gets serious and turns to Sofia. "Dear one, we come from the same spirit, you and me. So when I go, I am giving my house to you."

Sofia is stunned by this. A rare, genuine smile grows large across her face. "Really?"

Estella smiles back at her. "Yes, this will be my promise to you."

Sofia grabs her grandmother and hugs her tightly. "*Gracias,* Abbi."

Estella hugs Sofia back. "But let that be our little secret for now."

Just past sunset, Memo's electric bike cuts across a street busy with traffic. He has Sofia sitting side-saddle just in front of him. He's going fast, and Sofia is enjoying the ride. "Where are we going?"

"You'll see," Memo says with a crazy smile.

They arrive at the world headquarters of his outdoor furniture business in the parking space below his Aunt's apartment. "More furniture?" Sofia asks.

"No, no. Tonight we are going upstairs to my aunt's place. *Vamos,*" Memo says, grabbing her hand and heading toward the building.

"Why are we going to see your aunt?" Sofia asks.

"We're not. We're going to see her apartment. She's in Texas with her new boyfriend."

Sensing a setup, Sofia slows down. "Wait."

Memo turns. "What?"

"I'm not so sure this is a good idea."

But Memo remains confident. "*Sí, lo es.* Because this is where we are going to live."

Sofia is more irritated than shocked by Memo's presumptuous statement. "Where are *we* going to live?" she asks.

"She told me she is moving out but will keep the lease if we want to rent it from her."

Sofia shakes her head, convinced this must be a ploy to get her upstairs. "You're just making that up," she says.

Memo looks at Sofia seriously. "No, I told her about you and how I feel about you. She knows I am serious. She wants to help. She said we could live here for free for a few months until I have enough money to pay."

"But Memo," Sofia resists.

"*Vamos*. Just five minutes," Memo says with a nudge. "I'll be good. I promise the moon."

Sofia thinks about it for a minute, then drops her resistance.

The apartment is on the top floor and is well-kept. It has a view of a park and part of downtown. It only has one bedroom, but the living room is large, and the kitchen is clean. Sofia is impressed. "Can't you see us here?" Memo says as he tries to hug her.

Sofia pulls away from him. "No, not really."

"I can," Memo says as they walk into the bedroom.

In the bedroom, Memo plops on the bed. Sofia looks out the window. Her smile disappears when Memo motions her to join him. "No way," she says.

Memo sits on the side of the bed and grabs her around the legs. "All you gotta do is let yourself believe."

Sofia struggles to get away from him. "Believe in what?"

"Believe me when I tell you we can make it here."

"Ha!" Sofia says, pulling away.

"I'm a serious *mujer*," Memo pleads. "I'm going to work my *culo* off. Then, I will make my business 'big big' and make you and the kids happy as coconuts on the beach!"

Sofia almost laughs. "Me *and* the *kids*?"

"*Sí, vamos*, Memo says with romantic eyes. "I'm ready."

Memo tries to grab her again. She jumps away from him with a giggle. "You're out of your mind. Get away."

Memo gets on his hands and knees and starts to crawl after her. "*Ellos dicen,* this is the land of opportunity. If it is, let us not waste the opportunity right here, *mi amor*."

"You said you were going to be good."

"*Cambié*, I changed my mind!"

"No! Stop!" Sofia says with a sudden seriousness.

Memo doesn't slow down for a second. He chases after her on all fours. Sofia stays just ahead of him. When they are next to the bed, she picks up some magazines and hits him over the head. "I'm serious," she says. "Stop!"

Memo stops. He feigns like he is hurt and crawls back to the bed, where he lies silent and holds his head.

Sofia suddenly becomes concerned. She moves to the bed. "Did I hurt you?" She gets onto the bed beside him and tries to see if he is genuinely hurt. Memo takes his hands off his head and looks at her thoughtfully. "I know you think I'm *un poco loco*, but it's only because *te amo*. I love you so much."

Sofia looks into his eyes. Memo looks back at her with a vulnerability she has never seen before. Sofia takes a deep breath. "I've decided I am going back to El Salvador with my grandmother."

"You always say that," Memo sighs.

"No, this time it is for real."

Memo gets a suspicious look on his face. "Really? How is that?"

"Memo, she is going to give me her house."

Memo is shocked. "*¿Segura?*"

Sofia nods with assurance. "She told me today."

Memo suddenly realizes this might happen. "No, c'mon. *No te vayas.* You can't! I can't even think of living here without you."

Sofia stares at him for a long moment. "Then why don't you come with me?"

"Back to El Salvador?"

Sofia smiles hopefully. "*Sí.* Why not?"

Memo doesn't have to think. He already knows the answer. "Because this is my dream, to live here."

"We'll have a place to live without rent or anything," Sofia says with conviction.

"But what about my furnitures?"

"There are still plenty of rich people in El Salvador," Sofia assures him. "You can still sell your benches to them!"

"But how would we even get there?"

Sofia smiles. "We're going to fly."

"And you have money for that?"

"Not all of it," Sofia says, "but I have a job working for a rich old Americano."

"You do?"

"Yes. Maybe I could show him a picture of your bench. Maybe he will buy it so you can buy your plane ticket."

Memo thinks about this but somehow can't get his head around it. "But I love it here. In a big country, dreams stay with you. Bruce Springsteen. The Rock. Iron Man!"

Sofia gets angry and starts to pull away. "Ok then, just take me home."

Memo reaches for her. "No, wait."

Sofia turns. "What?"

Memo closes his eyes for a moment, then makes a decision. "Sofia, I love you. If going back to El Salvador is what will make you happy, then I will go with you."

Sofia is shocked by this sudden turn. "Really?"

Memo nods. "I don't want you away from my sight—ever. And if that means going back, then our big country will be little El Salvador."

Sofia giggles, "OK, but it is a secret right now. Don't tell anyone!"

Memo holds his index finger up to his mouth. "My lips are closed tight with staples from the devil himself."

Sofia suddenly gets a big smile on her face. For the first time, she truly believes Memo loves her. Memo pulls her toward him. She doesn't resist, and their lips come together passionately. Memo pulls her further into the bed until she looks up at him. He kisses her again and reaches for the first button on her blouse.

9

GANG BANGERS

Ana waves with a smile as Jack pulls up in front of her tiny home on Cherry Tree Avenue. Sofia, standing next to her, does not smile.

"Good morning, ladies," Jack calls from inside the car.

Ana nudges Sofia with some motherly advice. "If you want to get paid, just be nice and do your work, understand?"

Sofia forces a fake smile at Jack and then starts to walk toward the car. "Yes, Mama. I understand."

Sofia walks to the car's passenger side but gets in the back seat instead of the front. Ana enters the backseat on her side. As soon as she is in, she slaps Sofia on the knee as a reminder to sit up front.

Sofia takes a deep breath, but Jack looks in the mirror and says coldly, "It's okay. Just stay in the backseat."

Sofia glances at Jack. She can tell by the tone in his voice that he is already being mean, letting her know he doesn't want her in the front seat next to him. Sofia turns to her mother with a false sense of triumph. "He wants me to stay in the back."

Jack doesn't attempt to chit-chat with his workers. He silently heads towards Main Avenue, but Ana nudges Sofia to remind her about something. Jack can sense something is coming and asks, "Is there a problem?"

Sofia gives Jack a phony smile. "No, no problem. My mom just wants to know if you can stop at her friend's house for a minute."

Jack frowns. "Stop at a friend's house?

"Yes, stop at the friend's house," Sofia says with irritation.

Jack slows the car. "For what?"

"She's picking up some food."

Jack glances at Ana and then back to Sofia in the mirror. "Food?"

"Yes. Food. For our lunch."

Jack thinks for a moment, then angrily says, "Why can't you just bring food from your own damn house?"

Frustrated, Sofia shakes her head and tells her mom Jack does not want to stop. Ana is surprised but doesn't push the demand. She shrugs as if to say, "No lunch for us today." But Sofia isn't quite so fatalistic and turns back to Jack. "Is there something at your house we can eat for lunch?"

Jack sighs as he usually does with great displeasure. "OK, to the friend's house. Which way?"

A few minutes later, Jack pulls to the curb next to an old, neglected house. Some old, broken-down cars are in the driveway, and junky-looking toys and boxes are in the front yard. Ana gets out of the car and heads for the house, leaving Jack and Sofia alone in the car.

Jack just shakes his head in disgust as he looks around the neighborhood. "I remember this area from a long time ago. It used to be a nice part of town."

Sofia looks out her window, but she doesn't have the memories that Jack has to make any comparison. She turns to her phone to see if Memo has texted her. He's left her a selfie of himself with a big smile next to a new concrete bench.

"If you put some paint on that house," Jack says, "it would be a nice home. But then, you people would just trash it again."

Sofia just rolls her eyes and turns to her phone, responding to Memo with a smiley face emoji that has red hearts for eyes.

Jack looks in the mirror. "Why do you guys get food here? Why don't you just go to the grocery store like everybody else?"

"We don't eat the food from the stores so much. Her friend makes real food, like from El Salvador."

"Are you saying American food is not real?"

Sofia forces a smile. "It's just not what we eat. And it's cheaper."

Jack then turns his attention to a group of four teenage Latino boys coming down the sidewalk. Sofia sees them, too. She lowers herself in the seat so they won't see her, but it's too late. One of the boys catches sight of Sofia and then nudges the other boys to take a look. Seeing their old classmate Sofia sitting in the backseat of a Caddy with a white chauffeur is interesting to them.

"Sofia is that you?"

Sofia looks away, not wanting to respond. One of the boys sees this and gets a little more aggressive. "No, that's not Sofia. That's Olivia Rodrigo and her Americano chauffeur."

The boys giggle a bit then the short one takes it up a notch. "Maybe she's just out turning tricks."

The boys laugh, but Sofia doesn't find the joke amusing. Without looking at them, she holds up a middle finger in the window.

The boys stop. "Hey, what is that for? You can't take a joke?"

Sofia ignores them. Jack watches apprehensively as the boys move closer to the car.

"Roll down the window and do that. See what that gets you."

Sofia continues to ignore them. The guy talking knocks on the window. "Hey, I'm talking to you, *Tardo*."

At this point, Sofia explodes with anger. She opens the door and lurches out at him. "Don't call me that," Sofia says forcefully as she pushes the boy. The boy jumps back with a laugh.

"Watch out," another boy giggles. "Dumb dumb is on the warpath."

"Hey," Jack yells as he slowly and painfully climbs out of the car. "That's enough."

The lead boy turns his attention toward Jack. "You lost or something, old man?

Jack isn't intimidated. "She's a hell of a lot smarter than you think. Just take a step back."

Insulted by Jack's remark, the boys don't move. Instead, they go into gangster mode. "You calling us stupid, *viejo*?

Jack is angered but tries to calm the situation. "Why don't we just give each other a free pass today? We'll be on our way in a few minutes, so you guys just move along."

"Free pass? There is no stinkin 'free pass' here. Everybody got to pay—especially old Uber drivers. And right now, you owe ten big ones for parking here."

Jack laughs at the boy as if to say, what a joke. "Ten dollars?"

"That's right. Otherwise, this ride might not be looking too good in a few minutes."

Jack thinks about this for a second. "You touch my car, and we'll see who ends up not looking so good."

Jack reaches under the front seat and pulls out his big police security nightstick. He raises it as if to say, don't mess with me.

The boys glance at each other and lose a bit of their gangster pose. They step back, but then one of them picks up a rock and holds it behind his head, ready to throw.

Sofia steps between them. "*Para*, Luis. Enough already!"

Luis keeps the rock behind his head. "Who is this *cabrón*?"

"He is military, and he is mean. Don't mess with him."

Luis looks at Sofia, then back to Jack. He doesn't know what to do. He glances at his friends nervously just as Ana reappears, speaking Spanish. "Oh my god! What is going on here?"

Luis quickly lowers the rock. *"Nada."*

Ana frowns at the boy. "It better be nothing. Otherwise, I will discuss this with your mother later."

The boys suddenly become boys again, and the situation quickly de-escalates.

Ana continues toward Jack's car. "Move out of my way so I can get in the car."

The boys obey.

As the car drives away, Sofia pulls herself together and looks up to see Jack looking at her in the mirror. It might be a look of understanding, or concern, or just general sympathy—she isn't sure. She just knows he has seen a part of her she isn't comfortable with him seeing. She looks away at her mother.

Ana is angry and scolds Sofia. "How many times do I have to tell you? Don't talk to them. They're pandilleros."

Sofia frowns. "No, they're not. They're little boys just pretending they are tough."

Ana lifts a finger to lecture Sofia. "Little boys pretending to be pandilleros are more dangerous than real ones."

Jack, who continues to pay close attention to what is going on, asks Sofia, "What is she saying?"

"She's just talking about pandilleros, the gang guys from MS-13."

"Yeah, I heard about those guys," Jack says cautiously. "But I thought they were only in El Salvador."

"There are some around here," Sofia says as if it is common knowledge.

"Really? Around here?"

"Yes. Why not? This is where they come from."

"What do you mean, this is where they come from?"

"They started here in America before they went to El Salvador."

"What? That's not true."

"Yes, it is! You didn't know that?"

"That's just an excuse to blame us for your problems."

"Ask your phone if you don't believe me."

"Ask my phone? What?"

In frustration, Sofia lifts her phone and says, "Hey, Google, where does the gang MS-13 come from?" Within seconds, the phone's robotic voice announces, "The Criminal gang known as MS-13 or Mara Salvartrucha originated in Los Angeles, California, in the 1980s."

Before Jack can fully absorb the information, Sofia adds, "They started here, and then they came to El Salvador, and then my family had to come here to get away from them. *¿Comprendes?*"

"Don't talk to me like that."

"What did I say?"

"Knock it off with the snotty attitude."

Sofia gives in. "Okay, okay."

They ride in silence for a few minutes until Jack returns to the gangs. "The gangs in El Salvador come from the U.S. I find that hard to believe."

"Believe what you want," Sofia says without looking at Jack. "My family is scared of them, but I'm not. I think they are all dumb and stupid."

It's partly cloudy with a chance of rain when the cleaning team gets the day's work assignments. Sofia is assigned to the kitchen windows that face the backyard and told she is to clean them inside and out, and that includes the glazed French doors that contain six window panes each. Although unhappy with the notion of rubbing so many windows with years of pesky streaks, Sofia sets about her job without complaint. Meanwhile,

Ana heads upstairs to take on the bathroom with a tub of cleaning products, and Jack recedes to his man cave with a mission of his own—an internet search for a new place to live.

Jack sits in front of his dusty old PC and prepares to type "Condos Jersey Shore" into the search bar, but is distracted by something else. After ensuring no one is watching, he opens up a private browser window and types in "CIA Gangs of El Salvador." A few seconds later, he lands on a "World Factbook" page presented by the U.S. Central Intelligence Agency, where he learns El Salvador gained its independence from Spain in 1821 and sits on the Pacific coast of Central America, surrounded by Honduras and Guatemala. It is the smallest country in Central America.

Immigrants from El Salvador came to the United States in two waves. The first wave came as a result of the civil war that occurred between 1979 and 1992. The second wave came and is still coming due to criminal gangs, including MS-13. The civil war was fought between the right-wing military-led junta government and a coalition of left-wing groups known as the FMLN. America, fearing communist insurgency, backed the military government. This, in turn, led to a whole basket of human rights abuses, including death squads, massacres, and disappearances.

Scared families, fearing for their lives, headed north to the U.S. border seeking asylum. Many ended up in Southern California. With them were a lot of children, ripped from their lives in El Salvador, much like Sofia. Some adapted, and some didn't. Those who didn't became alienated. Then, some of the alienated kids started little cliques or "clicas" to hang out together.

At first, these little clicas were just headbangers—fans of heavy metal music. But over the years, they drifted into criminal activities that landed many in jail. Once in prison, they came under the influence of the highly developed Mexican gangs. By the time the Salvadorans got out of jail, they were carrying the master playbook on how to build a gang and prosper, courtesy of the Mexicans.

Jack sits back and looks away from the computer screen as he sips coffee. He wonders how all this has escaped him. He does remember Oliver North and the whole Iran–Contra episode under the Reagan administration. But this whole thing going on in El Salvador was pretty much off his radar. He turns back to the computer screen to learn more.

As the Salvadoran gang problem grew in Southern California and other parts of the U.S., the American authorities devised a plan to deal with it. First, they tightened the laws on expelling refugees from the U.S. and then started deporting as many gang bangers as possible. This strategy was beneficial for the U.S., but it was a disaster for El Salvador. When these tattooed thugs found themselves back in El Salvador, they just rebuilt their gangs inside their home country. And as they soon discovered, the government in El Salvador wasn't strong enough to do much about it.

Over the following decades, the gangs in El Salvador invaded almost every aspect of daily life. Any law enforcement that attempted to stand up to them met a horrific end. It was a nasty situation made worse by an insulated, ambivalent upper class and a collection of idiotic politicians who made deals with the gangs to get endorsed for election.

By the late 1990s, the situation had become so bad it set off a new wave of refugees heading north. But this time, the migrants were not running from war. Instead, they were running from gangs being managed, ironically, from prisons inside the U.S. The majority of the stateside Salvadoran gangs remained in California, but a small contingent of those made their way to the East Coast and are now active, on a smaller scale, in New York and New Jersey.

Jack exits the CIA page and attempts to go back to real estate searches, but he just can't maintain his concentration.

Instead, he remembers stories from his grandfather about the gangs of New York and how miserable it made life for the old man there in a neighborhood called Five Points. It was notorious for being an overcrowded, dangerous, and disease-ridden slum. After further thought, Jack can't help but think his family and Sofia's family are not that different.

Arriving back in the kitchen, Jack finds Sofia cleaning the windows on the backdoor as the intermittent sun fills the backyard with some momentary color. Latino music plays softly from Sofia's phone while she tries to rub one of the more stubborn streaks on the glass. There is a playfulness to her rhythm that Jack has not seen before. After stopping to watch for a moment, Jack says, "Wow. I haven't seen so clearly through those windows in years."

Sofia is caught off guard by Jack's sudden appearance and turns down the music. "These windows were very dirty," she says.

Jack steps closer with an impressed look on his face. "I thought it was just my eyes going bad."

Sofia turns back to admire her work but suddenly sees a strange animal crossing the backyard. "What is that?" Sofia asks with excitement.

Jack steps up next to her. "That's a red fox."

Sofia watches it as it slinks away. "You have a fox?"

"No, he's wild. There are a few around here."

"Where does he live?"

"I don't know. It probably has a den around here somewhere."

"You are not afraid of it?"

Jack laughs. "No, not at all. They don't bother anybody, and they love eating mice and small rats. Good to have around, actually."

Sofia's eyes move from the fox leaving the yard to a flock of small birds grabbing seed from a bird feeder. "What kind of birds are those?"

Jack glances toward the feeder. "Those are European starlings."

"Starlings," Sofia repeats as if she had never heard the name before.

"Yeah, they look like they are running out of seed. The squirrels probably raided the feeder this morning. You want to help me fill up the bird feeder?"

"Sure," Sofia says.

The bird feeder is an old-fashioned tall wooden box with a wide ledge where birds can perch and grab seeds from a small trough. Jack unhooks it from the tree and places it on the ground so they can refill it. Sofia scans the backyard and notices there are lots of birdhouses and feeders. "You have a lot of things for birds."

"Those all came from my mother. She loved birds. She could tell you the name of almost any bird by just listening to it."

"Really?"

"Yeah, like that one calling from the tree. Do you hear that? That's an American robin. It's got a very unique song."

Sofia listens and smiles. She's impressed. "Wow. Is your mother the reason you know so much about birds?"

"Yep. My mother even worked part-time at a bird rescue center. She was going to build her own bird rescue facility here, but she never finished it."

Sofia looks over at the remains of the half-built aviary. "Why do the birds need to be rescued?"

"People find injured birds all the time around here. But a

big part of it is taking pet birds that people don't want anymore."

"People throw away their birds?"

"Well, the truth is, a lot of people buy birds, like parrots, and don't realize they live for 75 years. So, the birds end up living longer than the humans. So they need a place to go."

Sofia thinks about this as she studies the abandoned aviary. "Do you have to go to school to do bird rescue?"

Jack turns to Sofia, a bit surprised, and quickly decides to exploit her interest. "Yeah, but you'll need to finish high school first."

Sofia quickly picks up on the unwanted counseling and grows serious. "Maybe in El Salvador when I go back."

Jack can't help himself. "Do you think going back to El Salvador is realistic? I mean, what are you going to do, just rub your ruby slippers together?"

Sofia turns defensive. "My grandmother and I are going back. Even my boyfriend is coming."

"But exactly how are you going to do that?" Jack asks sarcastically.

Sofia's temper flares. "I saved all the money from my *quinceañera*. We just need a little more. We are going to fly in a plane."

"What is a quincynora?" Jack asks with displeasure.

"It's a special party for when a girl turns 15," Sofia lectures. "All the people who come to the party give you money."

Jack gets the picture but still isn't convinced. "I think you're going to need more than some envelopes with party money," he says with new grouchiness in his voice.

This pushes Sofia over the edge. "Well, at least we are trying —which is more than you."

"Excuse me? What does that mean?" Jack says.

"You just gave up!"

"Gave up what?"

"Your house. You're just going to sell it! No fight. No yelling. Just sell it."

Jack suddenly finds himself on the defensive. "Look, you don't know what's going on here, so don't be so damn presumptuous. It's insulting and disrespectful."

Sofia holds her tongue but stares at Jack without blinking. Jack can see her disappointment in him, and once again, he is befuddled by this young girl's ability to get under his skin. "You better get back to work," he finally says for lack of anything else to say.

Sofia frowns. "I'm done here," she says defiantly and walks off.

10

THE DREAM

A gentle breeze drifts up off the bay and through the dark trees in Jack's yard under a waning crescent moon. Jack crawls into bed just before midnight for what he feels will be a night of peaceful sleep. But not long after he drifts "away with the fairies," as his grandmother used to say, he has a fitful dream where Sofia regretfully appears. They are in a burned-out tropical jungle surrounded by homeless people. Sofia is just staring at him with her angry but sad eyes. Jack turns to his doctor, who is also in the dream. "Is this what happens when you are homeless?" he asks the old doc. "Yes, but there isn't much I can do at this point," the doctor says sadly and tries to put a blood pressure cuff around Jack's arm. A group of policemen appear and start chasing Jack and Sofia while firing machine guns. Jack leads Sofia into an old house where they take refuge, but the police surround it and keep shooting. The fugitives run from room to room, trying to hide from the bullets, and finally find a small space inside a closet. Jack asks Sofia for her phone so they can call the police and negotiate a surrender. But Sofia resists. "We didn't do anything." Jack sticks his hand out for the phone. "It's either surrender or die. Give me the phone." Sofia refuses, screaming, "Screw you," and slams the phone on the floor so hard it breaks in pieces with a thunderous crack and wakes Jack from his nightmare.

As Jack lies awake in his bed, his mind fills with thoughts of Sofia and her unwavering determination to fight for her home. It makes him wonder why he doesn't seem to have the same fire in his belly. Is it simply the diminished vitality of old age, or is there something more profound at play? Maybe this isn't just the "takeaway" period of his life, but a period when the whole of the family heritage is taken away by fate, or destiny, or whatever force it is that does such things. But maybe fate has nothing to do with it. Maybe it's just the twists and turns of life that brought him to the pitiful position he is in. His thoughts then drift back to the past.

When Jack was still a teenager, his dad took over the family real estate business and raised it to new heights by branching into commercial properties. That's when they built the pool and guest house. It's also when they bought the family boat, a big cabin cruiser known as a Hatteras 53. It was named the "Ha' Penny" after a bridge in Dublin and meant to signify the virtues of frugality. Pop often said he paid for his trip to America by walking a mile out of his way to avoid the bridge that charged a half penny to cross.

When Jack's father, Sean, was getting older in the late 1960s, he wanted Jack to take over the family business, but Jack thought it was more important to fight for his country in Vietnam. He wanted to do the right thing, make his mark, and come home a hero with medals to prove his worth. Then, he would be ready to step into the real estate business. Dad was not happy to hear about this, but Jack already knew he was more a product of Pop than his father. And he knew Pop would encourage him to attend to his patriotic duties before making money.

It took three years, and Jack did establish himself as a worthy warrior, but when he finally came home, he didn't receive the hero's welcome he expected from his fellow citizens. Instead, he came home to long hair, war protesters, draft dodgers, yippies, and hippies. There was black power, women's rights, civil rights, and gay pride. The new heroes of the land were the "flower power" types who braved the mud of Woodstock, not the tiger cages of Southeast Asia. Being part of the military meant you were part of the "establishment" and unwilling to "turn on, tune in, and drop out." There wasn't special early access for active military to airplanes or even an occasional "Thank you for your service." Most greetings were frowns or occasional two-fingered peace signs.

Many returning soldiers couldn't escape their military uniforms fast enough, but not Jack. Instead of going with the flow, he rigidly stuck to his principles and angrily refused the new counterculture. Like his grandfather, Jack's values leaned more toward conformity, tradition, and, above all else, patriotism. To him, this new "hippy movement" was self-indulgent and unpatriotic. It represented a liberalism that was eroding traditional American values.

Instead of joining the family business, he re-enlisted in the Marines. It was a massive disappointment for his father, who wasn't as conservative as Jack or Pop. He angrily warned Jack there was no money in the military. But Jack refused to listen. He wanted to yell "love it or leave it" as loudly as possible and be with others who agreed. Unfortunately, there was no social media or conservative news to help organize the young conservatives of the day, so it was either wear a hard hat or join the military. Jack stuck with the military.

Looking back now, Jack can see how that road may have

brought him to where he is, but it wasn't the low pay that placed him in financial straits. It was a sweet smile from a young flight nurse named Camille Carter. He was on patrol during his first tour with his platoon in Vietnam when they got caught in an ambush. A grenade exploded only a few feet from Jack, and hot shrapnel ripped through his leg and neck. The next thing he knew, he was on a stretcher being carried through the jungle. A medevac helicopter created a hurricane as it touched down in a clearing. Jack was shoved in and quickly lifted thousands of feet in the air with a bright-faced flight nurse smiling down at him. "What's your name, soldier?" she asked.

"John O'Mally," Jack said as he winced in pain. "You?"

"Camille," she said, pulling out an IV bag and needle.

"Nice to meet you, Camille. My friends call me Jack."

"Nice to meet you, Jack. You pass out back there? You know what day it is?"

"I don't think I blacked out. It's Tuesday."

"Nope," She joked.

"It's not Tuesday?"

"Nope," Camille said playfully. "Today is your lucky day. It doesn't look like that shrapnel hit anything important, but you get a little shot of feel-good anyway."

Under the influence of morphine and a playful, beautiful blonde from Florida, Jack spent the next 30 minutes of his ride blabbering away about himself like never before. He was putting out all his beliefs, hopes, and dreams like he was discussing the weather. He told Camille things he had never discussed with any woman. He even told her about his desire to find a woman just like her, have some kids, and make a real home. "You married?" he asked her.

It wasn't the first time Camille got a marriage query during a medevac flight, but Jack had something that attracted her. She confessed she wasn't attached to anyone and asked him if he could handle the daughter of a Southern Baptist preacher. Jack thought she was just putting him on, but she assured him it was true. "Women like me come with some baggage." Jack wasn't sure what she meant by that, but it didn't matter. He was already smitten.

After the morphine wore off and the reality of his injuries set in, Jack's thoughts about Camille cooled. He did make some attempts to find her, but getting information on female flight nurses was next to impossible. Over time, he forgot about his magical helicopter girl. Then, three years later, he ran into her again on his second tour of duty at Camp Lejeune in North Carolina. He was at the medical center and stepped into a crowded elevator. Standing in the front, he could hear the conversations behind him, and in the middle of it all, he recognized a voice he had thought about many times. He turned around, and there she was. Her hair was a different color, but it was her.

"Camille?" Jack asked.

Camille looked at him for a second, then got a big smile on her face.

"You remember me?" Jack asked. "Vietnam medevac flight to Natrang?"

Camille smiles with recognition. "Shrapnel to leg and neck, right?"

"Yep. That's me."

"Wow," Camille laughed. What are the odds? I take it you made a full recovery."

"Yeah, no problems," Jack beamed. "Just here for a general physical."

"You stationed here?" Camille asks.

"Yeah. What about you?"

"Yeah, for a while anyway. I'm teaching now."

The elevator reached Camille's floor first, but Jack didn't

hang around. He exited the elevator with her and followed her down the hall. "Can I talk to you for a sec?"

Camille slowed, told her colleagues she would catch up with them, then turned to Jack. "What's up?"

Jack fidgeted nervously. "I just want to let you know I tried to look you up back in Nam. Just couldn't find you."

Camille smiled. "For real?"

"Yeah. Scouts honor. I really did."

"Yeah, well, they kept us flight nurses under tight security. Too many wounded warriors looking for love."

"Tight security is putting it lightly. They made it impossible."

Camille became a little more playful. "How hard did you try?"

Jack thought about it for a minute and decided to go along with her playfulness. "Well, it took a couple of years, but I finally tracked you down."

Camille laughs. "Good one."

The attraction these two felt toward one another was still alive, and things developed rapidly. A little over a year later they walked down the aisle together. The only ripple in the relationship came when Jack was ready to propose and wanted to follow the old conservative tradition of asking her father's permission. This was when he discovered Camille was not the daughter of a Southern Baptist preacher. Instead, she was the daughter of a hard-drinking bowling alley owner in Panama City, Florida. Camille explained the deception as something the military forced upon her. She told Jack they didn't want the flight nurses giving out personal details to soldiers under care. At first, she tried to explain that to her patients, but it never went well. So, she then started to make up the details of her personal life. It seemed harmless since she rarely saw any of her patients again. And the one about being the daughter of a Southern Baptist preacher kept the boys more respectful.

Jack accepted the explanation and didn't pursue it further, but he should have. Camille, it turned out, was a bit of a pathological liar, and all her playfulness covered up the fact that she did not have much backbone in the character department. She had little conviction in her own beliefs and just went along with whoever she was with. If she was with a soldier, she was like a soldier. But if she was with a hippy, she quickly became a hippy. She could talk down marijuana with a cop just as easily as she could smoke a joint with a rock musician.

Once Jack realized how impressionable Camille was, he nicknamed her "Chameleon." It came off as a term of endearment at first, but it became more serious over the years—especially after they had their kids. Jack hoped the kids would force her into adopting strong parental values, but even that did little to give her much bearing. She was more like a playmate to her kids than a mother. This forced Jack to be the authoritarian of the family. But every time he lowered the boom on bad behavior, Camille would huddle with her children and play the victim with them. It created a chasm in the family, with Dad on one side and Mom and the kids on the other.

When orders came through that Jack's logistical skills were needed at a reserve training base in Miami, Florida, Camille and the kids were thrilled. Jack hoped it might improve the family bond, but things merely deteriorated faster. As Jack soon learned, southern Florida was racially diverse and morally sketchy. It had a lot of sunny glitter on the outside, but scratch the surface, and you encounter greed, hedonism, and hollowness. Even life inside the gates of the Marine base was affected. The parties were wilder. Substance abuse was everywhere. Sexual escapades and sexual harassment were rampant. The line between duty and personal indulgence was blurred. And the lack of integrity was everywhere..

At home, it was even more horrifying. Jack could barely get his golf clubs unpacked before his wife and kids were getting swept up in the "anything goes" atmosphere. If his son J.J. wanted to go punk, Camille would buy him the hair dye to make his head pink. If his daughter Beth wanted to take belly dancing classes, Camille would buy them both outfits and sign up for classes. When Beth showed a preference for black boys, Camille would make quiet little jokes with her about black guys having a bigger "you know what." Jack protested loudly and warned of "consequences," but his words fell on deaf ears.

Over time, Jack's frustration with Camille merged with his frustration over the increasing liberalism he saw everywhere. He became such a reactionary that it earned him a nickname on base that was only whispered. It was S.O.B., but it didn't mean Son of a Bitch. It meant "Son of Bunker," as in "the Son of Archie Bunker," the popular right-wing television character from the hit show *All in the Family*. But the joke came to a screeching halt when J.J. died at the tender age of 19. He and his friends ate some magic mushrooms one night and decided to go water skiing in the dark. It was all a big, fun, magical mystery tour until J.J. tried to ski close to a boat filled with teens and spray them with his wake. J.J. misjudged his maneuver, hit the boat, and flew across the bow, hitting his head on the windshield and falling back into the water on the other side. All the other kids were so out of it from various forms of substance abuse that no one moved quickly enough to rescue J.J., and he ended up drowning. The tragedy brought Camille to her knees and justified everything Jack had warned her about.

Hoping to make a fresh start and overcome the tragedy of losing J.J., Jack decided they should move back to the family home in New Jersey. He had to retire from the Marines to do it, but there was no way he could stay in South Florida. Camille and Beth offered no resistance and soon found themselves in Atlantic Highlands, under the thumb of Jack, who became more inflexible than ever. He started dictating which television shows could be watched and which could not. He controlled their clothing, hairstyles, and who they socialized with. Anything that did not agree with his standards was banned. And to make sure the "liberal circus" did not invade the neighborhood, Jack started his own Neighborhood Watch group.

Jack got a job as a salesman for Allied Food and Fragrances and did quite well. He earned a good salary and had no problem maintaining the home, but his little family was slowly disintegrating. Beth confronted Jack one day and suggested he get some psychological therapy. She was convinced Jack's dictatorial behavior was coming from the deep guilt he felt from not saving J.J.

"Oh really," Jack responded defensively. "Is that what you think is going on here?"

"Yes," Beth said without much sympathy. "And now you're overcompensating by trying to save Mom and me, and the whole world from, I don't know what—the big bad wolf?"

"It's better for us here," Jack responded with authority.

"Why?" Beth asked sharply.

Jack looked her straight in the eye. "It's a better community. There's more integrity here."

Beth couldn't help but laugh at the irony. "Seriously? Atlantic Highlands? The town known for rum running? The wholesome community where Vito Genovese bought a house? The place where the KKK was once second in popularity to the fire department? Where my great-grandfather used to march with a white hood over his head?"

Jack quickly grew angry. "Pop was just trying to protect what he built from the criminals that invaded the place during prohibition—that's all."

Beth could only shake her head in judgment. "Dad, J.J. was just being a stupid teenager. He could have had that accident anywhere. His problem wasn't Miami. His problem was you. You never spent enough time with him."

The conversation struck a deep chord with Jack, but it

didn't get him to pick up the phone and call for counseling. It just made him double down on his resolve, which came straight from the mouth of his grandfather: "Never let your guard down. Stick to your convictions."

About a year later, Camille and Beth went out one day and never returned. Camille only left a note to say Beth missed her Jamaican boyfriend in South Florida and "I am taking her back to see him." Jack knew Camille well enough to know that Beth talked her into moving back to Florida. What he didn't pick up on was how the plan also included a divorce and a proposed settlement agreement that would force him to sell the Atlantic Highlands house and give Camille half the proceeds.

Once Jack overcame his anger, he decided not to sell the family home but instead sell all his stocks and drain his savings account to buy Camille out of her half. The plan worked, and he saved the house, but it left him on the edge financially. When he had his accident, that was all it took to push him over the cliff and place him into the situation he is in now.

Realizing he has little chance of sleeping at this point, Jack gets out of bed and heads to the bathroom to dose himself with a home concoction of sleep aids, including some cold and flu medicine and a tab of antihistamine. While doing this, he glances at himself in the mirror. He can't help noticing how old he looks, but at the same time, he senses a power that comes from all the deep lines and wrinkles that mark his lifetime full of experience. On the outside, he looks like a pretty tough old bird, and maybe that is what Sofia is confused about. If he's so tough, why is he giving up on his house so easily?

By the time Jack reaches his bed again, a small flame has come to life inside his gut. "Maybe Sofia is right," he thinks. He saved the house once before. Why couldn't he do it again?

Maybe he could find some work? Or perhaps he could do an Airbnb thing? Or sell some stuff—like the family boat? No, not the boat. But there has to be a way. A new sense of hope fills his head. He tells himself that all he really needs is a little "can do" attitude. That's when the echoes of another old expression used by his grandfather comes to his lips: "Not without giving it socks." In other words, "Not going down without a fight."

PART II

11

DAWN'S ROSY CHICKEN FINGERS

Jack gets up just before dawn, puts on his golfing clothes, and heads for the driving range at his golf club. Reclaiming a piece of his old life will help him prove his re-energized prowess. With a smile, he looks toward the golden horizon and says, "Dawn's rosy chicken fingers." It comes from when his daughter Beth gave him a copy of The Odyssey by Homer and said he would like it because it was about a badass soldier. Jack dove into the book eagerly, but when he found out it was a giant poem, that was the end of that. As he later joked with his daughter, "I never got past dawn's rosy chicken fingers - a play on the book's famous epithet. "Over the years, it became an often repeated pun between father and daughter anytime they saw a sunrise together.

Jack pulls out his driver and grabs the handle carefully. He takes a slow and shallow swing to see how painful it will be. He is surprised at how well it goes. He then places a ball on the tee very carefully, as if it holds all his burgeoning plans going forward. Gone are the fears of where he will go and what he will do. In their place, is a "mission notebook" that Jack has filled with a detailed strategy to win not just the battle, but the war itself. First, he will expand the scope of his clean-up operation and slow it down as much as possible. That will buy him some time with Fitzy, his financial advisor, and Mia, his pesky real estate agent. Next, he will turn over every rock and investigate every nook to come up with the money he needs to accomplish the mission. At the top of the list is "Beth loan." He will contact his daughter about repaying the money he gave her. He will also investigate how to Airbnb his guest house and look into selling the family yacht.

After taking a deep breath and exerting maximum concentration on the ball, Jack takes a swing. The head of the club connects solidly but not forcefully. The ball does not fly very far, but it heads straight out toward the 50-yard sign. Jack is encouraged. On his next swing, he puts a little more of his back into it, but this time, a little too much. He suddenly freezes and grabs his back as the ball dribbles off the tee. "God Damnit!" Jack yells in frustration.

The parking lot lights at Gulfstream Health and Fitness are just coming on when Jack arrives. He pulls into his usual space next to the bike rack that no one ever uses.

"Hey," Juan says happily in his usual mangled English when Jack enters the club. "How are you?" He sticks his hand out to shake.

"Good," Jack says, extending his own hand. "How's Sofia and your wife?"

"Good. Good," Juan says.

"Tell them I have more work for them," Jack smiles. But this goes beyond Juan's English comprehension.

"Yes, yes," Juan says, not wanting to show his lack of English.

Inside the steam room, Big Lou, Bobby Brown Sheets, Vlad, and some other guys are up to their usual banter when Jack enters. They can see Jack has a new attitude. He seems more erect and walks more quickly. Jack steps up to the thermometer on the wall and holds up a bottle filled with cold water. "Anybody mind?"

"No, hit it," Lou says.

Jack pours the cold water on the thermometer. It's a hack the men use to trick the system into producing extra steam.

"You're in a good mood today," Lou says. "What's up?"

"Guys," Jack says as he sits down, "I need to raise some money. Maybe you guys can help me with some ideas."

Big Lou is a little surprised and curious about this. "I never knew you as a man who needed money."

Jack smiles sheepishly. "Yeah, well, I didn't know that either until my financial advisor kindly informed me. The medical bills from my accident pushed me a little too far."

Big Lou still looks surprised. "Aren't you covered by the VA? You're a vet, aren't you?

"Yeah, but I went private. I thought the insurance from my company would cover it. Wrong."

Lou shakes his head. "Oh fuck, you musta got raped?"

Jack lets out a short snort of a laugh. "Dry anal raped is more like it."

"Jesus," Lou thinks. "What about your house? Can you get a second mortgage?"

"Already up to my eyeballs in a third."

Lou can't believe what he is hearing. "Where the hell did all your money go?"

Jack looks down. "Buying my ex-wife out of her half of the house was a big hit. And I guess that loan to my daughter to start a record business didn't help."

Lou looks over at his son, then back to Jack. "Holy shit, a freak'n record business? You know that went belly up."

Jack nods in agreement. "That's what it's looking like."

"I know the feeling," Lou says with another glance at Bobby.

"Jeez, bad luck," Vlad says.

Big Lou leans a little closer to Jack. "I know somebody who can help collect on that."

Jack looks up at Lou. "You know, my sales and logistics background might be useful to a man like you. Or maybe somebody you know? "

Lou gets a weird look on his face. "Jack, no offense, but you're a little old. And the people I know probably wouldn't work with a 'Mick.' You know how it is."

Vlad doesn't understand this. "Mick? What's a Mick?"

Lou shakes his head as if to say this Russian guy knows nothing. "When the Irish first came to America," Lou says, " a lot of them had names that start with Mc, names like McFlannagan or McNeil. So people started referring to them as Micks."

Vlad thinks about this. "So, if I want to go to McDonald's, I can say I want to go to Micks?"

Brown Sheets giggles. "No, that's Mickey Ds."

"How come not Micks?"

"Don't be a dumbass," Lou says. "McDonald's isn't Irish."

Vlad shakes his head. "America is big racist country."

"So go back to your Russian rat hole if you don't like it," Lou barks. He then leans toward Jack. "Seriously, you know what I would do if I were you?"

Jack looks up like he may be getting a real lead.

"I'd go on one of them dating sites for older people," Lou says. "Lots of rich widows out there looking for a man."

Jack gets an ugly look on his face. "Not a pleasant thought. Besides, I'm not in very good condition to be somebody's Romeo."

"Hey, who knows?" Lou smiles. "Maybe you can find an old nurse with a purse. Know what I mean?"

Jack thinks about it, then remembers his mission statement reads, "no rock unturned." He turns to Lou. "I'll put that one on my list."

The door to the steam room opens and Robert enters. Lou frowns. "Shut the door. You're letting the steam out."

Robert greets the group without acknowledging Lou's insult. He takes a seat and turns to Jack. "How did it go with the cleaning team this time? Better?"

Jack gives Robert a look like, let's talk about this later. Robert looks around, then leans closer to Jack. "Sorry."

Lou and Vlad listen to all this, then look at each other, confused. "What's this about a cleaning team?" Lou finally asks.

Jack stays calm. "I'm cleaning up my house in case I have to sell it."

Brown Sheets picks up on what is going on before his dad. He sees an opportunity for revenge. "Who is this cleaning team?"

Jack keeps his head down. "It's a service called none of your business."

Brown Sheets looks over at his dad, enjoying the sweet taste of revenge. "He's using illegals," he says to Lou. "Guaranteed."

Lou looks at him strangely.. "Get out of here. Jack would never do that."

Bobby holds his ground. "Ask him."

Lou turns to Jack with growing suspicion. "Jack? You hiring illegals to clean your house?"

Jack, realizing there is no escape from the truth, takes the bull by the horns. "You know Juan, the guy who works here?"

"Yeah."

"It's his wife and stepdaughter."

Lou thinks about it for a minute. "They got papers?"

Jack glances at Robert as he borrows Robert's line. "They're working on it."

"Told ya," Brown Sheets says with a goofy smile.

Lou can't believe his ears. "Jack. Jack. What are you doing? You letting 'Commiefornia' pull you to the dark side?"

Jack stiffens. "He doesn't have anything to do with it."

"He doesn't?" Lou asks. "Then why is he talking like he's their pimp?"

"Relax," Jack says with an edge in his voice. "It's just a temporary thing."

Lou frowns and gets philosophical. "I thought we had an understanding that we were going to do something about this shit, not participate in it. I mean, this thing we are working on was your idea. Look at what you are doing. These people come up here, steal jobs from good tax-paying Americans."

"Uh, that is highly debatable," Robert says aggressively. "America has always relied on migrant workers for labor."

"I wasn't talking to you," Lou barks. He then turns to Jack. You shouldn't be hiring these people. Did you talk to Midge about her husband who works for ICE?"

"Yeah," Jack replies. "It's not her husband. She's not married. It's her cousin who works for ICE."

"Did you get his phone number?" Lou asks.

"No."

"Why the hell not?" Lou demands.

Jack gets angry. "You better get down off that attitude, or we're going to have a problem here."

Lou stares at him for a moment, and then Vlad interrupts. "How much do they charge? Maybe come clean my house. Russian wife getting too old to clean."

Lou snorts at his question. "What the fuck is going on around here?

Vlad sneers at Lou. "And your Italian wife? She keeps the house clean? Or you get help?"

Lou doesn't know how to answer this. "As long as the house is clean, I don't ask."

Feeling a sense of hypocrisy in the air, Jack and Robert

share a look. Then, Robert asks, "Should I let Ana know when you want them back?"

Jack nods his head affirmatively. "Yeah. Next Tuesday will do."

"Shame on you," Brown Sheets says.

Jack glances up. "Did you ever tell Robert the story about when your dad took you out hunting for black bears? You know, when you got your nickname Brown Sheets?"

"*Vaffanculo*, Jack."

12

OPERATION BRASS TURTLE

Ever since she was a small child, Sofia always had a piggy bank of some kind. She always liked keeping a small coin or two to look at when she didn't have much else to do. It made her think of things she could do with those coins—mostly where she could go and what she would do. Her current place to tuck away her riches is the little airline pouch she got at the churchyard charity. It's the one airlines handout to business-class customers with a full complement of personal items, including the sleep mask Sofia uses to blind herself to the world. It is filled with all her quinceañera money and whatever small income she has gained—including her small salary from cleaning Jack's house. At present, she is very proud to tally a grand total of four hundred and twenty dollars, which is almost enough to buy two one-way airline tickets back to San Salvador.

Sofia can already hear the sounds of her past in her ears, from the cows and goats outside her window to the cackle of parrots overhead and the distant sound of the river where she learned to swim. She can smell the earthly perfume of freshly tilled soil and the whisper of ripe oranges, limes, and mangos.

She can also feel the tingle of her *abuela's* kitchen in her nose, filled with the spice of chiles roasting on an open flame and the aroma of coffee floating throughout the house. The symphony of all this fills her spirit with a smile. Her dream of returning home to a life that used to be will soon come true.

At Jack's house, Sofia is gathering cleaning supplies when Jack approaches her with news that he is expanding the scope of the house cleanup. Sofia accepts the news positively as it means more money for her. But she's curious what the reason is for the new scope of the project.

"Can I tell you a secret?" Jack asks her.

Sofia is a bit shocked that Jack would be this intimate with her. With a slight edge of suspicion, she consents. "Okay."

Jack looks around to see if anyone else is in earshot. "I've decided I am going to do my very best not to sell the house."

Sofia is surprised by the news, but it makes her curious. "I don't understand. Why?"

Jack looks at Sofia and chooses his words carefully. "Well, I could tell you how much the place means to me and how I can't imagine living anywhere else, but the truth is, it's because you were right."

Sofia can't believe her ears. Is Jack really giving her credit for something? "Me?"

"Yes," Jack says with a bit of a smile. "You kinda inspired me when you said I was just giving up. What you meant was I was giving up too easily. And you're right. So, I've come up with a plan to stay right here and sleep in my own bed in my own house until they pry it from my cold, dead hands. It's called 'Operation Brass Turtle.'"

Sofia, slightly weirded out by all this, thinks for a moment. On the one hand, she's feeling some pride and gratitude for the praise Jack is giving her, but on the other, she is concerned this might interfere with her own plans. "Does this mean we will not be working here anymore?"

"No, no," Jack says with a wave of his hand. "Not at all. You just keep doing what you are doing, only do it slower."

"Huh?"

Jack winks with a look of conspiracy on his face. "The longer you take, the more time I have to keep that 'For Sale' sign off my front yard. Know what I mean? I've got a whole list of new things for you to do."

Sofia quickly grasps the concept but remains cautious. "And you're going to pay us the same as usual?"

"The same. Can you explain this to your mom?"

With a half-smile, Sofia shrugs and confidently replies, "Sure, I can tell her that."

As part of "Operation Brass Turtle," Sofia and her mom are tasked with cleaning out the unused bedrooms in the house, boxing up all the personal items found within, and taking them all to the garage for storage. "But take your time and pack the boxes carefully," Jack tells them. "Make sure each box is clearly marked as to where it is coming from and what is inside it. Sofia, please help your mom with that and make sure it is all written in English."

Moving at the pace of a sloth, Sofia takes on the bedroom that was formerly occupied by Jack's daughter, Beth. Sofia assumes Beth has been gone a long time, but Jack never got around to cleaning out the stuff she left behind. Some clothes are still in the closet, a few posters on the wall, and a pile of CDs on a shelf next to a CD player.

Sofia starts by just looking through the clothes in the closet. There are t-shirts with the faces of black hip-hop artists from the early 2000s, like Dr. Dre, 50 Cent, and Jay Z. She also left some ripped jeans, sweatpants, and dark high-top sneakers with big bright stars. After fingering through the clothes, Sofia becomes curious about this girl and turns back to look at the posters on the wall. They too have a hip-hop theme. There's one that is filled with bright tropical colors that shows a boom box dominated by the words "HIP HOP BATTLE FESTIVAL MIAMI." As for the CDs stacked on top of a small table next to a desk, they are more of the same. There is music from Rick Ross, Flo Rida, Trina, and even Vanilla Ice. Some promotional materials from the Los Angeles Recording School promise a quick route to a degree in music production.

The bed is made but has not slept in for a long time. Sofia sits on it to see how soft it is. She likes the way it feels. After sensing Beth and what she was like, Sofia lies down on the bed and looks for more clues about the mystery girl and what happened to her. Did she get married and move away? Did something happen to her? And what would it have been like to be her and live in this house?

Ana suddenly sticks her head in the door. "Oh my god! What are you doing?"

Sofia rises from the bed slowly. "What happened to Jack's daughter? Do you know?"

Ana frowns. "No, and it is better we don't know."

Sofia defends her curiosity. "Why not?"

Ana infuses a little more motherly authority into her voice. "We are here to work—not to get involved in his personal life."

"But he said to go slow."

Ana grows frustrated. "That doesn't mean to lie around in bed. Did you clean out the desk yet?"

"No."

Ana points at the desk. "Well, do that, then I want you to go to the supermarket with Jack and make sure he gets the right spray cleaner this time."

Ana leaves as Sofia sits at the desk and opens the drawers. She starts to pull things from the top drawer and place them in the box but then stumbles across an unsealed letter-size envelope with the handwritten word "Dad" on it. Sofia opens the envelope just enough to see a piece of paper inside. Looking around to ensure her mother is gone, Sofia quietly removes the paper and discovers it is a short, handwritten letter.

Dad, I know why you wanted to bring us back here, but this isn't our old home. This is your old home. And I don't fit here. If you really believe in what America stands for, then you should support me for who I am, not who you want me to be. I fell in love with a beautiful black man who loves me, and I am sorry you can't accept that. I hope we can someday find a way to be in the same house again. But till then, goodbye.

Sofia is intrigued by the message but unsure what to make of it. After a second reading, she puts the letter back in the envelope. But now she doesn't know what to do. Did Jack read this? Did Beth not give it to him? Or did Jack just leave it here after reading it? Sofia goes to the window to see Jack working on the birdfeeders in the backyard. She thinks for a moment, then decides not to pursue it. She throws the letter in the box with all the other items from the desk.

13

ANGEL WING

Later in the day, Jack's Cadillac slowly winds through the tree-lined roads near his home. The mission is "Destination: Grocery Store" to get spray cleaner—the one in the yellow bottle with bleach—not the blue one without. Sofia hasn't yet graduated to the front seat. Instead, she remains in the back, focused on her phone, smiling at some texts from Memo. Flying hearts and sparkling kisses dance across her screen.

Sofia sends Memo a picture of Jack. "This is Jack. I showed him pictures of your benches," she taps. "He likes them."

Memo responds with an animated, happy face. "When can I see you?"

Sofia looks up at Jack. "*Jefe*, what time do you think we will finish today?"

Jack doesn't look back at her. Instead, he has his eyes glued to the rearview mirror. "Probably by 4:30."

Sofia looks back to see what Jack is looking at—a late-model Porsche SUV that is tailgating them.

Jack keeps his eye on the car. Sofia barely has enough time

to send an answer to Memo before Jack suddenly erupts in anger. "Hey asshole, read the bumper sticker," he barks.

Jack puts on his brakes and slows down. The Porsche gets even closer. Sofia looks back and forth but says nothing. Suddenly, the Porsche crosses into the left-hand lane and zooms past Jack. Jack sees a dad driving with his teen daughter in the front passenger seat. The Porsche pulls back into the right lane, then slows to give Jack a taste of his own medicine.

"Oh, come on," Jack laughs. "You want to play that game?" He flips on his high beams and rides right up on the tail of the Porsche with a look of satisfaction. "Okay, have it your way! See how you like it!"

Sofia watches the action closely. She isn't scared by it. On the contrary, she seems more perplexed than anything else.

Without warning, the Porsche driver slams on his brakes and forces Jack to do the same. But Jack knows this move. He quickly jerks his car to the right and passes the Porsche on the shoulder, "Dumbshit," Jack yells as he passes the Porsche. Sofia watches the car go by, then turns around to see what the Porsche will do. The guy in the Porsche hits the gas, and the chase is on.

"He's coming," Sofia says.

Jack looks in his mirror. "Is your seatbelt on?"

Sofia looks down and sees it is not. She works quickly to fasten it.

The Porsche comes screaming up from behind and moves to pass Jack. But Jack swerves into the left lane to block it. The Porsche backs off and then tries to pass on the right. Jack steers to the right. They go back and forth for a few rounds; then the Porsche takes it over the edge. The driver gets around Jack by driving up on somebody's lawn.

"This guy is crazy," Jack says. He checks on Sofia in the mirror. She seems excited. Jack hits the gas and prepares to pass the Porsche, but the road suddenly widens into two lanes when it meets a divided highway. The Porsche stops in the right lane at a red light, and Jack pulls up and stops in the left lane next to it. The occupants of both cars check each other out without lowering their windows.

"I knew it," Jack says. "Ahab the Arab."

Sofia catches the eye of the young girl in the car. There is no sympathy between them. They just stare.

When the light turns green, Jack turns left, and the Porsche goes straight.

"Sorry about that," Jack tells Sofia. "When people drive like that, I can't control myself."

"You said a lot of bad words," Sofia complains from the back seat.

"Yeah, sorry."

"And you're a racist."

Jack looks over to see if she is serious. She is. He smirks at her sarcastically. "Like you aren't?"

"No, I'm not."

"Kid, everybody is a racist. It's just a matter of who admits it."

"That isn't true."

"It isn't? What do you think about black people? You think they are the same as you?"

"No."

"Then you're a racist."

"But I don't hate black people like you do."

"I don't hate black people. Where did you get that idea?"

Sofia holds her tongue and looks out the window as Jack enters the grocery store parking lot. Jack produces a handicap placard and hooks it on his mirror. "While we're here, I want to get some bread and milk too."

"Okay," Sofia responds.

They exit the car and head for the store, but Sofia suddenly points to the side. "Look!" Jack turns to see the Porsche pulling into a parking space not far away.

"Is that them?" Sofia asks.

"Yeah, they must have come in from the other side."

The Porsche driver and his daughter exit the car. As they head toward the store, the daughter spots Jack and Sofia. She points them out to her father. Jack turns to Sofia playfully. "C'mon, let's go before these two try to steal our basket."

Sofia looks back at Jack and smiles. It's still game on. Jack starts moving as fast as he can, considering his physical limitations. Sofia has to slow down for him. Behind, she can see the Porsche people closing in on them. Jack suddenly commands. "Look, there is no way I can keep up. You go ahead, grab a cart, and get started. "I'll catch up."

Sofia suddenly loses her confidence. "But I'm not sure what kind of bread or milk you want."

"You just get the damn bleach cleaner. I'll get the food. Go. They're catching up."

By now, the Porsche people know that Jack and Sofia are still engaged. The daughter breaks away from her father and rushes toward the shopping carts, but Sofia gets there first. Sofia grabs a cart and heads inside with her competitor not far behind. The girl's dad rushes past Jack without looking at him and races into the store.

Inside the store, Sofia jogs up and down the aisles looking for the cleaning supplies. The other girl and her father do the same in pursuit of whatever they came for. Sofia comes across an employee and asks, "Do you know where the house cleaner stuff is?"

"Cleaning supplies—aisle six, on the left."

Sofia heads off for Aisle 6 as the Porsche people stop for help. "Organic dog food?"

"Aisle nine, on the right."

Sofia reaches the cleaning supplies and frantically looks for the products her mother wants: "SpotX All Purpose Cleaner" with Lemon Breeze scent and "Bonaire Wood Polish" in a 32-ounce bottle. She finds the brands quickly, but there are so many variations. It makes it hard to know which one to get. She looks around for Jack, but he is nowhere to be seen. Carefully she reads the labels and then makes a choice. She throws the bottles in the cart and races toward the front of the store.

As Sofia passes an intersecting aisle, she sees the Porsche people also racing toward the front with dog food in their cart. When they see Sofia, they pick up the pace. Sofia speeds up as well.

Both Sofia and the Porsche people reach the checkout lanes at the same time. The father and daughter scan the area and find an open lane. The dad pushes the cart forward, smiling at Sofia as if to say, "You lost." But Sofia notices something that they don't. The cashier they picked is turning off her light. So Sofia grabs the bottles from her cart and runs for another open cashier.

The cashier greets the dad and daughter with, "Sorry, I'm closed," from the cashier. They both look frantically to the left and right. They see the lane next to them with a light on. Dad yanks at the cart in that direction, but just before he pulls into the lane, Sofia cuts him off and places her items on the conveyor belt.

"Excuse me," Jack says from behind. "I'm with her."

Jack is in an electric cart holding a carton of milk and a loaf of bread. Both dad and daughter are forced to step out of the way.

～

Jack and Sofia giggle as they leave the store. "So you saw the light go out," Jack says as if he is about to write up a military debrief report.

"Yes, I think I was just lucky."

"That was more than luck. You took in the information and adapted to the situation. You dumped the cart when you realized it would slow you down."

Sofia shrugs, still exhilarated by the win. They reach the car, and without thinking, she gets into the front seat. Jack continues. "I've seen a lot of soldiers with half your wits get ahead in this man's world, so don't underestimate yourself."

Sofia thinks about this for a minute, but something else catches her eye. On a grassy knoll bordering the parking lot is a flock of Canada geese—ten of them, all fully grown, their long black necks uncoiled. Their black heads, with signature white bands on the cheeks, are busy poking at the short green blades of grass. They seem oblivious to all that is going on around them.

"Look," Sofia says with some lingering excitement in her voice. "*Gansos.*"

Jack looks, then gives her the correct English name, "Canada geese."

Sofia instantly rebels and defiantly informs Jack of the Spanish name, "*gansos de Canadá.*"

"God damn poop machines are what they really are," Jack growls. "Cows with wings."

"Can we feed them?"

"They don't need any food," Jack says.

"But I want to."

Jack thinks for a second, then gets an idea. "If you want to feed Canada geese, I've got a better place."

A few minutes later, Jack turns into a hamburger place. Sofia is confused. "Why are we going here?"

"Hold on, you'll see." Jack passes the drive-thru lane and proceeds toward the back parking lot, which borders a big patch of trees. Jack drives until he spots what he is looking for. "There you go," he says, pointing. In front of them is a parked car. Next to the car is a family of Canada geese, all gleefully eating up leftover bits of hamburger meals being thrown from the car window.

Sofia laughs. "Look at them."

Jack points to the side. "There's another family of geese coming out of the forest into the parking lot."

Sofia rolls down the passenger window. The Canada geese take this as a cue and head straight for Sofia's window. Jack grabs the loaf of bread he bought and hands it to Sofia. "Don't give them too much. You don't want to give them angel wing."

Sofia excitedly rips open the bread. "What is angel wing?"

"If they eat too much bread, they get this thing where their wings get deformed, and it can make it hard for them to fly."

"Is that true?"

"Yeah, true."

"How do you know that?"

"How else? My mother."

Sofia takes a loaf of bread and tears little pieces off. She throws out a single piece. The mom and dad compete for it. Dad wins and leaves nothing for anyone else. Sofia scolds the bird and then tries to drop a few more pieces for the goslings and their mom. This time, Dad doesn't get anything. Sofia laughs, then throws a bit directly at Dad.

"Why do you like these birds so much?" Jack asks.

"I don't know. I just like how they go where they want. I like how they come here in the winter, but they can go back to Canada whenever they want."

"Not these birds."

Sofia turns. "What?"

"These birds live here year-round."

"No, they don't."

"Yeah, they do. If you come here during the summer, these same birds will be here. Scouts honor."

Sofia is perplexed by this. "Why?"

Jack laughs, "Look around. They have a nice big forest here with a lake in the middle. And right next to that is a fast food place with people throwing french fries and hamburger buns at them all day long."

Sofia thinks about it. "Serious?"

Jack smiles. "They have a better life here. Why leave?"

Sofia turns and studies the birds more closely. The little goslings look happy to her. Jack watches Sofia for a second. "You know, you have what it takes to make it here. Maybe you should think about going back to school."

The suggestion angers Sofia. "Maybe you should think about calling your daughter to apologize for being a racist."

Jack is bolted in place. "What?"

"I saw the note she wrote you when I was cleaning out her room. You didn't like her boyfriend because he was black. You were mean to her, and she left."

"Do you really think any of that is your business?"

"No, but me going to school. Is that any of your business?"

"Guess not," Jack growls. "Not worth the bother."

"Besides, I'm going back to El Salvador. There is no point."

Jack scoffs at her. "You keep saying that, but I still don't get it. I mean, where are you going to live?

"We're going to live in my grandmother's house."

Jack stares at Sofia for a moment. "But didn't they sell your grandmother's house?"

Sofia's face suddenly grows concerned. "No."

Jack looks skeptical. "Are you sure about that? I mean, everyone left, right? It's just sitting there empty?"

Sofia tries to remain confident, but a look of fear invades her face. "Yes, my grandmother even told me she is giving the house to me when she passes away."

Jack realizes he has gone too far and decides to back off. "Well, I could be wrong. What do I know?"

He turns back to start the car, but it is too late. The damage has already been done. Sofia has a worried look on her face.

Back at Jack's house, Ana is still working on the second floor when Sofia comes up the stairs with a stern look on her face. "Did Abbi sell her house?"

Ana looks at her daughter curiously as Jack appears at the bottom of the stairs. "What is this all about?"

Sofia stays calm. "I just want to know."

Ana still can't understand what is going on but decides to tell her daughter what she wants to know. "Yes, we sold everything. The land and the house."

Sofia suddenly looks shocked. "No, no. That isn't true!"

Ana is growing frustrated with all this. "What do you mean it isn't true? Of course, it's true."

"Abbi told me she has the house."

"How else were we going to pay for the whole family to come up here? We needed the money."

"Does Abbi know you did that?"

"Of course, she knows. What is this all about?"

Sofia is shattered. She turns away from her mother to hide her pain, but Ana walks around in front of Sofia. "What's the matter?"

Sofia has tears in her eyes. "But she said she was going to give the house to me."

Ana puts down her cleaning things. She grabs Sofia by the shoulders. "How many times have I told you Grandma is not well in her mind? She has a disease that makes her forget things. I warned you to stop playing along with all her schemes to go back home. This is why!"

Sofia looks profoundly defeated. "This means I can't ever go home again."

Ana doesn't respond with words, but the truth hangs in the air. She looks down at Jack, who is watching from the bottom of the stairs, then tries to hug Sofia, but Sofia pulls away. "Leave me alone."

Estella is sitting on the front porch when Jack's Caddy pulls up. Sofia gets out of the car immediately and heads toward the house while Ana receives their pay in the car. Estella smiles and opens her arms to Sofia. "Come give me a hug, my dear."

Sofia silently obeys and stoops to hug Estella. When they separate, Sofia holds her gaze on Estella. She thinks about saying something but then decides there is no point. Sofia smiles as best she can and disappears into the house.

"Is something wrong?" Estella asks as Ana arrives at the front porch.

Ana smiles sadly. "No, mamá. Everything is fine.

Just as the skies grow dark, Memo is in the parking space under his aunt's apartment. He hits the switch on an extra work lamp to help him finish pouring a new bench. Then, out of the corner of his eye, he senses someone approaching. It is Sofia. He stops work with a big smile but quickly notices Sofia is not in a good mood. "You okay?"

"No," Sofia says as she steps up in front of him.

"What is it?"

Sofia says nothing, crumpling onto the floor. Memo quickly removes his work gloves and gets down on the floor next to her to hold her. He doesn't ask any questions for the moment. He just lets her grab him and bury her head in his chest.

14

A SPECIAL OFFER

A few weeks later, as the days grow shorter and colder, Jack arrives at the health club at his usual hour with a bag in hand. So far, he has been able to keep the For Sale sign off his lawn due to his cleaning crew being out of action since Sofia's meltdown. He's also been making progress with his fundraising campaign. He's managed to get himself familiar with the Airbnb rental service and set up an account on a senior's dating site. He's even started some good conversations with some of the lonely ladies there.

In the locker room, Juan empties a laundry hamper full of dirty towels and prepares to take it to the laundry. When he sees Jack, he smiles sheepishly. Jack heads for his usual locker and asks, "Sofia? Okay?"

Juan frowns a bit with little emotion in his eyes. "*Más o menos*," he says.

Jack nods, neither smiling nor frowning. "Tell her she still has a job at my place when she is ready."

Juan clearly doesn't understand what Jack is saying, so Jack lets it go. He drops his bag on the floor, sits on the bench between the lockers, and undresses.

Inside the steam room, Big Lou is on his usual perch using a spray bottle to infuse the steam with some eucalyptus oil. As he does this, Vlad continues his rant of the day. "You want to know how to fix the immigration problem at border?"

"Yeah, let's hear it," Big Lou says.

"You just get the military—put them place where people come through wall. Then they shoot anyone they see coming in."

Lou laughs. "That would get the word out."

Bobby Brown Sheets thinks about this with a strange look on his face. "But what about the kids coming through?"

Vlad thinks about it. "Collateral damage."

Bobby is incredulous. "Seriously?"

Vlad gets serious. "Hey, just go ask those pilots from World War II. When they were dropping all those bombs on Germany, did they worry about kids?"

Lou nods approvingly. "The man has a point."

The door opens, and Jack comes in. Big Lou brightens up. "Hey Jackie Boy, good news!"

Jack sits in his usual place. "Yeah, what's that?"

"Midge gave me the mobile phone number for her cousin who works for ICE."

Jack looks up, curious. "She did?"

"Yeah, his name is Tony. Turns out he's a paisano. He said he would take a meeting with us anytime we like. He likes the idea."

All eyes fall on Jack, but Jack keeps his gaze on the floor and says nothing. The small tile squares on the floor suddenly look different to him. He thinks about asking if they cleaned them recently.

"Did you hear what I said?" Lou asks.

"Yeah, I heard you," Jack replies flatly, without looking up.

"That's good news. Don't you think?"

"Maybe," Jack says for lack of a better response. What once

seemed like an act of patriotic duty to him no longer feels like it has any honor in it. He can't help but wonder why it suddenly seems so loathsome.

"Whatya mean, 'maybe?' This guy could put the fix in for us, and we'll be a real thing."

"Yeah, but who is he? He could be the janitor for all we know."

Lou leans toward Jack a bit. "Well, then, why don't we take a little run up to his office in Newark and find out?"

"Not right now," Jack says. "I've got too many things going on."

Lou's voice is edged with anger. "Like what?"

"Still trying to raise cash. Are any of you guys interested in buying a boat?"

"Here we go again," Lou snaps. "You and the freak'n money problems. Enough already."

Jack shakes his head. "Sorry," he says almost sarcastically, then mocks the Italian with a flamboyant hand gesture. "It's what it is."

Vlad shows some interest. "Boat? What kind?"

"Cabin cruiser. Hatteras 53. It's worth 200 grand. I'm willing to sell for 100."

Vlad shakes his head. "Too much gas. Sailboat better."

"Well, I don't own a sailboat, unfortunately."

Lou thinks for a minute. "Look, with an offer like that, you'll be able to sell it. Just bring your phone with you to Newark, and you won't miss any calls. What's the big deal?"

"The big deal is I don't want to go, alright."

"Why not? You were all for it a couple of weeks ago?"

Jack feels cornered. "I'm a little sensitive to people being pushed out of their homes right now."

"But Jack, you're a real American. The people we are targeting are illegal and should not be here!"

"I hear what you are saying, but I'll let you guys handle it," Jack says.

Lou isn't going to let him off the hook that easily. "Jack, we're at 35% spic and span on our way to 50. We're going to be the minority soon."

"You don't need me."

"The hell we don't. You set up the Atlantic Highlands Watch. You know how to do this shit. We need somebody with street cred!"

"Now is not the time," Jack says as if it's his final word. He gets up from his seat, tightens his towel, and then leaves. Lou shakes his head and stews for a moment. "Freak'n Commifornia," he says.

"I leave Russia because of communists," Vlad says. "If America turns communist, wife would say, okay, let's move back Russia, get away from these Marxists and Mexicans."

A few minutes later, Jack is just about ready to head home when Lou comes from the steam room. Jack stiffens, ready for a fight, but Lou has a smile on his face. "Okay, Jackie Boy, how about this offer?"

"I'm all ears," Jack says, zipping up his bag.

"I'll buy your boat in exchange for you coming to the meeting."

Jack laughs at the offer. "100 grand for me to go to the meeting."

"That's right."

"What's the catch?"

"There is no catch. If the boat is worth what you say it is worth, it will be a win-win. You make some money, and I make some money. All I'm asking is a favor to come to the meeting."

Jack thinks about it for a moment. He's still very suspicious. "And what are my obligations at this meeting?"

"Just go and listen. I'll do the talking. If you don't like what you hear, then that's the end of it. Swear to Jesus."

Jack stares at him for a moment. "I don't believe you. With you Dagos, there's always a catch."

Lou leans closer to Jack. "Okay, well, how about this? Ever since this California guy shows up, you start losing your marbles. I had a good partner in my activism until that guy came along. Then, next thing I know, you're hiring illegals to clean your house."

"You want the job?"

Lou holds up a hand. "Just let me finish. Now, I know you got problems with money right now. You're worried about losing your home. And all that probably got you distracted or whatever. So what I'm thinking is, if I help take some of the pressure off and get you going again, then you will come back to your senses. Is it wrong to look out for my pal Jackie Boy, even though you're a freak'n mick? Huh? C'mon, whatya say?"

Jack thinks about this for a second. The money for the boat would allow him to get his life back to normal. He opens up to the idea ever so slightly. He looks at Lou and shakes his head. "Damn Wop."

"That's the spirit," Lou smiles. So you in?"

Jack turns to the door. "I'll think about it."

"Think about it? What's to think about? C'mon!"

Jack turns and heads for the door. "I have a date with a rich divorcee."

Lou is frustrated. "What the hell?

"It was your idea."

"I know," Lou replies, "but you're going six different directions at once. You're selling your boat; you're not selling your boat. You're chasing after rich bitches. What the hell?"

"Hey," Jack says wisely. "Most battles are fought on multiple fronts simultaneously. It's the only way to win a war. Why should this be any different?"

Lou frowns. "Now I'm sorry I told you about that."

Jack shakes his head. "We'll see how it goes."

Lou gets a serious look on his face. "Thing like that is gonna take some time. In the meantime, you have my offer. You can always buy me back out if you strike it rich."

Jack smiles. "I'll let you know."

Lou cocks his head a bit. "Hundred cash, Jacky Boy. One hundred big ones—cassssshhhhhh."

Just at this moment, Robert Mathews comes in the door. He senses something is up. "Hey Jack, everything alright?"

Lou frowns at the sight of Robert. Jack smiles. "Yeah. Any tips on senior dating?"

"You're going out on a date?"

"Yep, with profile number 60234—Ms. Helen Dupont."

Robert smiles. "Nice. Hey, I talked to Ana. She said she's sorry. Maybe next week."

Jack shakes his head. "Yeah, I know. Sofia is still down for the count."

Robert shrugs. "We could always try to find another helper who speaks English."

"No, it's fine," Jack says, unperturbed. "I can wait."

15

SWEET HELEN

Helen Dupont, Jack's hook-up from the senior dating site, lives in a large estate home on the banks of the Navesink River. The driveway to reach the house is longer than the road through Jack's entire neighborhood and ends with a circular extension just in front of a sprawling house accented by two Range Rovers and a Mercedes AG Coupe.

Jack pulls up in front of the home, feeling intimidated by the enormity of the place. But at the same time, there is a solidness about it that appeals to him. It looks like a place that harkens back to a time of lineage and legacy. Its stone walls stand like a symbol of enduring Anglo family values—the kind Jack likes. Inside, he imagines walls covered with classic portraits displaying faces of honor, duty, and respect.

Before Jack reaches the broad oak front doors, dressed in khaki golf pants, a white shirt, a gray sweater, and a dark blue blazer, he has a feeling that he might have found a gold mine. Not a gold mine in the sense of the money he is looking for, but the unexpected treasure of finding a place whose owner might share his principles of maintaining tradition and guarding against the "circus" at the gate.

A black housekeeper answers the door. "Hello, I'm Jack O'Mally, here to see Helen."

The housekeeper smiles warmly, opens the door, and invites Jack into the foyer. It's a spacious open room with marble floors and a winding staircase. "She is coming now," the housekeeper says with a Jamaican accent. She then turns and leaves Jack there to wait.

Jack can't help but marvel at how fast he connected with Helen. Being the gearhead he is, it didn't take long to learn what to click and which way to swipe. No sooner did he get online than he started getting "likes" from women. When Helen popped up, it stated she was looking for a "breath of fresh air" and a "real man." She said she liked "upscale restaurants, art museums, theater, and adventure of any kind." She had a pretty face with high cheekbones and a big smile. Her profile said she was 59. They hit it off so well in the app that Helen decided to forgo the standard "meet somewhere" for the first in-person date. She knew Jack was a stand-up local guy with his own home and trusted he wasn't a weirdo. She suggested he just come to pick her up.

Jack admires the high ceilings from the foyer, but his attention is interrupted by two richly dressed young women and an eight-year-old girl who appear and head for the front door. The taller woman is white, but the shorter one and the little girl are black. The white woman puts an arm around the black one. "Call me as soon as you get there so I don't worry, okay?"

"I will," the black woman says. They see Jack and smile.

"Hello," Jack says.

"You must be the 'famous' Jack," the taller woman says. "My aunt is excited to meet you."

"Well, I..." Jack stutters. "I'm looking forward to meeting her, too."

When the women reach the front door, the taller one opens it but doesn't follow the black woman and the girl outside.

Instead, they embrace and give each other a long, romantic lesbian kiss. "Bye, my love," the taller white woman says, stooping to hug the small girl. "Take care of your mom and make sure she keeps her seatbelt on. Don't be on your phone the whole time."

"Okay," the young girl says sheepishly.

"Bye, Mama," the black woman calls out to the housekeeper.

The housekeeper appears again and waves to her offspring. "Likkle more, bless up."

"Bless up," the black woman says with a flawless Jamaican accent.

Jack is unnerved but has little time to react before a new figure appears at the top of the stairs. "Hello, Jack," Helen says from the stairway as she descends. She stands a tad shorter than Jack, has an impressive thin body, and takes each step with poise and elegance. She's dressed like an older "Gucci hippy," complete with expensive bell-bottom jeans, a big brown leather belt, and a flowery blouse accented with a leather vest with tassels on it.

Jack smiles and stupidly waves at her. He's more intimidated than anything else but beset by a bolt of regret as he takes in her "rich hippy" vibe. He and Helen never talked politics online, which now looks like a mistake.

"Aunt Helen, you look gorgeous," the tall white woman says. "I always love that outfit on you."

"Hi, Helen, bye, Helen," the black woman says as she heads for the car.

"Bye, ladies," Helen waves. "See you next week," she says as she turns to Jack. She looks him up and down and seems happy with what she sees. "I've enjoyed our conversations online so much. You were very sweet. How's your back?"

Jack reaches around and rubs his lower back. "Still a work in progress, but one day at a time."

"Yeah, I heard about your fall," the younger woman says. "I can't imagine what you have been through."

"I'm sorry," Helen says. "I should have introduced you two. Jack, this is my niece, Alexia."

Jack puts out his hand. "Nice to meet you."

Alexia accepts. "Likewise."

The conversation is interrupted by a car horn from the top of the driveway. It's a late-model black BMW driving toward the house. Alexia and Helen share a nervous look. Helen then turns to Jack. "Jack, would you mind if we just go right now? Otherwise, things are about to get rather unpleasant."

Jack realizes something is wrong and immediately turns for the door. "Okay, got it. Let's go."

Alexia stays in the doorway, ready to slam it shut as soon as her aunt enters the car. But unfortunately, Helen doesn't get to Jack's car fast enough. The BMW comes to a screeching halt, and the male occupant jumps out.

"Fucking bitch," he says after pulling a cigarette from his mouth.

Helen tries to stay calm. "Roger, please, don't make a scene."

Roger pulls another drag off the cigarette as he stomps closer. "You think I'm some kind of toy? You just think you can play with my emotions and tell me to get lost when you get bored?"

Helen holds her ground. "Roger, I did not get bored with you. But, I told you, I just don't want a gigolo."

"Don't call me that," Roger says, flipping his cigarette butt at her. It hits her on the arm, and sparks fly.

"Hey," Jack says, stepping between Helen and Roger. Jack lifts his cane.

Roger smirks at Jack. "Oh, what are you going to do? Hit me with your cane?"

"I will ram it through your right eyeball and watch you bleed out from the back of your head. You want to try me?"

Roger looks over at Helen. Helen just cocks her mouth a bit. "He's a veteran of two wars. I think he means business."

Roger backs down. "Screw it," he says and turns back to his car. "Good luck, asshole. She's going to eat you alive, just like she did me." He starts to cry as he gets in his car and speeds off.

Inside Jack's car, Helen grabs his arm. "I'm so sorry to put you through that, Jack. This online dating is hit and miss."

"No worries," Jack says as he starts the car.

Helen smiles at him. "I can't tell you how good it is to be with a real person for a change—not one of these needy babies looking for a breastfeeder with a big checkbook."

Jack swallows hard with guilt but tries to make light of it all. "Yeah, well, I was going to ask if you could help with dinner?"

Helen suddenly looks fearful. "Seriously?"

Jack smiles. "Sorry, that was a bad joke."

"Oh, sorry. Sometimes my sense of humor is out to lunch," Helen says as she lightly slaps her own head. "I mean, we aren't even going to dinner. Duh!"

Jack smiles at her self-deprecating humor.

The destination for the night is an art gallery opening on the backside of town. The gallery is part of an old warehouse that has been converted into a metal and concrete attempt at being ultra-hip. It's called "Impasse." On this particular night, it is the place to be. The valet line is filled with expensive cars. Inside, servers offer trays of wine and hors d'oeuvres to well-heeled art patrons who have arrived for the party. The hors d'oeuvres are a variety of small dishes, including deviled eggs, crostini, shrimp cocktail, and stuffed mushrooms. The guests mingle and chat as they check each other out. The atmosphere is festive and lively.

By the time Jack enters the gallery's front door, his mood

has changed. Unlike before, he seems more somber. Helen looks at him curiously. "Everything alright?"

"Not really," Jack says.

"What's the matter?"

Jack is already punishing himself. He can't understand why he would have fallen for such a stupid idea as finding a rich woman online. Seeing that crazy guy in front of Helen's house made him realize that every low-life in town is already in this game. The thought that he is just another one of them is something he wants to fix. "I need to tell you something," he says stoically.

"What?" Helen asks, befuddled.

Jack tries to find the words just as Memo, working as a server, shows up with a tray of wine.

"Any wine for you," he says, smiling at Helen.

"Yes, thank you," Helen says as she sweeps a glass from the tray. "Jack, are you having wine?"

When Helen mentions Jack's name, Memo takes a closer look. His smile suddenly grows larger. "You are the Jack Sofia works for!"

Jack looks back at Memo, whom he has never seen. "You know Sofia?"

"Sofia is my girlfriend. I recognize you from the pictures on her phone!"

Helen looks at Jack curiously. Jack turns to her awkwardly, attempting to dispel any suspicion of impropriety. "Sofia and her mother work for me." Helen seems to accept his explanation as Jack turns back to Memo. "How is she doing?"

Memo saddens. "Not too happy right now. But hopefully, I can make the sunshine come again tomorrow."

"Hope so," Jack says. "She's a good kid."

"She is my everything. I leave no rocks turned over for her! Hey, did she send you pictures of my furniture designs?"

"Yes," Jack says. "Very unusual."

"It's something very artful," Memo smiles proudly. "I think you will like it?"

Helen turns to Memo. "You are a furniture designer?"

"Yes," Memo beams. "I'm working on a whole collection of outdoor furniture. Take a look at the pictures on his phone."

Helen is impressed. "I'm actually looking for some pieces for my pool area. "Can we see the pictures, Jack?"

Jack shrugs and pulls out his phone. He moves to his camera roll, and there it is, the latest picture. It shows the "La Sofia" bench and has Memo's contact info.

Helen gets a big smile when she sees it. "That is beautiful. I don't think I have ever seen anything like it. Jack, can I forward this to my phone?"

"Sure," Jack says and hands his phone over to Helen. Helen hits the share button.

"Thank you," Memo says. "I'm creating tables and chairs too."

Helen continues to look at the bench with admiration. "I am so impressed with this."

Another woman's voice suddenly cuts through the crowd. "Impressed with what?"

Jack looks up to see Mia, his real estate agent.

"Hey Helen," Mia says and then turns to Jack with a surprised look. "Jack? What are you doing here?"

"I'm with her," he says, nodding toward Helen

"Wait, you two came here together?"

"Uh, yeah," Jack says for lack of anything else to say.

"Oh my god, this girl is my best friend forever," Mia laughs as she and Helen hug. "How do you two know each other?"

"We just met online," Helen says.

Mia looks from one to the other and then suddenly giggles. "Who wrote the algorithm for this computer match? Holy shit."

"What?" Helen asks defensively.

"Girl, if you were one of the protestors at Kent State way

back when, this is the National Guard soldier who would have shot you."

Helen looks over at Jack, then back to Mia. "I'm not so sure about that. I think this man marches to the beat of his own drum."

"You've always been a woman of faith," she laughs. "So, anyway, let me see this thing you are so impressed with."

Helen points to the picture on the phone. "This young man designs custom outdoor furniture. Isn't it wild?"

"Wow, cool," Mia says, checking out the bench. "Where do you sell your stuff?"

Memo smiles sheepishly and nods toward the photo. "I'm selling online right now. It's very exclusive—only to special people."

The nearby catering manager watches all this and shouts, "Memo!" Memo turns to see the manager throwing her hands up as if to say, "Get to work."

"Sorry," Memo says. "Gotta go. My contact info is on the picture. Please, you can share it like peanut butter shares with jelly. Bye."

"You know Jack," Mia says. "Something like that in your backyard would add a little pizazz to the place. Are we making some progress over there? I haven't heard from you for a while."

Jack suddenly becomes very uncomfortable with the direction of the conversation. "Mia, I need to talk with Helen. Can you give us a minute?"

Mia and Helen share a glance. "How intriguing," Mia says to Helen. "I'll be by the bar, girlfriend."

Jack escorts Helen to an outdoor patio and puts down his wine. He becomes stiff and determined. "Sometimes, on the battlefield of life, you can be lured into things."

Helen smiles at Jack. "Yes?"

"You can find yourself down a blind alley and wonder how you got there."

All this amuses Helen. "Yes?"

"But the important thing is, once you find yourself there, you have to stop, accept your situation, and recalibrate."

Helen smiles. "You really are a military man. So what's this all about?"

"What I am trying to say here is I made a mistake. As you are about to find out from Mia, I'm on the verge of losing my home. My pursuit here was somewhat financial."

The message suddenly becomes clear to Helen. Her smile fades quickly. "I see," she says with disappointment.

"I'm sorry. It was stupid of me."

Helen thinks about this for a minute. "I appreciate your honesty."

Jack nods rigidly. "Would you like me to take you home?"

"It's okay," Helen says after thinking about it. "I'll get Mia to take me home tonight."

"Sounds like a deal," Jack says, feeling slightly better. "But one favor."

"Yes?"

"Mia is my real estate agent, no need to rock the boat with her. She doesn't know I am trying to keep my house off the market."

Helen nods affirmatively. "I get you."

They share a smile. Jack sticks his hand out to shake. Helen accepts it warmly. He is ready to leave it at that, but Helen has stirred something in him. He leans in and kisses her on the cheek. Helen accepts it warmly.

"Nice meeting you, Jack," she says.

"Nice meeting you," Jack says humbly and turns to leave.

"Uh, Jack," Helen calls.

"Yes?"

"I think you're right. Sometimes, we can get lured into things without thinking. But I like the way you manned up. You owned it."

"I'm just sorry it didn't work out."

Helen thinks, then makes up her mind and stumbles with her words. "Look, I don't know about you, but if you want to make a fresh start, well, I'm game. Just give me a call sometime. We can try again. You've got my number."

Jack smiles. "Okay, that would be nice."

Jack heads out the door as Mia and a group of women gather to look at pictures of Memo's furniture. Sally, the wife of the gallery owner, is very impressed. "Very much in the 'brutalist' style. This would be perfect for the back patio. Who is this young man?"

Helen points to Memo, who is nearby. Sally motions him over. "Is this your work?"

"Yes, those are my things," Memo says with a smile.

"Your work reminds me of Isamu Noguchi from Japan. Would you call yourself a brutalist?"

"That is a word I never know, but you can call me 'Memoist' if that makes the smile come."

One of the other women in the group looks up at Memo curiously. "Where are you from?"

"I'm from El Salvador," Memo says proudly.

"Central America," the woman says. "I've been to Costa Rica. It's very beautiful."

"El Salvador is very beautiful too," Memo smiles. "Just a little bit up north."

"What is your opinion on the immigration problem?" The woman asks bluntly.

"Nancy, really?" Sally says. "We don't need to discuss that now."

"It's okay," Memo says. "If you want to know my opinion, I will give it to you."

"Is there a solution?" Nancy asks.

"Well, my solution is very simple," Memo says. "And very, very good too!"

"And what is that?"

"If you want to solve this problem, you have to think out of the bag."

"Do you mean outside of the box?"

"Yes, sorry," Memo says, embarrassed by his mistake. "Out of the box."

"Okay," Nancy smiles. "I like out of the box. Let's hear it."

"Well, the first thing you do is get together with Guatemala and invite them to become the 51st State of the United States."

"Why on earth would we do something like that?" Nancy laughs.

"Because if they agree, you can make Guatemala the best place to go for your asylum request. The Mexicans would go south instead of north. And the Central Americans would not have to go any further north than that to start the process."

"Why would Guatemala ever agree to something like that?" Nancy frowns.

"Money," Memo smiles. "All those billions of dollars they spend on building walls could go to Guatemala."

"You think the Guatemalans would be open to something like that?"

Memo smiles. "Never hurts to ask the pineapple which way the sun is shining."

All the women stare at Memo blankly. They can't tell if he is serious, kidding, or crazy.

16

SUICIDE MISSION

Retreating to his man cave at home, Jack grabs his "mission notebook" and crumbles into his big chair. Inside the notebook, he looks at his list of money-raising projects and scratches out "rich woman" with a sad look on his face. Next, his eyes fall on "Beth loan." This one is painful enough to make him pour himself a shot of rye in a stout, fat whiskey glass engraved with the Marine Corps motto, "Semper Fi." On the backside of the glass there are three horizontal lines to measure the pour: "Cakewalk," "Outnumbered," and "Suicide Mission." Jack pours it up to "Outnumbered." He pauses, thinks about it, and continues the pour to "Suicide Mission." He then sits back down with his glass and stares at the picture of his daughter Beth as he takes the first drink. He remembers a T-shirt she gave him once. It said, "Dads and daughters, not always eye to eye but always heart to heart." Jack checks his watch, calculating the time difference between New Jersey and California. It's still early out there. He takes a deep breath, pulls out his phone, and searches his contacts for "Beth."

Beth doesn't pick up. Instead, the call goes to voicemail.

Hearing her voice makes Jack uncomfortable. He starts to cancel the call but stops and forces himself forward. "Beth, hello, this is Dad. I need to talk to you. Please call me."

Jack hangs up and puts the phone down. He takes another sip of his whiskey and flicks on the TV. It's his usual conservative news channel, with his favorite evening host ranting about how climate change has nothing to do with the rising tide of homeless refugees worldwide. Instead, he blames it on inept liberal politicians who don't have the backbone to tell people, "No, you can't live in flood zones next to the ocean! No, you can't live on hills prone to fire and mudslides! No, you can't be complete idiots!" Jack quickly mutes the sound, then picks up the phone again. This time, there is no ring. Instead, it goes straight to voicemail. Jack hangs up and sends her a text message instead. "This is important," he types. "Please call me." He then un-mutes the television and listens to more angry commentary from his favorite host.

Suddenly, the phone rings. It's Beth. With little emotion, she asks, "Are you okay?"

"Hello to you, too," Jack grumbles.

Beth doesn't soften. "What's up?"

"I'm calling about the loan. Any chance you might be able to start paying me back? It's been years."

Beth sighs. "Look, Jack, we're struggling right now. I'm working at Burger King just to make ends meet, and PuzzleMe is still working on the album."

"How long has he been working on that thing?"

"It takes time. He wants to get it right."

"God damn, Beth, I put a lot of money into your record business. It's been years."

"Jack, I told you," Beth says with growing anger. "We needed more investment, and you bailed on us. So now I have to work for months just to afford some studio time."

"Stop calling me Jack. I'm your father."

"Father? Seriously? Doesn't a 'father' have some obligation to show up at his daughter's wedding?"

"I was angry."

"Angry about what? The loan or the fact that I married a black guy?"

"Can we not get into this now? I'm in a serious spot with the house. If I can't pull it together quickly, I will need to sell it."

Beth pauses for a long moment. "Well, maybe it is time for a change."

"Just like that," Jack growls angrily. "Our family heritage? Your inheritance?"

There is a long pause on the phone. "It's only filled with bad memories for me. Why would I want it."

"Don't say that. You're being silly."

"No, Dad, I'm not. I've adopted a new family, a family that makes me happy. And by the way, you have a grandson."

Jack is stunned by this. If he felt like a turd warmed over after his date with Helen, he's now fallen into Dante's seventh layer. "Congratulations," he says, void of any emotion. "And 'PuzzleMe' is the father?"

"Yes, Dad, you are the proud grandfather of a beautiful mixed-race boy, Keiran."

"Karen?"

"No, Keiran, K-E-I-R-A-N. It's Irish-Gaelic for dark-haired."

Jack says nothing. He doesn't know what to say.

"That's what I thought," Beth mutters. "You know, the thing I never understood about you? You're a big right-wing 'America first' kind of guy and a 'land of opportunity' cheerleader. Why don't you understand it doesn't work if it is only for a few people? It only works if everyone participates. America was founded on that principle. You'd think a George Washington fanboy would understand that?"

"It's not that simple, and you know it."

"You go around blaming everyone else for your problems, but you never stop to think maybe 'you' are the problem?"

"Enough!"

"You want everybody to live in a world that no longer exists. And when they refuse, you undercut the very principles you claim to be defending with all your hate."

"I don't hate!"

"You ever hear the expression, 'Our unity is our diversity'?"

"That's a gross oversimplification of a very complex issue."

"You can't go back to Blue Bayou, Jack. "I'm done arguing with you. We'll start sending money when we can."

Jack laughs. "Right. When PuzzleMe solves his riddles."

Infuriated by this remark, Beth just hangs up.

Jack slowly puts down the phone and takes a long sip of whiskey. He looks around the room. It would be nice to think it is always darkest before dawn, but dawn may not be showing her rosy chicken fingers over this house again—at least not while it is his. He pulls out his list and scratches out "Beth loan."

17

BIRDS AND BABIES

At the top of Cherry Tree Avenue, the street Sofia lives on, is a small Winter King Hawthorn tree that someone planted long ago. Every fall, its branches fill with bright red-orange berries. The berries will sit there for months untouched. Then, on no particular day, at no particular time, a flock of robins will show up en masse to strip the tree clean in a frenzy of eating. Once the berries are gone, the birds will disappear just as quickly as they came. Most people pay little attention to the event, but when Sofia comes across the scene, she stops to watch. She smiles at the frantic antics of the birds, and as usual, her mind turns to the same thought. Where do these birds come from, and where do they go? She wonders if they have a home somewhere or if they just keep moving forward like a group of Latino immigrants, tree to tree, neighborhood to neighborhood, town to town. She assumes it is a latter. These creatures must have no home except for the flock itself. It reminds her of her own family.

The desert was hot and harrowing when Sofia crossed it the first time she came to America. But the second time she came, it wasn't the desert that was the obstacle. It was Ricki. After a long, dangerous journey to the U.S. border, they reached the Rio Grande. On the north side, they could see American Border Patrol agents waiting to take them into custody, and this is how the family wanted it. They knew the INS would not separate families with special needs children. Once they could prove they had a place to go, the family would be released pending a court hearing to determine if they would be granted asylum status. It could take years for the hearing to happen, but in the meantime, they could not be deported and would be safe. All they had to do was wade across a shallow part of the river and surrender themselves to the border patrol agents.

Everybody was eager to wade across the shallows except Ricki. He didn't want anything to do with it and refused to put a toe in the water. Roberta and Arnell kept telling him it was okay, but he kept backing away, telling everyone he just wanted to go home. Finally, somebody came up with a raft he could ride in, but he didn't want to do that either. He started rocking back and forth on his feet and yelling, "You're killing me! You're killing me!"

Sofia was hot and tired at that point. Watching Ricki hold them up was making her angry. Estella was exhausted and needed rest, but she hung in there and tried unsuccessfully to convince Ricki to cross. It wasn't until Arnell made a game out of it and got Ricki up on his back that they could proceed. Once Arnell was in the water, Ricki screamed and kicked, but Arnell acted like it was fun. "Don't look back! If you do, you'll turn into a pillar of salt. Don't look back!" As Sofia followed Arnell across the river, she kept looking at Ricki and telling herself she would never have children. But now, just a few years later, here she was on her way home from the drugstore with a pregnancy test hidden in her pants.

Once back at the house, Sofia quietly heads for the bathroom and locks the door behind her. She then lifts her shirt and pulls out the pregnancy test. But instead of reading the instructions in the package, she grabs her phone and scrolls through some videos on Youtube. There are mountains of clips on the subject of pregnancy, including listicles like "10 Signs You Are Pregnant" and "15 of the Earliest and Weirdest Pregnancy Symptoms." But there is also a massive collection of videos about how to take a pregnancy test. She clicks on one by a registered nurse and props the phone on the window ledge with the sound turned down very low. The nurse holds up a box like the one Sofia bought. "So what does this test measure?" The nurse asks as if lecturing a class. "It is going to look for a hormone in your urine called HCG, which stands for human chorionic gonadotropin, and it is a hormone produced by the placenta."

Sofia opens the box and yanks out the test, then fast-forwards the video to the instructions. "You will need a pregnancy test," the nurse says, holding up the box. "You'll need a cup to catch your urine. And you'll need a timer, either your watch or your phone."

Sofia follows the instructions without any trouble, then lays out the test strip. "So what we are going to do is add three drops of urine right here," the nurse continues. Sofia follows along, barely getting the three drops in before there is a knock at the door.

"*Necesito usar el baño*. When are you coming out? " Ricki says from the other side of the door.

Sofia rolls her eyes in frustration. "*Okay, dos minutos Ricki.*"

In the video, the nurse explains how to read the results. "If at two minutes or so there is only one line, then you are not pregnant. But if there are two, that means you are going to have a baby! Congratulations!"

Ricki leans on the door. "You are only watching videos."

"Please," Sofia says with growing frustration. "Just give me a minute!"

Sofia shuts off the video and gathers all the packaging as

the test strip slowly reacts to the urine. She slips all the packaging back into her pants, grabs the test strip, and waits for the results.

"Sofia, you okay?" Roberta asks from outside the door. "I have a very anxious little boy who wants to get in there."

"Just a minute," Sofia counters with obvious irritation in her voice. When she turns back to the test strip, the results start to appear. Within seconds she can see there are two lines—not one. As she suspected, she is pregnant. Sofia looks up from the test strip and stares at the wall in front of her. Fear is not one of her vices, but in this instant, she is petrified.

Outside the bathroom, Roberta patiently waits with Ricki, stroking his hair to keep him calm. "Sofia?" The door suddenly opens, and Sofia appears with a strange, panicked look. Roberta picks up on it immediately and wonders what is going on. "What's up?"

Sofia quickly moves past Roberta and Ricki. "I can't talk right now."

"Ok," Roberta says and curiously watches Sofia head down the hallway.

Sofia leaves the house and races down the sidewalk in a state of shock, disbelief, and fear. She does not care which way she is going. She just needs to walk and walk quickly. She is overwhelmed with anxiety and completely clueless about what she should do next. Should she keep this a secret? Or should she go to her family for support? She didn't expect this to happen, but now that it is happening, everything has changed. She happens upon a small park filled with moms and kids and quickly walks to a bench across from the swing sets. After watching the kids with their moms for a moment, she turns to her phone for some answers. The first thing she discovers is that there is a TV series called "16 and Pregnant." Oddly, this provides her with a slight bit of comfort knowing she isn't the only 16-year-old who has stumbled into this briar patch of thorny issues. Everything else she finds just promotes the notion that she should see a doctor right away, regardless of whether or not she wants to keep the baby. Then, there are tips on how to use Abortion-Finder.org. This last entry stuns her. She gives up on the phone, watches the kids playing for a moment, then lowers her head with a deep sigh. After a few deep breaths with her eyes closed, Sofia suddenly looks up again. She raises her phone and sends a text to Memo to meet her ASAP.

Half an hour later, Memo stands patiently at the prearranged rendezvous spot by the river, next to the bridge, eagerly awaiting Sofia's arrival. Today, he seems to be in an exceptionally cheerful mood, and his attire reflects this; he is adorned in his one-of-a-kind prison-striped bib overalls and a bright red Marvel Comics t-shirt, both of which are splattered with dusty cement.

Sofia appears in the distance, her eyes fixated on Memo. With determined strides, she briskly walks towards him, her expression devoid of any warmth or joy. As she approaches, Memo's smile widens, and he extends his arm in a friendly wave. However, to his dismay, Sofia doesn't reciprocate the gesture. Instead, she marches up to him with an air of urgency and uses both arms to forcefully slam him in the chest. The impact of the sudden blow catches Memo off guard, and his smile swiftly transforms into a mix of shock and concern. "*¿Qué pasa?*" he exclaims.

Sofia gets right to the point. "*¡Estoy embarazada!*"

"You're pregnant? What?"

"I'm going to have a baby."

Memo stares at Sofia for a long moment. "Are you sure?"

"Yes, I'm sure."

Memo can't believe his ears. "And it's like... mine?"

This infuriates Sofia, and she slaps him. "Of course it's yours! What do you think?" She then starts hitting him uncontrollably. Memo cowers away from her and tries to protect himself by falling to the ground. As he lies in the reeds and stares back up at her, towering over him with a look of fear and fury, he suddenly realizes it is a historic moment. His fearful expression slowly transforms into a big smile.

"What are you smiling about?" Sofia asks, infuriated by his insincerity.

Memo rises as his eyes dart from side to side at their surroundings, trying to etch it all in his mind. "I want to remember everything from this moment. Where this happens. What is around us. This is the most blessed day of our lives. *¡No puedo creerlo!*"

"So you are happy about this?" Sofia asks seriously.

"Of course I am happy! *¡Estoy emocionado!* Aren't you?"

"No," Sofia says.

Memo suddenly gets worried. "I don't understand. Why are you so angry?"

"I'm not angry."

"Well, you don't seem very happy, *seguro.*"

"I'm scared," Sofia says.

"Scared? *¿Por qué tienes miedo?*"

"I don't know. I'm just scared!"

In that tender moment, Memo's eyes catch a glimpse of the insecurity that has violently overwhelmed Sofia. Without hesitation, he gracefully moves closer, bridging the distance between them. His gentle hands find their place on her upper arms, a silent gesture of reassurance. With a gaze that speaks volumes, Memo locks eyes with Sofia, his sincerity palpable. His voice, soft and soothing, carries the weight of his unwavering love. "Sofia," he begins, his tone a blend of comfort and conviction, "there is absolutely nothing to fear. *Yo te amo*. I love you more than the big of the sun." As the words leave his lips, a promise hangs in the air between them. With unwavering determination, Memo declares, "I will never take a step in any direction that doesn't go *para nosotros*, for us. You, me, and the baby."

Sofia listens closely and looks for any sign of insincerity. "Are you sure?"

Memo smiles, "Never more sure in my life!" He turns, looks around, and grabs one of the reeds growing on the river's shore. He breaks it into a short length and then makes something out of it. "I didn't plan like this, but just for now, please take this." Sofia looks at him curiously, not sure what he is up to. But then he suddenly kneels before her and holds up a small ring he has made out of the reed stem. He holds it out to her. "Sofia, you will marry me?"

Sofia is overwhelmed by a tempest of mixed emotions. It frustrates her, and she backs away with tears in her eyes. "No, no, no. Don't do this."

"I know it is a lot. But sometimes, you have to let life happen the way it wants. You know what I'm say'n? This is all meant to be!"

"No, I'm not ready for all this!" Sofia moves away from Memo and heads for the area under the bridge. Memo rises and follows her.

"Don't go," Memo calls after her. "No like this. Let me talk with you!"

Sofia moves faster, but Memo is faster than her. She starts to run. He starts to run. She runs faster. He runs faster. When it looks like he is about to catch up, she turns sharply toward the river bank. Memo follows her as she zig-zags to keep him from grabbing her. Just before she reaches the water, she looks over her shoulder to see where he is. It causes her to misjudge her distance to the shoreline and accidentally tumbles off the high bank face-first into the water.

Oddly enough, the tumble into the water feels familiar to her. It reminds her of jumping into the river back home. She hears herself and her friends giggling, calling out to each other under the water. But then Memo's hand grabs her firmly. The laughter stops as he pulls her to the surface. She suddenly realizes how cold the water is and gasps for air.

"Are you okay?" Memo asks emphatically as he pulls her back to the river bank.

Sofia looks at him, feeling strange and disoriented. "*Sí*, I'm okay."

"*Segura*—you sure?"

"Yeah. But this water is freezing!"

"Well, it's winter. That's what happens in these months."

Sofia giggles a bit. Something about the shock of the cold water has cleared her confused emotions. She feels strangely relieved. Memo looks over at her and sees the small smile that comes with the giggle. "Well, looks like I'm not the only crazy one around here. Sofia, the people say, *es una chica loca!*"

Sofia smiles and grabs him as if to get his help, but instead, she pushes him into the water. Memo screams as he goes in, and Sofia laughs with delight.

A cold winter sun shines through the windows of the apartment owned by Memo's aunt. Sofia is sitting up in bed, covered in blankets, with a white towel wrapped around her head. She is sipping hot chocolate and looking around the apartment with fresh eyes as Memo prepares some hot tea for himself. "Did you change something in here?" Sofia asks.

"No. It is the same as always from the beginning of time."

"Looks different to me," Sofia says.

Memo finishes preparing his tea and sits on the bed next to her. "You see things differently because you have finished your five-year mission to explore strange new worlds. Now you are going where many women have gone before—to be a mother."

Sofia checks her feelings. "Stop talking silly."

Memo becomes more serious. "So then, please tell me what you are honestly feeling."

Sofia thinks for a moment, then without turning to Memo, she says, "What I am honestly, truly, really feeling now is…"

Memo waits for the rest of the sentence, but it doesn't come. "Is…what?"

Sofia holds her breath for a moment, then turns to Memo with sheepish eyes. "I'm feeling like I want to have this baby."

Memo lights up with a big smile. "That's perfect because so do I!"

"No, seriously. I really want this baby—like, you know—I really want to do this. Is that weird?"

"Why would you think it is weird?"

"Well, you know, most girls my age around here get abortions."

Memo quickly puts his index finger over Sofia's mouth to keep her from saying anything else. "Please, don't even speak about that. It is your choice, but know it would make me sad to the rest of my days."

"Don't worry. I won't do that. I don't want to do that. Happy?" Sofia asks.

"Yes! Yes! If the world is the size of my thumb," Memo says holding up his left thumb, "I am happy as my whole hand."

Sofia giggles at his crazy metaphor, then gets serious. "I think what scares me is how are we going to do this? I mean, we have nothing."

"No, no," Memo replies with raised hand. "I told you *no te preocupes*—don't worry. I got this more covered than a tent on the beach."

"With what, your new multi-million dollar bench busi-ness?" Sofia asks.

"*Exacto, mujer*. That lady your boss introduced me to? She called again. She wants three benches. She's making a deposit tomorrow!

Sofia is surprised by this. "She wants three?"

"Yes, she buys two for her backyard and one for the art gallery I was catering. Nice huh?"

"Really?" Sofia asks with growing excitement. How much is she paying for them?"

"One thousand dollars!"

"One thousand for all of them?"

"No, one thousand dollars each!"

"You kidding?"

"No. That is the price."

Sofia thinks about this for a moment, then looks around the apartment. Memo watches her closely and curiously. "What?" he asks. "What are you thinking in that beautiful *cabeza* now?

Sofia gets a lump in her throat but knows what she wants to say. Finally, without looking at Memo, she lets out the slightest giggle. "So, I guess this is going to be home for us."

Memo looks around the place as his heart fills with hope. But is he hearing her correctly? "If we don't go back to El Salvador..." he says cautiously.

Sofia looks at him carefully. She knows this is a big moment. "I think it's better for the baby if we stay here."

Memo can't believe his ears. "No puede ser... Did you just really say that?"

"*Sí*. Like you say, you can't ride a bike backward to go forward."

"*Dilo de nuevo*—Can you say it again?"

"No."

"Say it again! I'm not sure the walls heard you. They are not smiling yet."

Sofia shakes her head and gives in. "I said it is better we stay here! Okay, did they hear that?"

"Loud and ultra-clear. Like in the dishwasher!"

Sofia puts down her hot chocolate and grabs Memo. They hug and giggle until Sofia pulls away. "How am I going to tell my mom?"

"I don't know," Memo giggles. "Let's ask the little one." He puts his ear on Sofia's stomach. "Hey, you in there! How you want us to tell the world, you come here. In the person? Facebook? What's that you say? You want parade! With a marching band! Okay, and some jets flying in the sky! *Sí, ¿por qué no?* You got it, *hombre.*"

Sofia giggles but then lovingly slaps Memo on the head. "I'm serious. She is probably going to freak out."

Memo lifts his head and looks at Sofia. "I think we just need to get your family to see this the best way. We just need to say we did not kill anybody—we created somebody!"

18

THE BIG ANNOUNCEMENT

On the following Saturday afternoon, the same day that clocks all across the country will be turned back one hour for the winter, Sofia and Memo arrive on the electric bike at the family house on Cherry Tree Avenue. In the backyard, last minute preparations are underway for a triple birthday party for Roberta, Ricki, and Angelica, who, as luck would have it, all have birthdays in the same month.

The entire backyard is filled with folding tables, each decorated with festive tablecloths and balloons that read "happy birthday" in English. The back walls of the house are decorated with purple and silver streamers. Just in front of the back door is a long serving table filled with large silver food trays covered in foil. To one side are three BBQ grills manned by older Latina ladies, hair pulled back in tight buns, preparing the *"carne."* To the other side are small containers holding plastic utensils, large pitchers of juice, and bowls of multi-colored gelatin covered in plastic wrap. In between is an assortment of Salvadoran foods like pupusas, yuca frita, empanadas, tacos, beans, fried plantain, and lots of picante. There are even chocobananos for dessert.

"I'm nervous," Sofia says with a tense look on her face.

Memo, showing a bit of nervousness himself, asks, "You sure you want to show what is behind door number three?"

Sofia glances at him as she starts to question her decision. "I think so."

"If you want I can tell them," Memo responds.

Sofia's eyes widen. "No, please don't say anything until after I make the announcement, okay?"

"*Sí, seguro* for sure, *mi amor.*"

Before they can dismount the bike and head for the back-yard, Father Giovanni Fontana, locally referred to as Father Vinny, appears carrying a white gift bag. He's a kind-looking Italian Catholic priest, complete with white collar. He's in his fifties but looks trim and fit. "*Hola Sofia,*" he smiles.

"Hi Father," Sofia responds with a sudden look of dread on her face.

"Everything okay?" Father Vinny asks, sensing her nervousness.

Sofia tries to bury the tense look on her face. "Yes, yes. Sure. Good to see you."

"Good to see you too," Father Vinny smiles. "Well, I'll see you in the back for the big announcement."

Both Sofia and Memo look surprised. "The big announcement?" Sofia asks nervously.

"Yes," Father Vinny smiles. "The big announcement about Ricki and Angelica's first communion. It's coming up soon!"

"Oh yes," Sofia says, relieved. "That's right. They're really excited."

Father Vinny heads toward the back, leaving Sofia and Memo alone. Memo takes a deep breath and giggles as he looks at Sofia. "This is like going to confession!"

Sofia gathers her courage. "We didn't kill anybody. We created somebody, right?"

"Yes, that is the general's idea," Memo says, trying to show confidence.

"Okay, let's go." Sofia says.

In the back, Ricki sees Father Vinny and explodes with excitement. "Father Vinny is here! *Padre Vinny!*" Ricki yells to alert the others. He then gives the priest a big hug that almost smashes the bag of gifts.

"How are you, Ricki? Careful with the gifts. You don't want to break them! And Angelica, my sweet angel, how are you?"

Seconds later, Ana, Juan, and Roberta arrive to greet Father Vinny and welcome him to the party. "I'm so happy you were able to come," Ana says with a big smile.

"I haven't missed one of your big birthday parties yet," Father Vinny smiles.

"Welcome, welcome!" Juan says with a hand extended.

Just as Ana turns back to get Father Vinny something to drink, she sees Sofia coming from the driveway. "Hi Mama," Sofia smiles sheepishly.

Once out of earshot from Father Vinny, Ana frowns at her daughter. "Now, you show up?"

"Sorry Mama," Sofia says. "What do you want us to do?"

Ana asks, "Us?"

Sofia turns back and waves Memo into the backyard. "I invited Memo."

As soon as Memo appears, tension fills the air. Ana frowns, puts down the meat tray, and moves toward Memo aggressively. "You are pretty bold to come here right now."

Memo smiles sheepishly. "I know you are still angry about the tattoo, but I have a problem. I can't say no to Sofia. I'm sorry. But look, I have one too!"

Memo pulls back his shirt to reveal his tattoo. Memo's tattoo is small but dramatic. "Mine is an eagle," he says proudly. "I want to write next to it, 'The eagle has landed.' You like it?"

Before Ana can fully react, the rest of the family quickly gathers to join the conversation. Ricki, who knows and likes Memo, leaves Father Vinny. He runs up to Memo, puts an arm around him and does not let go. Angelica stays with Father Vinny but waves to Memo with a shy smile.

"Let me see that," Arnell demands. Memo pulls back his shirt obediently.

"It doesn't have anything to do with a gang," Memo says. "Please don't worry about that."

Sofia reaches out and grabs Arnell to pull him back. "Arnell, please."

Juan, the second oldest next to Estella, smiles at Memo but offers a few words of caution. "Look, it's just that we haven't known you for too long, and well, you know."

"I understand, "Memo says. "I'm just not that kind of guy. I'm an artist."

"Artist?" Arnell pipes in sarcastically.

"And a businessman!"

"Yes, he is! "Sofia adds. "He's starting a company that will sell furniture."

"He's in a gang," Arnell says, making up his mind.

Juan stays calm. "Sofia is a lot younger than you. We don't want her marking up her body."

"Oh my god," Sofia cries. "Will you stop!"

"He's 19!" Ana interrupts.

"Ah," Memo smiles. "But I just turned 19, and Sofia is almost 17. So we're only two years and a couple of months different."

"I don't think he should be here," Arnell states.

"Arnell, he is my guest."

"Well, it's not your party!"

"Well, if he can't be here, I don't want to be here."

Memo suddenly holds up a hand to make peace. "It's okay. I will go."

"No!" Sofia shouts. "If you leave, I'm coming with you."

"Stay, "Memo says to Sofia. "You will disappoint Ricki and Angelica. Just remember, sometimes we have to drive over the rocks before we get to the sandy beach."

Sofia is about to blow when suddenly, a yell comes from the other side yard. *"¡Hola! ¿Llegamos temprano?"*

Appearing from the driveway is "Commiefornia" himself, Robert Mathews with his Japanese wife, Sandra. Sandra Mathews is shorter than Robert, but has beautiful flowing black hair. She is well-put-together with a white silk blouse, high waisted black trousers and a pair of flat sandals. With only a few delicate pieces of jewelry and only a touch of make-up, she comes across as sophisticated and intelligent. Both Robert and Sandra are smiling as they enter with gifts in hand.

Juan and Ana both turn away from the conversation with Memo and move to greet the special guests with big smiles.

"Heyyyyyy!" Juan waves as he approaches them. Ana also waves and follows Juan.

Memo watches the scene curiously. "Who is that?"

Sofia forces a smile and waves at the visitors. They recognize her and wave back. She then turns back to Memo. "That's Robert and his wife, Sandra. My mom works for them."

Memo is surprised. "And they come here for a birthday party?"

"They're weird. They're from California."

"You think they would want to buy some outdoor furnitures from me?"

Arnell turns back to Memo. "Weren't you on your way out?"

"Yes, yes. I'm leaving," Memo smiles. "I'm leaving, but..." He stops before finishing the sentence and glances over at Sofia. "What about the announcement?"

"What announcement?" Roberta asks with sudden curiosity.

Arnell also becomes curious. "You have an announcement?" he asks loudly.

Arnell's loud voice attracts everyone's attention. Ana and Juan turn back toward Sofia and Memo. Even Father Vinny tunes in on the situation.

Sofia tries to summon the courage, but she just can't find it. "Yes, we have something to tell you, but not right now."

Ana, sensing something important is going on, looks back and forth between Sofia and Memo, asking, "What is all this about?"

"I'll tell you later," Sofia says and then turns to Memo with a defeated expression. "C'mon, I will walk you out."

Arnell starts to reach out for Sofia but doesn't want to create a scene in front of Robert and his wife. "You stay here," he tells her quietly.

Sofia turns to Roberta with a look of, help me. Roberta grabs Arnell by the arm. "It's okay, honey. She's just walking him to the front." Arnell stands down.

Back at the front of the house, Sofia escorts Memo to his bike. "I'm sorry, Memo," Sofia says, shaking her head, "I just can't do it right now. You see what it is like? Both those guys act like they are my father, and neither of them is even close! I was afraid of what they would do to you."

"I think your mama was right to come here," Memo says. "But she left you back in El Salvador for too long. So your sister became more of a mother to you. Her husband is just trying to fill in as a daddy man."

"Yeah, probably," Sofia says sadly. "I don't know how to tell them."

"It's okay, *mi amor*, we will find a better time. Maybe just tell your mama first so me, father man, don't get killed by the daddy men."

Sofia giggles, her mood lightening. "You always make stuff funny. How do you do that?"

"I don't know. Something is wrong in the brain."

"Great, my baby's father is brain damaged."

Memo smiles. "Maybe, but that will not stop him from coming now."

Sofia kisses Memo warmly to say goodbye. "Nothing stopping this baby."

Memo pulls her in for a second kiss. "I love you."

Sofia pulls back and looks at Memo. "I love you too."

Memo's eyes grow wide. "Whoa. Truth?"

Sofia shakes her head with a smile. "Double Truth."

When Sofia appears at the party again, Robert and Sandra are at the table with Father Vinny, Estella, Juan, and Ana. Robert hopes Sofia will stop by and say hi, but Sofia barely notices him. Instead, she walks straight to the DJ station and takes the phone playing the music away from Ricki. "C'mon, you guys, let's dance." She then cranks up some Salvadoran pop music. She moves with her niece and nephew out into some open space and starts jumping around. Sofia laughs at some of Ricki's crazy dance moves.

"So, how is Sofia these days?" Robert asks in Spanish with his thick American accent. "She looks happier than the last time I saw her."

Father Vinny, who is also watching the dance floor nods his head. "I was just thinking the same thing."

Juan and Ana share a glance, then turn and watch Sofia dancing with the kids. They then turn back to each other with a curious look.

19

OLD PICTURES

The morning after the birthday party, Ana waits patiently until Estella goes outside to feed the chickens. Once she is sure the coast is clear, Ana calls out to Sofia. "Sofia, come here. I need to talk to you," she says. Sofia, intrigued by the sudden seriousness in Ana's voice, quickly makes her way to the small basement suite they share. As Sofia enters the room, she notices Ana closing the door, creating a sense of privacy and intimacy.

Ana sits on the edge of their modest bed, her eyes filled with a mix of sadness and determination. She reaches under the bed and pulls out a stack of old photo albums. With trembling hands, she flips through the pages until she finds the pictures of her brothers. "Sofia," she begins, her voice dropping to a whisper, "I have something to tell you. Something I've kept hidden for a long time."

Sofia's curiosity grows stronger, and she leans in closer, her full attention on Ana. "What is it?" she asks.

Taking a deep breath, Ana reveals the truth that has burdened her for years. "The story you've always been told about my brothers Carlos and Tomas... it's not entirely true," she says solemnly. "They weren't both killed in the war."

Sofia's eyes widen in shock, her mind struggling to process what she is hearing. "What do you mean?" she stammers.

Ana then reveals a story Sofia has never heard before. One day, during the war, when Tomas was 17 and Carlos was 16, some soldiers came to the house and told Estella they were taking the boys to conscript them into the battle against the communists. Estella begged them not to take the boys and pleaded she needed them to help with the family's meager farm. The commander took pity on Estella and told her she could keep one of the boys, but the other would have to go. It was up to her to choose. Estella agonized over the situation and ended up choosing Tomas. He was older and stronger than Carlos. She figured Tomas would have a better chance of surviving.

The look on Tomas' face when Estella made her decision was a mix of shock and horror. She tried to hold on to her boy and tell him how sorry she was, but the soldiers pulled him away and took him off to a truck outside. Tomas became a soldier and was allowed to come home occasionally, but he was never the same. His sense of betrayal never left him. After a while, he stopped coming home altogether. Estella later learned Tomas was killed in battle.

Fearful that the same thing could happen to her younger son, Estella arranged for Carlos to go north and seek asylum in the United States. He ended up living in Los Angeles with Estella's cousin, Enrique. But Enrique was a hard-drinking man who didn't treat his family well and treated Carlos even worse. Carlos drifted into a gang and followed the usual path to jail, followed by deportation back to El Salvador. But once back home, he met a woman and fell in love. They had a child together, and Carlos decided to leave the gang. But the gang wasn't about to let that happen. Instead of letting him go, they killed him. His wife fled with their child and has not been heard from since.

"From then on, our family was a constant target for the *pandilleros*," Ana said. "They wanted to make sure all their members understood that leaving the gang was dangerous for them and their families. "I've never told you this, but when I was pregnant with you, I was stabbed by a gang guy just because I was Carlos' sister."

"They stabbed you?" Sofia asked in disbelief.

"Yes, very close to the womb. It almost killed you."

Sofia was shocked. "How come you never told me about this?"

Ana just shook her head. "Why fill your head with such a horror story? Life has been hard enough for you already. But now I think maybe you are ready. I know you think I abandoned you, and I know you are angry with me. But I came here looking for a safer place for us to live. I just want you to understand."

Sofia stares at her mother for a long moment, then leans in for an embrace. It's a connection that has been elusive for so long. In this moment, the barriers that have separated them melt away, and they truly reconnect for the first time since Ana left El Salvador. As they finally release each other, Sofia and her mother look into each other's eyes, their connection stronger than ever before. "Mama, I have something I want to tell you, too," Sofia says softly.

"Okay, tell me," Ana says with a rare softness in her voice.

Sofia starts to speak but it is hard to get the words out. She hesitates.

"What is it?" Ana asks, growing more curious. "You keep saying you have an announcement."

Sofia reaches deep in herself and finds the strength to release the words from her mouth. "I'm pregnant."

Upstairs, the whole family hears a loud shriek coming from the basement suite where Sofia and Ana are. Ricki and Angelica are the first ones to run for the stairs. Ricki pushes on the closed door at the bottom of the steps and finds Ana on her feet staring at Sofia with a look of disbelief on her face. When she sees Ricki and Angelica, she rushes toward them. "Not now," Ana says forcefully as she pushes them out and closes the door. The kids don't try to open the door again but they don't go back upstairs, either. Instead, they lean in and place their ears on the door to hear what is going on inside just as Roberta shows up to join them. "What's happening?" Roberta asks. The kids put fingers to their mouths, silently telling Roberta to be quiet.

"How did you let this happen?" Ana asks desperately.

Sofia remains on the bed, not showing any signs of grief. "It just happened—almost like it was supposed to happen."

Ana starts to pace. "Don't act foolish, This is very serious. You've broken my heart. You know good girls don't sleep with a man until they are married where we come from. How could you do this?"

At this point, Sofia finds her inner strength. She stands from the bed and moves closer to her mother with a look of confidence. "Mother, you were unmarried and just sixteen when you had Roberta."

"Yes, and look at me now," Ana cries. "I clean houses. We didn't come all the way here so you would end up doing the same thing. I wanted a better life for you and you've gone and ruined it with that crazy boy!"

"Once again," Sofia says calmly. "Memo is not crazy. He's a talented artist who is starting to make a lot of money. And he really, really loves me. He's already proposed like three times and has a place for us to live. He's got it together."

Ana stares at Sofia for a moment, wondering if she should believe all this. "How's he making money?"

Sofia grows more positive. "He's selling his benches to all these rich Americanos for like a thousand dollars each."

"And he has a place for you two?"

"Yes, an apartment near downtown. It's big!"

Ana is still upset, but she is calmed by what she is hearing. Her curiosity grows. "So, you would stay in New Jersey?"

"Yes."

"No more talk about going back to El Salvador?"

"No. We think we will be better for the baby if we stay here and just move forward."

Ana is stunned by Sofia's sudden maturity. She knows she can't just cave in to the idea of a baby, but secretly she now feels a great sense of relief. She reaches out and grabs Sofia by the shoulders and looks deep into the young girl's eyes. "And you are sure you want to have this baby."

"Yes."

"And that's it? Just take care of the baby and cook for Memo?"

Sofia is surprised by her mother's question but proudly announces that she has thought through this as well. "Not just that. I've decided I want to be an ornithologist too."

"What is that?" Ana asks.

"That's what they call people who work with birds," Sofia explains. "I want to work with birds."

Ana shakes her head in near disbelief. This transformation that has overcome her daughter is shocking. But wisdom tells her the pregnancy has forced Sofia to grow up. And despite the terrible stigma against teen pregnancy, perhaps in this case, it is a good thing - not just for Sofia, but for the whole family. It will be the first "Americano" born in the family.

"Okay," Ana finally says. She then walks over to the closed door and opens it to reveal the hidden snoopers. The group now includes Arnell and Estella. "Well," Ana says, turning back to Sofia. "Go ahead and tell them."

Sofia stares for a moment. She knows they already know, having heard her discussion with Ana, but she can't hold back the proud smile that sweeps over her face. "I'm going to have a baby!"

Ricki and Angelica get excited and run to hug Sofia, but the adults are not sure what to think—especially Estella. Estella's expression darkens immediately.

20

MORNING SICKNESS SURPRISE

The first real snow of the season has finally graced the ground, blanketing Jack's backyard in a pristine layer of white. Though it measures only a few inches, its presence is enough to transform the landscape into something from a classic Norman Rockwell painting. And with the arrival of the snow, there is a sense of change in the air. It's as if nature itself is signaling the start of a new chapter for Jack, but bringing with it the mystery of what comes next.

Inside his cozy man cave, Jack sits ensconced in front of his computer with a down vest wrapped snugly around him. In an effort to combat his heating costs, he has turned down the thermostat. As he nurses a steaming mug of hot tea, he grapples with the task of creating an Airbnb listing for a short-term rental "near the beach." Just as he is about to add the finishing touches, Jack's phone lights up with an incoming call from his semi-Irish friend and unofficial booking agent for Sofia and Ana, Robert Mathews. "Good news," Robert says. "You're cleaning team is back and ready for action."

Jack is pleased by this information. With a hint of concern and curiosity, Jack inquires, "Is Sofia feeling better?"

"Yes, I think she is on to new horizons," Robert coyly speculates.

"I can imagine," Jack responds with a hint of friendly sarcasm. "When do they want to come up?"

"They're ready whenever you are. Ana mentioned tomorrow."

"Okay then," Jack snickers. "I guess I better get the place cleaned up for them. Ana gets pissed off when the dishes aren't washed."

"Oh, yeah. I know what you mean. She does the same thing to us. My wife, Sandra, always likes to joke, "We better clean up, Ana is coming!"

"They're actually good people when you think about it," Jack says philosopically.

Robert is pleasantly surprised by Jack's sentiment. He thinks it might have something to do with Jack's love life. "How did it go with your online date?"

Jack rolls his eyes. "Beautiful gal, but I got off on the wrong foot with her."

"Sorry to hear that, Robert replies. "What happened?"

"Long story for another time, Commiefornia."

Robert laughs. "Oh now you're going to start calling me that too?"

"I'll see you at the club," Jack says with a smile. "Tell Ana I will be by to pick them up at the usual time tomorrow."

Cherry Tree Avenue is much quieter than normal when Jack turns onto the street. The coating of white snow softens the whole setting by covering over the scars of an immigrant invasion. Jack assumes the Latino inhabitants of this block, whose thin blood is more accustomed to tropical temperatures, remain indoors next to heaters or fires and contemplate why they decided to live in such a cold place. When Jack nears his destination, he sees Ana, Sofia, and the two kids standing in front of their little house on the sidewalk. He pulls up with the window down. "Good Morning."

Ana smiles at Jack. Sofia also smiles, appearing to be in a good mood. "Good morning."

"I see you have some fans to send you off today."

Sofia points to the kids. "This is Ricki, and this is Angelica. They are my niece and nephew."

"Hello," Jack waves, sensing something odd about Ricki.

Angelica waves sheepishly at Jack, but Ricki grunts and heads for the backdoor of Jack's car. Ana waves at him to stop. " Ricki, wait!

Ricki stops and turns around, wondering why Ana has stopped him. Sofia asks Jack, "Would it be alright if we bring Ricki and Angelica with us today? Their mom had to work today, and there is no one to watch them?"

Jack's polite smile suddenly turns into a frown. He thinks about it for a second, then scratches his head. "But who will watch them while you guys are working?"

Sofia stays firm. "They'll be quiet—just watch TV or something."

Jack sighs in resignation. He thinks to himself how it is always the same with these people. They don't think ahead. They don't plan. Everything just happens, and they all act like it is normal. And what is odd is he's starting to accept it. He nods with reluctant approval. "Okay, hop in."

Sofia takes the front seat while the rest get in the back. She smiles at Jack. He smiles and asks sarcastically, "Are we stopping for food today too?"

"Yes, at the house."

Jack figures as much. He shakes his head and heads down the street.

Once on the road, Ricki rolls down the back window and

throws an empty candy wrapper out. Jack notices this and pulls off to the side. "Did you just throw something out the window?" Ricki looks around at the others in the car but doesn't answer Jack. "I don't know how it is in your country," Jack scolds, "but in America, we don't litter. Do you understand English?"

"Yes, Sofia answers, "he understands English, but..."

"There is no 'but' about it. Ricki needs to get out and go pick that up."

Ricki looks more confused than ever. Angelica quickly comes to his aide. "I will go get it," she says.

"No, Jack barks. "He was the one who threw it out. He should be the one to go get it!"

"But Jack," Sofia says softly. "He's special needs."

"Special needs? What are you talking about?"

Sofia leans in quietly. "He's autistic."

Jack suddenly figures out what is going on. "Oh, sorry. I didn't know." He thinks about it for a minute, then opens his door and starts to get out.

"No, I will get it," Sofia says. She jumps out of the car and runs back, looking for the wrapper.

Jack glances at Ana in the rearview mirror with an apologetic look. Then he turns to Ricki more politely. "No trash throwing, okay?" Ricki looks at Jack and smiles. He takes an entire candy bar out of his pocket and throws it out the window with a loud snort of a laugh.

Once inside his home, Jack sits the two little ones on the living room couch and turns on the TV. It's on a conservative news channel, of course. Angelica looks at the TV politely and seems to resign herself to the fact that this is what she will be doing for the next five hours. But Ricki knows what he wants to watch and isn't shy about letting the world know.

"I want to watch cartoons!"

Angelica tries to calm him down, but he remains agitated. Jack looks to Sofia for help.

"He wants to watch cartoons in Spanish," Sofia says.

Jack frowns. "I don't think my cable package has that."

"I'm pretty sure you do. It's on basic cable. Can I try?"

"Can't he watch them in English?

Sofia looks at Jack as if to say, "Seriously?"

Jack realizes he's not being sensitive to the situation. He gives in and hands the remote to Sofia. She quickly finds Spanish cartoons and turns up the volume. "He likes them a little loud."

Jack just shakes his head. He turns toward the kitchen and leaves Ricki and Angelica in peace.

"Here, I got this stuff for you," Jack says to Sofia as she walks into the kitchen.

Sofia looks at the pamphlet on the table. It has information about an online class for people interested in taking the GED.

"Do you know what the GED is?" Jack asks.

Sofia is pleasantly surprised. "Yes, I know what it is. So you went out and got all this for me?"

"Yes. I just thought. You know…"

Sofia studies Jack curiously. It feels strange that he would care enough about her to do this. On one hand, she feels like Jack is just another guy who wants to act like her father. But on the other hand, nobody else thought to get her something that would help her like this. She studies the paperwork for a moment. "So it's like a test."

"Yes," Jack says, sensing she is interested. "You study for the test, and if you pass, they give you the equivalent of a high school diploma."

"Yeah, this might be good now that I'm going to stay in New Jersey."

Jack is pleasantly surprised by this. "You decided against going back to El Salvador?"

"Yes."

Jack looks curious about this. "Why?"

Sofia smiles at Jack. She tries to find just the right words to let him know about the bun in her oven, but then she is interrupted by Ricki who comes into the kitchen. He's hungry and goes straight to the fridge, opens the door, and looks for something tasty.

"Ricki, that isn't our food," Sofia says.

Ricki stops, looks at Sofia, then at Jack.

Jack waves a hand and moves toward the fridge. "No, it's fine. You want some apple pie?"

Ricki looks at Sofia to explain. *"Pan dulce de manzana,"* Sofia tells him.

Ricki agrees to try it, and when he does, it brings a big smile to his face. He steps up to Jack and puts an arm around him to show his pleasure. Jack smiles at him stiffly, waiting for Ricki to let go. But Ricki doesn't let go. He just stands there with his arm around Jack. Jack looks to Sofia for help.

"Ricki, you're missing your cartoons. Don't you want to go watch?"

Ricki remembers he was watching cartoons and leaves with his plate of apple pie. Jack moves to return the pie to the fridge. Sofia holds up her hand to stop Jack before he puts the pie away. "Can I have some too?"

Jack is surprised by this. Sofia usually prefers her regular Salvadoran stuff. "Sure. You want to heat it up?"

"Yeah, sure, Maybe it will help my stomach."

"What's wrong with your stomach?"

"I'm a little nauseous," she says, holding her stomach. "I think it might be morning sickness."

Jack gets a curious look on his face. "Morning sickness?"

Sofia looks at him and realizes she has not told him yet. She smiles proudly. "Yes, I'm pregnant."

Jack suddenly freezes. "What?"

"I'm pregnant. I'm going to have a baby."

"You're kidding, right?"

"No, I'm moving in with my boyfriend Memo—the father—who told me to thank you for helping him sell three of his benches."

Jack hears nothing about the benches. This news that Sofia is pregnant lights him up like a candlestick, and not in a good way. It's more like a fireworks show gone bad.

"What in the living hell?" Jack erupts.

"I know," Sofia says sheepishly. "It wasn't planned, but we're both very happy."

"Not planned?" Jack asks as his face turns deep red. "You're only 16 years old, god damnit!"

Sofia is thrown off guard by the level of Jack's anger. Her family's support lulled her into thinking it was something she could be proud of. She didn't consider how differently an old Americano like Jack would see it. Nevertheless, she tries to keep her cool. "I know how old I am!"

"You're only 16!" Jack yells even louder.

Now Sofia becomes angry. "I'm almost 17!"

Jack paces the room like an angry lion, ready to pounce. "You shouldn't even be having sex at your age!"

"Really? How old were you the first time?"

"Don't you talk to me like that!"

"Don't YOU talk to me LIKE THAT!"

"Didn't your mother teach you anything? What kind of mother lets this happen? Ever hear of birth control?"

"You don't understand," Sofia shoots back with growing anger. "I want this baby. I want to be a mother."

Jack shakes his head. "Don't be stupid. You don't know what you want. You're just a kid."

"You don't know me."

"Oh, yeah? You're illegal! You're a high school dropout! And now you're pregnant! That's who you are."

"Why do you care, anyway?"

"Maybe I saw something in you—but no more. You've just gone from hero to zero."

"No, you are the zero," Sofia shouts back.

The yelling brings the kids back to the kitchen, as well as Ana. Ana asks Sofia "What's going on here?"

Sofia turns to her mother with real pain on her face. "He is angry with me for being pregnant and says you are a terrible mother."

Ana turns to Jack with a look of shock. She becomes upset and starts talking to Jack with a raised voice in Spanish.

Jack turns to Sofia. "What did she just say?"

"She said she wants to know why you talk so mean to me? She supports me because I know what I want and am happy. And she says that is a good thing!"

Jack turns to Ana. "No! This is a bad thing! Very very bad!"

Sofia translates to her mother. Ana turns back to Jack and speaks sternly to him.

Jack looks at Sofia. "She said she doesn't know what is important to you or what is not important. But she thinks the road you have taken in life has left you angry and alone in a big lonely house. She says she thanks you for all you have done for us, but she doesn't want to work here any longer. She wants you to take us home."

Ana takes off her cleaning apron and prepares to leave. Ricki suddenly dashes to the fridge for the rest of the apple pie.

"Ricki, no!" Ana yells at him. But he doesn't listen to her. Instead, he grabs the white pie box and heads for the front door.

Jack waves his hand sarcastically. "It's okay. He can have it. Take whatever you want!"

Sofia gives Jack a contemptuous glance, then grabs the Salvadoran food from the fridge.

Minutes later the front door bursts open, and a parade of unhappy people head for Jack's car. But blocking their way is a young Asian couple on their way to ring the front doorbell.

"Can I help you?" Jack asks angrily.

"Yes," the young man says. "We saw the Airbnb listing. Is it okay if we take a look?"

Jack becomes suspicious. "How did you get my address?"

The young couple look a little baffled. "It's in the ad," the woman says, holding up her phone to show proof. "We were in the car on Ocean Avenue and thought we'd check it out in person."

Jack checks and sees his address is indeed publicly posted on the ad. "Crap, how did that happen?"

"I don't know," the man responds. "But any chance we could still take a look?"

Jack takes another look at the couple. "No, not right now. I'm on my way out. Call me later," Jack says glumly. He then turns and gets in his car with all the others.

All the regulars are in the steam room at the Gulfstream Club when Jack Yanks opens the door and enters through the mist like a dark, menacing creature from beyond the wall. He sits down next to Robert and remains silent, with only the sound of steam hissing out from the nozzle on the wall near the floor.

"Everything alright?" Robert asks, sensing a disturbance in the force.

Jack sits silently for a moment, staring at the floor. Then without looking up he asks Robert, "Did you know Sofia was pregnant?"

Suddenly, the attention of all the others is on Jack and

Robert. Robert fidgets a bit on the hot tiles as if he is guilty for betraying Jack in some way. But on the other hand, it's not terribly sensitive to invade Sofia's privacy by announcing her pregnancy status. "Yes, I knew. But I don't know what you'd expect me to do, call you up and gossip about it?"

Jack thinks about this silently and looks around at the other guys. He realizes he is revealing too much of his feelings, but he is still too upset to care. "Unbelievable," he finally says, shaking his head. "And the way her mother is okay with it! She's like, Oh, so you are pregnant? Let's have pupusas for lunch today. Crazy!"

Robert wants to respect Jack's anger, but he can't help smiling. "You know about pupusas?"

"How could I not? They're always sticking pupusas, tacos, chocobananos, and god knows what else in my fridge."

Lou grows curious and asks, "Are you talking about your maid's daughter?"

"Yes," Jack responds.

Lou snorts. "She's probably like what, fifteen?

"Sixteen," Jack responds bluntly.

Bobby Brown Sheets, who has been listening to all this with a curious look on his face, leans in toward Jack. "I don't understand, why do you fucking care anyway? What's this girl to you?"

"She's nothing to me," Jack groans unconvincingly.

At this point, Vlad smiles devilishly and asks what everyone is thinking. "You sure you're not the father?"

Jack turns red with anger. "What kind of a god damned question is that?"

"Well, you know what they say about a man who talks 'pupusas' all the time."

"No, I don't," Jack says with anger. "Why don't you explain it to me."

"In Russia, there is old football saying, 'When the field has grass, it's ready for play.'"

Jack looks like he is going to stand up and deck Vlad, but then Robert tries to interject and not let things escalate any further. "Jack, I don't think it's so unusual that you would get upset about it. You obviously care for Sofia, and you are concerned for her welfare. There is nothing wrong with that."

"What kind of bullshit is that?" Lou scoffs at Robert. "Jack's just kicking himself for getting involved with these people. And you were the one who pushed him into it. Now he knows it was a mistake. Now he knows who they really are."

Robert, growing tired of being cautious around Lou, quickly asks, "Oh yeah, and who is that?"

Lou's face turns a vibrant shade of mobster purple. "These people are like mice in the basement. You can't be nice to them. They'll take over your house! They're like those kudzu vines you see crawling all over the trees along the highway. They're freak'n parasites, poisoning the blood of this town—this country—right in front of our eyes! That is who they are!"

Before Robert can respond, Vlad cuts in. "You know those white power guys, worried white race be replaced by color people? They are very stupid. They spend big money to buy militia outfits and go to protest. No! If they want not be replaced, they should just go home and make more babies! Idiots!"

At this point, Bobby Brown Sheets gets curious. "Who makes more babies? Blacks or Latinos?"

Vlad laughs. "Chinese!"

"My wife has just written a report about this," Robert says. "The fertility rate is highest among whites in America. Latinos are second, followed by blacks."

Bobby Brown Sheets shakes his head. "I don't believe you. Maybe once upon a time, but not anymore."

"No, it's true," Robert responds. "You can look it up."

Everyone falls silent for a moment as the steam generator kicks in after a brief rest. As a new cloud of vapor begins to fill the room, Robert giggles to himself. "Guys, you know what is ironic here?" he asks. "All of us in this room could probably go up to Ellis Island and find pictures of our ancestors who came here as immigrants."

"Yeah, that's right!" Lou bellows from his perch. "And we made this country what it is. Why should we now hand it over to a bunch of Incan half-breeds?"

Bobby Brown Sheets piggy-backs onto his father's anger. "They don't even know who these people are coming across the border. How stupid is that?"

Robert can't help but smile at the irony of this one. "You know why they call Italians, WOPS?"

"Careful," Bobby Brown Sheets says with a finger pointed at Robert. "You're getting into dangerous territory."

"I'm not trying to insult you as an Italian American," Robert says. I'm just trying to point out that when your ancestors came here, many of them had no identification either, so they pinned them with a note that said WOP, which stood for Without Papers. Why is that so different from today?"

Bobby Brown Sheets doesn't really know how to respond to this, so he turns to his dad. Lou doesn't know what to say either. So he defaults to "Why do you have to make a college class out of everything? It's annoying!"

"Let me make one last point," Robert says hurriedly, " and then I will shut up. First-generation immigrants are the lifeblood of the American Dream. I don't think we should try to change that."

Vlad nods in agreement. "Yes, I'm first generation immigrant! I give blood for American dream!"

"You are not," Lou snarls. "You're a Russian Jew and a computer geek. That's different."

Brown Sheets looks over at Vlad. "Didn't you say you used to watch Adams Family in Russian?"

"Yes. And Bonanza too. I love Bonanza's music. 'Dun Dun Da Dun Bonanza!' 'Okay, Adams family, let's go!'"

As the conversation drifts into small talk, Robert turns to Jack, hoping to say something under the radar. "I think what got you so upset had to do with, you know, the cultural divide. Ana is okay with the pregnancy because where they are from, they hold motherhood in higher esteem than we do. Teen pregnancy is more accepted in their culture."

"Jack, don't listen to that crap," Lou says, overhearing Robert. "That's like saying it's okay for some Ahab to come here and walk around wearing a bomb belt because that's what they do back home."

Jack shakes his head in frustration, concluding he should have never come here to blow off steam about Sofia. He starts to get up but Lou leans in. "Did you think about my offer—you know—about the boat?"

"Yep."

"Okay, so we're good?"

Jack thinks about it for a long moment, then turns to Lou, looking defeated. "If you want to come down to the marina and do an inspection, let's set something up."

Lou suddenly brightens. "That's good news, Jackie Boy."

21

THE HA' PENNY DEAL

The romantic notion that mornings are full of possibilities couldn't be further from reality at the Atlantic Highlands boat storage yard on this day. The skies are an oppressive winter shade of gray, seemingly devoid of any semblance of warmth or light. An unsettling howl permeates the air as it whips mercilessly across the shrouds and halyards of the sailboats taking winter shelter in the yard.

Amidst this dreary scene stands Jack, woefully under-dressed for the occasion. He shifts uncomfortably, his arms folded tightly crossed across his chest in an attempt to generate some warmth. Alongside him, his companions Big Lou and Bobby Brown Sheets share his misery, their faces etched with similar expressions of discontent. They huddle together just beside Jack's beloved boat, the Ha' Penny.

Resting upon V-shaped supports, the Ha' Penny is wrapped in a cocoon of white plastic shrink-wrap, giving her a ghostly appearance as her massive form looms over the yard. Despite her temporary slumber, her grandeur and impressiveness remain undiminished.

"Where the hell is your inspection guy?" Lou asks Bobby with an unexpected piece of phlegm in his throat.

Bobby looks at his watch and then around the yard, where nothing else stirs. "He said he would be here."

"When did he say that?"

"A couple of days ago."

"You didn't confirm with him last night?"

"No."

"How many times, I gotta tell you. Winners wake up in the morning with their ducks all lined up. You? You wake up every morning going, 'Where the fuck are my ducks?'"

"I do not!"

You don't? Well, I don't see no ducks. Jack, you see any ducks?

Jack points toward the front gate. "Maybe those are your ducks in that truck."

Bobby looks relieved. "That's gotta be him."

A rusted old Ford Ranger pickup pulls up with two men inside. A short Latino man with dark skin and a broad nose climbs out of the driver's side. "Hey, I'm Antonio, here for the pre-sale inspection," he says with a heavy Spanish accent. "You call for a dry inspection, right?"

Lou looks over at Bobby, angered by who Bobby came up with for the inspection. The guy is dark brown and looks illegal. "That's your duck?"

Bobby tries to cover his ass. He turns to Antonio. "You're not the one I spoke with on the phone, are you?"

"No, that's Larry, the owner of the company. I work for him."

Jack looks at Antonio. "You from Mexico or El Salvador?"

Antonio smiles. "Guatemala!"

Jack turns back to Lou with an ironic smirk on his face. Lou, already aware of what Jack is thinking, holds up his big hand. "Excuse me for just a second." He pulls Bobby away from the group where they can talk privately. "You got me in some real shit here."

Fearful but defensive, Bobby says, "I did what you told me to do. I didn't do anything wrong."

"Well you could've asked who they were sending down here for this inspection. I mean think about it. We came to buy Jack's boat so he will go to a meeting with us at ICE where we will ask for help throwing people like this Antonio and his buddy out of the country. But here we are working with them."

"Nobody has to know about this," Bobby says. "Besides, who else are we gonna get?"

Lou thinks. "I'm a man of principal. What I say is what I mean. You understand?"

"Yeah, I understand," Bobby says with respect. "You want me to tell them the inspection is off?"

Lou thinks for a long moment, then finally makes up his mind. "Fuck it. Let's just get this done. And you, you keep your mouth shut about this."

Once the order to proceed is given, Antonio turns to his partner in the truck and gives him orders in Spanish. The other man jumps out of the passenger side and grabs an old extension ladder from the truck's cargo bay. When Jack sees the ladder, he becomes concerned. It is all metal without protection. It could scratch the hull when they lean it against the boat. "Hey, you got any pads for that thing?" Jack asks the helper.

"*¿Cómo?*" The helper asks, not understanding the question.

"Sorry, he no speak English," Antonio says.

"Hey, if he's going to live in this country, he needs to speak English," Lou barks loudly.

Antonio laughs when he hears this. "Him? He's too stupid and stubborn like a mule. That's why we call him Burro." Antonio translates to his helper, and they both have a good laugh. The helper starts mimicking a mule. "Hee Haw, Hee Haw, Hee Haw."

Once the ladder is in place, Antonio and his helper climb up, cut their way through the shrink wrap, and disappear into the boat. Jack turns to Bobby. "Go with them."

Bobby frowns. "Me?"

"Yeah, keep an eye on them."

Bobby turns to his dad. "Seriously?"

"Yeah, 'seriously.' Get up there."

Bobby reluctantly obeys and starts up the ladder.

"And don't let them use the toilet," Jack adds.

Once Bobby is gone, Lou turns to Jack. "See, this is exactly the problem. This is why we have to be activists. We have to raise awareness to the point where we bring about some real mother fuck'n change. I mean deportations, protests, and lots of news coverage all over the goddamn place. The whole nine yards. You with me?"

Jack looks befuddled. He just can't accept "Big Lou" and "activist" in the same sentence. "It's freezing out here," Jack says. "Let's go sit in my car."

They head toward Jack's Cadillac. "We should also think about hanging some of those big banners," Lou says. "You know, like those Greenpeace kids. They know how to do that shit. Hey, maybe we could hire some of those little fruit cakes to help us out, you know, like freelance."

"What would you put on the banners?" Jack asks curiously.

"I don't know. Maybe something simple like, 'GET OUT NOW!' or just 'GO HOME!' You know, short and to the point."

Jack considers the message. "You know, a lot of those folks don't have a home to go back to."

Lou stops dead in his tracks. "I swear to Christ, I'm gonna put a fucking cap in the ass of that wack job Commiefornia. He's taken over your mind like that *'Portoricano'* took over Patty Hearst's brain! Enough already!"

"Hey," Jack roars to life with anger. "How many times do I

have to tell you, if you get up in my grill, we're going to have a problem."

"Grill? What the fuck is that? 'My grill.' Is that some kind of slang? I never heard you use slang like that before."

Jack has to think about this one. Lou is right. But never mind. Jack doesn't want to discuss it. "Get in the car," he commands Lou.

Lou holds up his hands. "Heyyy, what is going on with you? First, all this commie shit, and now you talk to me with so little respect. This isn't the Jackie Boy I know. Not even close."

Jack realizes he is being gruff but doesn't apologize. Instead, he just changes his tone. "Could you please get in the car?"

"No, I don't think so. I find your sarcasm insulting. I think I'll go sit in my own car."

Jack gives up. He opens his car door, gets in, and starts the engine. Lou turns, walks over to his late model Lincoln Town Car and does the same. A few minutes pass, then Jack looks in his rearview mirror. He can see Lou just sitting there staring at him.

After the inspection, Antonio, Burro, and Bobby climb back down the ladder. Jack and Lou leave their cars and meet at the boat without looking at each other. "Well, how much am I going to lose on this thing?" Lou asks.

Antonio wipes his hands. "Hull, superstructure good. Engines little old with *muy pequeño* leak in gearbox, but no bad. Deck and controls good. Maybe a couple stress fractures in rear deck, but more good than bad. I like the 'convertible' version like this boat. Good for fishing!"

"How much you think I can get for it? "Jack asks.

I'd have to do wet inspection, yes, but dis boat? Maybe 170–190. Is a good boat. Very popular. No make the 53 no more."

Bobby hands Antonio some cash. "Thanks, Antonio."

Antonio takes the cash and shakes everyone's hand. "Okay, if you want to do wet inspection out on water, just call Larry."

Once Antonio is gone, Bobby turns to his dad. "Papa, for what Jack is asking, you won't lose anything on this. Especially if you do the crypto exchange like I told you."

"Crypto. Crypto. What is with you young guys and cryptocurrency?"

Jack gets worried. "You're paying in crypto?"

"Calm down," Lou says, still upset from Jack's insult. "You get cash. He's just talking about selling it in crypto later."

"You wait, Papa. When you see how it goes, you're gonna want to buy every boat they got in here."

"Yeah, yeah."

"So, when do I get the money?" Jack asks.

Lou frowns. More disrespect. "What? You think I'm gonna try to stiff you?"

Jack gets a stern look on his face. "I'm not waiting till you sell it. I need mine up front."

"Okay, follow me," Lou says with anger. He turns and leads Jack to the car's trunk. Inside is a gym bag with a huge amount of money in it. "That's 100 big ones right there. Okay?"

"Okay," Jack says sternly.

"But seeing how I can't get the full 200 for the boat like you promised, whatcha say we take a little off what I'm paying you for it?"

Jack smiles with hostility and adds a mock Irish accent to his voice. "Ask me arse."

"What?"

Jack points to his ass and thickens his Irish. "I said, ask me arse! You might get a better answer."

Lou stares at Jack, thinking he should pull out a pistol and end this string of insults once and for all. But no, that was the old Lou, not the new Lou with a higher purpose. "*Fanculo*," he says, giving in. "One hundred large for Jackie Boy. It will be right here when we get out of the meeting with the ICE guy. We got a deal?"

Jack double-checks the arrangement. "So all I have to do is just be there, right?"

Big Lou holds back his temper. "Yep, that's it."

"You're doing all the talking. I just listen."

"That's what I said. Sweet and Simple."

Jack thinks. "So when is this meeting?"

"Tuesday. Can you do that?"

"I'm available."

Lou closes the trunk of his car. "Done." He sticks his hand out. Jack shakes without smiling.

22

HOPE AND FEAR

A dark military helicopter on a training exercise from nearby Fort Dix passes over Sofia's house like a black cat on its early morning rounds. Inside the little house on Cherry Tree Avenue, Sofia lies in bed, alone in the room, with her hands rubbing her stomach to feel the first signs of her baby. She doesn't know why, but the warm glow of a brighter life is giving way to a strange nervousness. Before her pregnancy, she could have cared less about her legal status in America. She didn't care about being undocumented, or being deported, or anything like that. But now that she has decided to stay, she worries about her ability to remain. For the first time, she is living with what millions of other undocumented migrants live and breathe every day of their lives—hope and fear.

Sofia attempts to dismiss her unease by focusing her thoughts on what they will name the baby. If it's a girl, she's set on the name Esperanza, but if it's a boy, she's undecided. She hopes Memo will suggest something other than his own name, Guillermo, not because she dislikes it, but because she yearns for something with more strength and character. Names like

Cayo, Anso, or even Lucho come to mind. She picks up her phone to look for more name ideas, but the sound of more military helicopters passing over her house pulls her to the window. She looks out to see a large flock of frightened birds take flight. Oddly, it reminds her of the day Arnell came to get her down by the river in El Salvador just before he put her on the bus to go north. There was something strange about that day too. She remembers how the birds took off when Arnell called her name. The connection between these two seemingly unrelated events sends a shiver down her spine. The echoes of that fateful day resonate within her, stirring a deep sense of unease and a haunting realization that life's patterns often weave themselves in mysterious ways.

"Sofia, are you awake?" Her mother calls from the top of the stairs.

"Yes," Sofia calls back.

"We have to leave in one hour."

"Okay," Sofia says. She gets up and goes to the communal closet where she fingers the hangers until she finds a particular dress. She pulls it off the rack and looks at it closely to ensure it is clean and wrinkle-free. Just then, little Angelica bounds down the stairs in a sleeveless white dress. She poses for Sofia, showing off the lace and satin dress with a proud look. "Entonces, what do you think?"

Sofia gets a broad smile on her face. "Oh wow," she says. "Today, you really do look like an angel!"

Angelica twists around a bit with a happy look on her face. "Yes!"

"What is Ricki wearing?"

"He has a white suit. Mama is helping him put it on now."

Sofia lays her dress on the bed. "Are you ready for your first communion?"

"Yes," Angelica proudly replies as she turns and heads back up the stairs.

Sofia turns back to her own dress and starts to put it on when her phone comes to life with a call from Memo. *"Amor,"* Memo says. "*¿A qué hora?* What time to be at the church?"

"Ten," Sofia says bluntly, continuing to work with the dress.

"You okay?" Memo asks.

"I'm not sure. I feel strange today."

"Are you sick?"

"No, I woke up fine, but now I feel like—I don't know. Nervous."

"Nervous good or nervous bad?"

"I'm not sure," Sofia says, giving up on the subject. "Are you coming over in your new truck today?"

"Yeah," Memo says proudly. "I'll come a few minutes early so you can check her out!"

"Okay, let me get dressed. See you then."

Not much later, Sofia emerges from the house wearing her church dress under a worn but classy winter coat. The soft, luxurious fabric drapes gracefully over her body, providing both warmth and a touch of glamour. To complete the refined look, she tastefully enhances her appearance with tinted lip gloss, a touch of mascara, light eyeshadow, and a hint of blush that accentuates her rosy cheeks.

Holding her phone up to her ear, Sofia talks to Memo as he comes down the street in a beat-up Isuzu Hombre pickup truck. The old vehicle, though showing signs of age and wear, has a certain charm to it. Memo pulls up beside Sofia, his face lighting up with a proud smile. "Wow!" he exclaims, gazing at Sofia in admiration. "Who is this beautiful woman who waits for me? You look more stunning than anything man knows."

Sofia lowers her phone as she blushes slightly at Memo's compliment. "You clean up pretty good too," she says.

Memo chuckles. "Not too bad for a farmer boy *campesino* from *el campo*, no?"

"That is one ugly truck," Sofia laughs.

"Yeah, but she can hold up three benches once at a time, and take us to the doctor!"

Sofia's amused expression quickly changes. "Doctor? What doctor?"

"Yeah, for prenatal care. YouTube is crazy about it and says it—"

"Memo, you're crazy. We can't afford that!"

"I have some money cash now, and if I no have enough we apply for public benefits."

The sound of those two words, "public" and "benefits," sends a chill down Sofia's spine. Not because it hurts her pride but because, in her house, it is considered a hazardous step into the system.

Sofia slips into the car to make what she has to say more private. "My mom would kill me if I go to a doctor."

Memo looks at her curiously. "Why?"

"It could get us deported. That's why."

Memo is more confused. "What?"

"They have secret ICE agents who hang around those clinics," Sofia says. "And if they find out you are illegal they will deport you."

Memo shakes his head. "Oh that's just crazy people making up stupid creepy pasta rumors. You don't believe that do you? Besides, your family is waiting for the asylum hearing, no?"

"No..."

"What? I thought all of you were waiting for a big court date?"

"My mother never started a process because she never got caught coming across. She has nothing."

"*Hijo*, she never calls an immigration lawyer?"

"No, too expensive."

"What about you?"

"Me, Roberta, Arnell, and the kids. We're in the system. They gave us a court date for an asylum hearing, but I don't think we went when we were supposed to."

"Shit! That's crazy, girl! *¿Estás Loca?* Why not?"

Sofia shakes her head. "I don't know. I mean, I thought I was going back to El Salvador, so I didn't ask."

Memo is stunned by this sudden news. *"Mierda,* shit man, that maybe makes it they have a deportation order out for all you guys."

Sofia's face remains blank. Suddenly, she feels stupid. "I don't know."

Memo scratches his head, trying to think. His pregnant girlfriend is an "immigration fugitive," and he has no idea how they could fix this. The laws are really complicated. *"Uy,"* Memo says. "All this is too much for my little truck!"

"We can have the baby with a midwife. My mom knows one."

Before Memo can answer, Estella comes out of the house and heads for the sidewalk. She too is dressed for church but doesn't appear to be headed in the right direction. Sofia rolls down the window. "¿Abbi! Where are you going?" Estella has a blank look on her face and does not answer. Sofia opens the door to the truck and goes after her grandmother.

Memo is confused. *"¿Qué pasa?"* He gets out of the truck and follows Sofia.

Sofia catches up to her grandmother and grabs her lightly by the arm. "Where are you going?"

Estella accepts Sofia's hand on her arm with a smile but does not stop walking. "I'm going home to Santa Marta. My parents are waiting for me there."

Sofia has never seen her grandmother at this level of dementia, but she wisely doesn't overreact. Sofia smiles at Estella. "Okay, can I go with you?"

Estella turns to her with a smile. "Yes, my dear girl."

Memo catches up but can't figure out what is happening. He looks at Sofia with a confused look. Sofia silently lets him know it is okay. Then, she turns to Estella. "Do you think he can walk with us for a while?"

Estella looks at Memo and smiles. "Yes, why not?"

"Great," Sofia responds as they walk. When they reach the end of the block, Estella stops and looks in both directions. She is confused about which way to go. Sofia pulls her gently to the left, working on a plan to walk her around the block and back to the house. "I think Santa Marta is this way."

Estella turns to the left but then suddenly appears to wake up. She looks around, confused. "What are we doing here?"

Sofia grabs her hand. "We're just out taking a walk. It's okay."

Estella suddenly looks sad and bewildered. "I'm lost. A lost old woman."

Sofia smiles. "You're with me—it's okay. Are you ready to go back now?

Estella looks at Sofia sadly and reaches out for some comfort. They hug for a long moment, then Estella lets go and looks at Sofia forlornly. "We can't go back. It's too late."

Sofia hugs her grandmother, fully aware of the gravity of their conversation. But instead of acknowledging the truth, she forces a smile. "You want me to make you some coffee when we get home?

Estella looks deep into her granddaughter's eyes and sees the unspoken truth. Accepting her fate, Estella smiles. "Yes. Why not?"

When they reach the house, Memo opens the door and offers it to Estella. Estella smiles at him knowingly. "Take good care of Sofia. She is very special to me."

"I will. More than anything beyond human possibility," Memo says.

Estella enters the house, leaving Sofia and Memo on the stoop together. Sofia turns sad and grabs Memo. Memo puts his arms around her but doesn't say anything. Sofia lets go and says, "I'll be back in a minute."

"*Sí mi amor.* Of course," Memo says warmly.

Memo returns to his truck and uses his phone to do some research about "public assistance" and how it works for undocumented people. Basically, Sofia wasn't far from wrong. To dissuade undocumented immigrants from becoming dependent on public assistance programs like food stamps and Medicaid, successive White House administrations initiated draconian policies to achieve those ends. Basically, the message was, "Use of public assistance programs will not only prevent you from gaining legal status but could also get you deported." The way they achieved this was by continuously widening the definition of what is considered a "public charge," which is someone dependent on the state for their well-being. In the old days, the term was mostly used for those needing cash assistance, like welfare. But over time, it steadily widened to include most forms of non-cash assistance like tax credits, housing subsidies, and all forms of healthcare. It even labeled people with chronic health issues as a potential "public charge" risk.

Exemptions from the widened definition of "public charge" include people who have refugee status, asylum seekers, and pregnant women. But many pregnant women don't take any chances. They avoid health clinics, fearful that rumors about ICE agents lurking there are true.

Memo tries to think about all this, but his thoughts are soon interrupted by the whole family emerging from the house. Ricki comes first with his communion suit on. It is all white with a shiny saffron vest. Following Ricki is Angelica in her special outfit, followed by Sofia, looking all grown up in her dress.

"Wow," Memo exclaims to the kids as he gets out of the truck."Who are you, people?" You people look more rich than Jennifer Lopez!"

"The kids want to ride in your truck," Sofia says to Memo. "Is that okay?"

"Sure, seguro," Memo smiles. "If it is more okay with mom and daddy man."

By this time, the rest of the family has appeared and head for Arnell's older SUV parked in the driveway. Ana, Juan, and Roberta return a wave from Memo. "It's okay by me," Roberta says. But Arnell doesn't give his blessing. He has some unfinished business with Memo. He walks over and gives Memo and the truck a suspicious look. Memo seems to know what Arnell wants to talk about but waits for Arnell to go first. Arnell stares at Memo for a long moment, but then skips over the baby issue and looks at the truck. "This yours?"

Memo smiles proudly. "Yes, just pay little cash."

Arnell looks suspicious. "Where did you get the money?"

The question angers Sofia. "Arnell..."

Memo cuts Sofia off so he can answer the question. He knows he is about to hit a significant milestone with Arnell. "You know the cement furnitures? The big business I start? I've sold four beautiful benches now. Things are crazy good and well!"

"It's true," Sofia adds. "You can go and see two of them at the art gallery."

Memo holds out his phone and shows Arnell pictures of the benches at the art gallery surrounded by rich-looking white people, including Helen Dupont, with Memo at the center. Another image shows a bench newly installed in Helen's extravagant backyard next to a pool. "Look at this one," Memo says proudly. "A lady with a big house on the river bought this one."

Arnell thinks about all this. He looks the truck up and

down, then turns back to Memo. He holds his hand out for a shake. "*Felicidades*—Congratulations."

Memo gets a huge smile on his face and accepts the shake enthusiastically. But before he can say anything, Ricki jumps in the truck and grabs the steering wheel. "C'mon, let's go! I want to go!"

~

The drive to church isn't very long, but it gives Sofia enough time to observe herself riding in the truck with her man and two kids. A slightly sarcastic smile lights up her face. "So, this is who we are going to be?"

Memo looks at her curiously for a moment but then gets the idea. "Yeah, hope so! *¿Por qué no?* Why not be the people from the next-door house?"

Sofia gets the pun and giggles a bit. She looks out the window and observes the homes going by. She sees a man shoveling snow with his son, a family getting in a car, and a woman riding with her child on a bicycle. But the uneasiness she's been feeling still lingers. "You really think this can be us for real?"

"Yes, of course. It's real for all these people. Why not us? *¡Sí podemos!* Yes, we can!"

Sofia thinks about it and looks at Angelica, all dressed up and looking so bright. She pushes herself to stay on the sunny-side. "Yes! Why not us? *¡Sí podemos!*"

Ricki picks up on the rallying cry and starts repeating the line over and over. "*¡Sí podemos! ¡Sí podemos!*" Then Angelica playfully joins in, as do Memo and Sofia. "*¡Sí podemos! ¡Sí pode-mos! ¡Sí podemos!*"

~

Holy Family Church is not very large but well-appointed. The structure is modern, but the design inside is old and classic. There is an altar at the front with a giant sculpture of Jesus on the cross at its center. From the front door, a long center aisle is framed on both sides by rows of wooden pews. Statues of Catholic saints line the walls.

As is the regular tradition, Ricki and Angelica are not the only kids to receive their first communion today. The ceremony is always held for a larger group of kids and their families. As a result, the church is almost full.

Ricki and Angelica join the other kids in a waiting room at the back of the church while Sofia and the rest of the family sit in the pews close to the altar. The kids are organized into a line, two abreast, by an older white woman with short hair and big wide-rimmed glasses. The woman instructs them to hold their hands up in a prayer position. As they do this, Father Vinny, dressed in a monastic robe enters. "Good morning," he says. "Does anyone have any questions?"

When no one raises a hand, Father Vinny holds up a small white wafer in his hand. "Today," he says happily, "you will be receiving the 'host' for the first time. Once you receive it, you'll be part of Jesus Christ and all of us who believe in him. It is a great day, isn't it?"

The group responds in unison. "Yes, father." Ricki and Angelica both glance at each other. From the look on Angelica's face, it's obvious she has never doubted the principles of the faith from day one and relishes this day as something extraordinary. Ricki, on the other hand, doesn't look like he connects with it.

Back in the main hall, the families wait for the procession to begin. Sofia turns to Memo and quietly asks, "Have you heard anything from your aunt about the apartment?"

Memo suddenly looks a little more serious. "Yes, but now let's wait till the communion passes to make this talk about it."

Sensing something is wrong, Sofia persists. "Why can't you tell me now?"

Memo hoped to hold this conversation off until later, but he knows he won't be able to. "Because where the news comes from is *malo*, bad," he whispers. "My Aunt said 'no' about the apartment."

Sofia suddenly gets a wide-eyed look on her face. "What? Why?"

Memo leans close to Sofia. "The Marlboro man got too *macho* and then she said, I need some space. Now, she *regresa*—come back here."

Sofia shoots him an angry look, then turns to exit the row.

"Where you going?"

"Out."

Memo excuses himself with a quick genuflection as he chases after Sofia.

Outside, Memo catches up to Sofia as she gets to the parking lot. "*Mira*, I'm sorry, Sofia. I thought she would say yes."

Sofia refuses to look at him. "I can't believe I believed you."

Memo tries to calm her down. "Well, it's no like I make it all up in my brains. I told you please, I need to ask her."

Sofia shakes her head as she looks around the parking lot. "What are we going to do now? We can't live with my mom and Juan."

"I'm going truly to find us something. I have a *muy buen* place to see tomorrow."

"How are you going to do that? We can't rent anything on our own. No papers."

Memo reaches out for Sofia and holds her. "Hey, you don't have papers, but I do. I have a work permit. I promise you, by the time that baby comes into this *mundo*, we will have our *casita*. It is going to be okay. No, it's going to be *mas de* okay. It's going to be beautiful like, *hermoso*."

Sofia stares at him for a long moment. Memo stares back

with as much confidence as he can muster. "You know what they say in the church there. They say faith is believing in *las cosas que no podemos ver*—things we can't see."

Sofia looks at him curiously. "What are you talking about?"

"What I am express to say is we have no seen the *casa blanca* on this hill that will be our home, but we know is there."

Sofia shakes her head in refusal. "Every time I believe in something, it always falls apart."

"*No esta vez*—not this time. This time I make so sure it stays together *como concreto*—like concrete."

Sofia lets her head fall onto his shoulder, her mind still full of doubts. Memo puts his arm around her. "C'mon, *nos vamos*. We will miss Ricki and Angelica to get the first holy wafer."

Communion has begun by the time Sofia and Memo return to the church. The kids have filed down the center aisle, two abreast, holding their hands up as instructed. Standing at the first step to the altar are Father Vinny and his attendants giving wafers to each child as they reach him.

As Angelica and Ricki near the front of the line, Sofia stares at Angelica for a long moment. Sofia feels almost jealous of how easy it is for Angelica to believe in it all. She looks around at the rest of her family and how frozen in the moment they all seem with no other thoughts, just like the saints standing along the walls. Sofia wonders why she can't be the same.

When Angelica and Ricki finally reach the altar, Angelica accepts her first holy wafer from Father Vinny with a solemnity that seems very mature for her age. On the other hand, Ricki accepts the wafer, puts it in his mouth, but then takes it out and scrutinizes it before sticking it back in and swallowing it whole.

23

FIRE AND ICE

It's a sunny and crisp day along the New Jersey Parkway. The traffic heading north is heavy but moving smoothly thanks to large trucks not being allowed on the parkway. Also helping the flow is the Driscoll Bridge, which moves 400,000 cars a day across the Raritan River with an expansive 15 lanes. On today's crossing, Bobby Brown Sheets, riding shotgun, turns to Jack, Vlad, and Robert Mathews in the back. "You ready? Here it comes."

"What coming?" Vlad asks with a confused look on his face.

"C'mon, Dad. Say it!"

Big Lou shakes his head, angry that Bobby is front-running him on their way to the ICE office, but he can't help himself. "Hey, you guys know this is the widest bridge in the world, right?"

"There it is," Bobby smiles. "Says it every time he crosses the bridge!"

The final arrangements for this operation were agreed upon in the steam room at the club the night before. Lou was dead set against Robert Mathews coming, but Jack was insistent Robert be included. He never really explained why, but Robert assumed it had to do with balancing the racial divide and having a witness who could help keep Lou to his word. The final arrangements required Robert to keep his mouth shut in the meeting and not discuss anything he saw or heard. Robert accepted the deal with the feeling of being inside some kind of mob operation. "So let me get this straight," he said with his best mobster imitation. "I go to the meeting and don't say anything, like Jack?"

"No," Lou said. "You're not allowed to talk, but Jack can say anything he wants. We just can't make Jack talk if he don't want to. Capeesh?"

"Capeesh," Robert said. "But what if somebody asks me a question?"

"Just keep your trap shut!"

Robert still didn't fully understand what the "big idea" Lou was pursuing was all about. It had a feel of buffoonery to it, but that is what worried him. Some of the most evil moments in human history started off looking like buffoonery—like the early days of Hitler. This comic little man with the strange half-mustache talking about making Germany great again must have seemed pretty silly at first. But then, for some unknown reason, people buy into the evil ideas of clownish figures like Hitler, and millions end up dead.

In Newark, the steam room vigilantes find street parking near the Peter Roding Federal Building on Broad Street, where the ICE field office is located. It's a tall, bland rectangular building in the typical federal style. It's sandwiched into a mixed neighborhood of old churches, ugly condos, and shabby brick office buildings. Inside, there are epic amounts of marble and harsh overhead lighting. The boys get through security without trouble and find their way to the ICE offices on the 10th floor. A few minutes later, they are led into a small office by Tony Martino, deputy director of program evaluations.

Tony is not a big man. His olive skin, dark hair, and brown eyes, accented by a well-trimmed mustache, make him unmistakably Italian. His white shirt with cufflinks is a cut above everyday office wear, and the suspenders let you know he is in work mode.

"So you're the famous Jack that Midge tells me about," Tony says with a smile.

Jack nods. "I don't know about famous, but yeah, Midge and I go back a long way. Is she okay? She left town."

"Yeah, her dad—my uncle—has Parkinson's. They decided it's time to move him into assisted living."

"Sorry to hear that."

"Yeah, he's not a happy camper. Doesn't want to move out of his home." Tony then quickly drops the subject before things get too serious. He turns to the other guys in the room. Big Lou sticks out his hand. "Lou Carpissi, concerned citizen."

Tony shakes hands with Lou, adding a slight nod to acknowledge their shared heritage. "A concerned citizen," Tony smiles. "Always helpful to have one of those around. *Benvenuta.*"

Tony also shakes hands with Bobby, Vlad, and Robert, and then the whole group takes a seat. Tony sits on one side of his desk, and the "gods of steam" sit on the other. Tony grabs a stack of his business cards and hands them to everyone. Jack is the only one to look at the card. He then puts it in his wallet.

"So what is this all about?" Tony asks. "You're having some problems with undocumented immigrants?"

"Yeah," Lou starts. "I don't know if you have been down to our area lately, but the place is overrun with illegals."

"Yes, Monmouth County has become a big destination lately. I'm not sure why. Someone is generously paying their way from Texas, or it's all those big lawns that need mowing."

Lou Smiles. "Well, Jack here, you know he organized the Neighborhood Watch in Atlantic Highlands, and they won national recognition. I think you were voted number one in the nation, am I right, Jack?"

Jack just smiles but says nothing.

"Jack built a whole network of guys who patrol the town. They're well-equipped with all sorts of high-tech gear. This team runs 24/7. It's amazing. "

"Are they armed?" Tony asks curiously.

"Not officially, but they can defend themselves if need be. Their biggest claim to fame is the gear. They have direct radio contact with the police."

Tony is impressed. He nods toward Jack.

Lou adds, "Always helps to have a military man in charge, right? Jack had a long career in the Marines."

"Sounds like the town is in good hands," Tony says. "How can we help?"

Lou smiles proudly. "So what we want to do is set up a group in my township modeled on Jack's Neighborhood Watch that focuses on identifying and reporting illegal aliens."

Tony gets a brighter look on his face. "Interesting idea."

Lou proudly adds, "We want to call it 'Illegal Watch of America' or just IWA."

"How would it work?" Tony asks.

"Simple. Our teams would focus on spotting illegals and gathering information like where they live or work. We try to get their names and anything else we can pick up."

Tony nods. "Okay. I follow you so far."

Lou lowers his voice for the next part. "Now, as you already know, there is no point reporting our info to the police because our town is a 'sanctuary' town. The cops won't get off their asses to do anything, so the idea is, we report the info directly to you guys because you have the federal authority to take action."

Tony thinks about this, nodding his head positively. "Nice," he says with a wry smile.

"So what do you think?" Lou asks confidently. "Are you somebody we could work with on this?"

Tony leans in a little bit. "Well, to be honest, it's not really my area. I'm part of the policy group. We just look at how the department works, you know, how it treats people once they are in the system."

Lou shrugs like a mobster. "Yeah, I understand, but you know people, right?"

Tony thinks about it. "Sure, but you know there is an 866 number you can call."

Lou raises a hand with a classic Italian flip-over. "Tony, I think we both know the system is there, and we know how well that works. What we're look'n for is some real help to get the job done, you know, 'grease the wheels' Jersey style."

Tony gets the message and thinks for a minute. "Okay, I hear what you're saying. Something like this falls under ERO— Enforcement and Removal Operations. I have some contacts in that department."

"Now we're talking," Lou says with a big smile.

"But here's the thing. This idea doesn't work if it's just regular folks waiting for their asylum hearing or stuff like that. ERO is looking for national security threats, criminal activities, and fugitives—like people with deportation orders. Now, if you come across something like that, and I can find them in our database, I could pass it on."

Lou wants to hug Tony. "Tony, you are starting to make me feel like a man doing something for his community."

Tony smiles. "I can see that. So, what have you got so far? Anything I could pass along?"

The boys all look at each other. They did not prepare themselves to move forward so quickly. There is an awkward silence in the room until Brown Sheets decides to take things into his own hands. Bobby tilts his head toward Jack. "Jack knows some illegals."

Jack suddenly turns red with silent anger. He looks to Lou and raises his hand as if to say, "Not the deal I agreed to. Don't go there."

Lou shoots a look at Bobby for being an idiot but then looks at Tony and sees they need something good to keep Tony interested. Lou turns to Jack slowly. "Hey, we're here. How about it? What about that pregnant girl you know? She's gotta be illegal as hell."

Tony hits the space bar on his computer. "If you give me her name, I can look her up and see if she is in the system."

Jack looks at Lou with rage in his eyes. "Leave her out of this."

Tony can see there is a problem, but he tries to help Jack along. "Jack, I don't want to interfere here, but this situation is classic. Young undocumented women often play the system by having what they call an 'anchor baby.' If the baby is born here, it is automatically an American citizen with all the rights granted to real Americans. Once that happens, it makes our job very difficult, if not impossible.

Lou is shocked. "Holy shit, is that true?"

"Yep," Tony nods.

"Holy crap! Jack, c'mon. We can't let her do this on the taxpayer's dime!"

Feeling cornered, Jack tries to find a way out without making a scene. "I don't think that citizenship thing applies to illegal immigrants," Jack says.

"Well, actually, it does as part of the 14th Amendment," Tony says politely. "It's called 'American Birthright' and applies to anyone born on US soil regardless of race or status."

"I knew that," Vlad giggles. "I know country better than you guys do."

Bobby, who seems blown away by all this, can't help

himself. "So any Mexican woman who wants can just slip over the border, have a baby, and it's an American?"

"Oh yeah," Tony says. "It's a popular trick known as birth tourism. We estimate over 300,000 a year are born to unauthorized immigrants."

"Three hundred thousand," Lou moans. "And they all have every right any real American has?"

Tony smiles sarcastically. "Yes, sir. This baby about to be born to this undocumented girl you mentioned? He or she could grow up to be president of the United States!"

"You gotta be shit'n me," Lou says in disbelief.

Tony raises his hands sarcastically, Italian style. "Land of opportunity!"

Lou turns to Jack and pleads with him. "Jack, c'mon. We have to get that little unborn son of a bitch out of here before it's too late!"

Jack looks like he is about to explode. But before anything happens, Robert speaks up. "There is an old famous saying in this country. I forget who it came from, but basically, it was, 'What makes America great is that anyone can grow up to be president.' Very famous."

Lou waves a hand at Robert. "Hey, did you forget our agreement?"

"Sorry," Robert says. "It was just an FYI."

Vlad suddenly lights up. "That was President Andrew Johnson who said that."

"You sure?" Robert asks.

"It don't matter who said that," Lou snarls. "When they wrote that, they didn't have three hundred thousand of these tourist babies being born." He then turns back to Jack. "So whatcha say, Jack?"

Jack thinks for a long moment, then stands. "You know what? I've changed my mind. I'm going to keep my boat."

Lou is stunned. "What?"

"I'm outta this deal."

Lou glances over at Tony feeling embarrassed, then back at Jack. "Jack, what are you saying?"

Too pissed off to be polite, Jack lets his anger show. "What I'm saying is, include me out."

Lou tries to stay cool. "Jack, you're embarrassing us here in front of Tony. Let's just talk about this for a minute."

Jack shakes his head. "About what? How good your word is?"

Bobby moves forward aggressively like he wants to hit Jack, but Lou holds him back and turns to Jack. "Look, you remember what Mike Tyson said, right? 'Everybody has a plan until they get punched in the face.' So, yeah, we had a plan, but this is a huge opportunity right here, right now, to make history. This may be the answer!"

"No thanks," Jack says with a sense of finality.

"Jack," Tony says, joining in. "We're not looking to hurt innocent people. We're just looking for the bad apples with warrants out."

"Yeah," Lou says, nodding to Tony. "Let's just try your girl as a test run. If she's clean, no problem."

Jack considers this for a moment. "Why don't you start by sticking your own name in there and see what comes up?"

"*Fottiti figlio di puttana,*" Bobby shouts angrily as he jumps to his feet. Lou grabs Bobby and forces him back down, but this latest insult is the last straw.

"You know what, Jackie Boy?" Lou says solemnly. "I think I'm done trying to work with you. If you wanna go play on your freak'n boat while my town gets taken over by illegals, be my guest. You're not a real activist anyway. You have no higher calling. No real passion. You ain't got what it takes. You're just a playboy with some walkie-talkies pretending to be tough. That's why this jack-off from California can come in and take over your mind. In your heart, you know you're weak. And that's the real reason you are losing your house.

Jack reaches the door and opens it. "You know what the first rule of holes in the military is?"

"No, what is it?"

"If you find yourself in one, stop digging. I'm taking the train home."

Robert jumps up from his seat. "I'll ride with you."

"Suit yourself," Jack says. And with that, Jack and Robert are out the door. Everyone left in the room looks at each other in embarrassed silence.

"I knew baby is his," Vlad concludes.

Tony shrugs. "When it comes to activism, you know what they say, 'Pioneers always take the arrows.' I like the idea and don't think you should give up on it. Don't forget to keep my card and give me a call if you come up with something."

Lou holds the card up and looks at it forlornly. His higher aspirations have quickly taken a back seat to revenge. He's no longer thinking about the personal rewards of activism; instead, he's thinking about how Carlo Rizza was killed in the original Godfather movie. He'd like to strangle Jack the same way—from behind with a garote made of piano wire. Once and for all, he will pin this Mick leprechaun to the mat for the ten count. And for sure, that baby is going bye-bye.

The commuter train ride home is a rather somber event for Jack and Robert. Jack isn't in the mood to talk, but Robert can't help himself. He wants to know what made Jack refuse to cooperate so vehemently. He keeps asking questions without any luck until they are almost at their stop. That's when Jack finally turns to Robert and says, "You remind me of one of those reporters on TV that sticks a microphone in a guy's face and asks, 'What are you feeling right now?' just as the poor slob is getting carried off after being hit by a car."

"Yeah, I admit it," Robert replies. "I am a bit of an ambulance chaser, but just the same, what are you feeling right now?"

Jack snorts and shakes his head. "I'm feeling like an idiot for giving up my last best chance of saving my house. That's what I am feeling.

"Why's that?" Robert asks, hoping for more. "I mean, why did you turn against those guys like that? The whole thing was your idea, right?"

Jack looked a little embarrassed. "Yes, it was, but that was before."

"Before what?"

"Before Sofia and her mom and that whole goddamn family."

In this tense moment, the seasoned journalist, Robert, understands the significance of maintaining silence. This strategic approach often prompts the subject to fill the void by speaking further. Jack, feeling uncomfortable in the ensuing silence, shifts uneasily before saying, "I had a conversation with my daughter over the phone the other night."

"Beth? The one living in California?"

"Yeah. She said a few things that got me thinking."

"Like what?"

"Just a lot of her lefty crap, but she reminded me of one thing. This country does have some founding principles, and as much as I have a problem with illegal immigration, I don't want to do things that undercut those principles, which I happen to believe in."

At this point, Robert is stunned. He never thought of Jack as a thinking man, but there it was, another side of this unique guy out on display. Jack can see Robert is baffled. "Okay, you happy now?" Jack asks gruffly. "Got your story?"

He then turns and looks out the window as if the conversation is over.

"No, no, wait," Robert says anxiously. "What are we talking about here? Are we talking about all men being created equal and having the right to life, liberty, and the pursuit of happiness? That kind of stuff?"

Jack turns and looks at Robert for a long moment before speaking. "You know, the first time Sofia was in my car, she didn't know who George Washington was. Do you know what is funny about that? Washington was the guy who said America was created for people like Sofia. It's supposed to be an asylum for people like her."

"So that means you're now in favor of undocumented immigrants being granted rights?"

"No, I didn't say that. I'm just saying we shouldn't be doing things that go against the basic principles we're supposed to stand for. Can we leave it at that?"

"Sure," Robert says. "Sorry, I didn't mean to pry."

"Yes, you did."

"Okay, guilty as charged. I'll shut up now."

Jack looks out the window. "Thank you."

Upon his return home, Robert tells Sandra about the amazing day he just had but postpones a glass of wine until after a computer fact-check on George Washington's stance on immigration. To his amazement, Jack is right about Washington. In a letter to a group of newly arrived Irish immigrants, Washington wrote, "The bosom of America is open to receive not only the opulent and respectable but the oppressed and persecuted of all nations and religions."

PART III

24

HOUSE FOR SALE

I t's a cold, quiet morning in Atlantic Highlands with only the distant sound of a bugle call coming from the Navy weapons pier out in the bay. Two Latinos pull up in an old truck in front of Jack's house and begin erecting a "For Sale" sign in his front yard.

Watching from the window inside his house, Jack feels embarrassed by the size of the colossal sign. It stands tall and proud, crafted from sturdy wood and adorned with an intricate border that proudly displays the logo of Mia Russo's esteemed real estate company. As he stares at the sign, Jack's mind drifts back to the moment he made the difficult decision to sell his beloved home—for the second time. He had hoped the call to Mia would be the most daunting part of the process. However, witnessing the physical manifestation of his decision, he realizes that the difficulties of the journey he has embarked upon are only just beginning.

To alleviate his renewed sense of loss, Jack embarks on a mission to separate what is trash from what he will take with him. Venturing into the kitchen, he places some empty moving boxes on the floor and places a large trash can next to them. His strategy is simple. Anything valuable and needed will go in a box. Anything unnecessary will go into the trash. "Just start with the easy stuff," Robert advised over the phone. "That way, you can build some momentum and get in the right mental space for throwing out the tough stuff."

Guided by the advice of his friend, Jack decides to begin his task by tackling a large bowl on the kitchen countertop. Jack picks it up and prepares to wrap it in packing paper, but inside it are the GED forms he tried to give Sofia. Jack takes the documents out of the bowl and prepares to toss them into the trash, but something holds him back. "Ah, for Christ's sake!" he says to himself. The chains of whatever it is about that girl still entwine him, refusing to release their hold. In a final attempt to quell his frustration, he reluctantly comes to a compromise. He'll put the papers in an envelope and drop them off at Sofia's house sometime when he's near that part of town.

In the man cave, Jack carries the papers to his desk, finds a manila envelope to stuff them in, then pulls out a piece of paper to write her a note and places it in the middle of his desk. He lifts a pen and thinks about what to say.

"Dear Sofia, I know you probably don't want to hear this, but the GED would be good for you. Sometimes we can blind ourselves to opportunity with our own..." Jack pauses, then changes his mind. He tears up the paper and pulls out another piece.

"Dear Sofia, I was going to throw this stuff out, but then I thought I would give it one more try. Sorry if I yelled at you. But I'm just trying to do right by you. You've been through a lot, and trust me, I know how rough it can be when you have your home and your whole life ripped out from under you. But don't let that stop you from being the best you can be. Yours Truly, Jack O'Mally."

Jack sits back and re-reads the note. He almost rips this one up too, but then changes his mind. "Ain't coming up with anything better than that," he murmurs. "Screw it." He stuffs the note in the manilla envelope with the GED papers.

Mid-morning at Jack's house arrives accompanied by two guests at the door. Mia, the real estate agent, and her good friend Helen. Jack is a little surprised to see them—especially Helen. She's not dressed up in her Gucci hippy look this time. This time, she looks more like the casual sporty type you'd see in an Athleta shop—slim polyester/spandex cargo pants with a wrap top under an inlet vest. "Hi, Jack," she says with a warm smile.

Jack looks slightly embarrassed, feeling frumpy in his old cleaning clothes, including his dirt-stained jeans. "Hi," he says back to her. "This is a surprise."

Mia gets a big Italian smile on her face. "We were in the neighborhood and thought we could discuss next steps if you have a few minutes."

Jack invites them both in. Mia's eyes dart around the house like a mouse looking for cheese. "It's looking better," she says happily. "You guys made some good progress."

"It wasn't easy, that's for sure," Jack says with a half grunt.

"Okay," Mia smiles, getting down to business. "Well, I first want to have an open house for other real estate agents. I usually like to do that mid-week if that is okay with you."

"Sure, whatever you think is best," Jack says with a perfunctory tone.

Mia is about to discuss her idea for a blind bid when her phone lights up. "Oh, sorry, guys. It's my son. I have to take this. I'll just be a sec."

Mia exits the room, leaving Jack and Helen alone. They look at each other in awkward silence. Jack, for lack of anything to say, just raises his eyebrows. Helen smiles back at him, raising her eyebrows to mimic him.

"So, how have you been?" Jack finally asks. "Everything good in your world?"

"Yeah, okay, I guess. You?"

Jack shakes his head. "Could be better, but what are ya gonna do?"

"I hear you. But hey, once you get on the other side of all this, I'm sure you will land on your feet."

"Hope so."

Helen asks, "Have you found a new place for yourself?"

"Got a couple of leads but nothing solid yet."

Helen thinks about this momentarily, then offers, "You know, if you want some company to look at places, I'm not that busy right now."

Jack is kinda surprised by this. "Really?"

Helen smiles. "Yeah."

"Okay," Jack says hesitantly, wondering if this means she is still interested in him.

"Actually," Helen says to clarify things, "I was hoping you would have called me by now for that fresh restart we discussed."

Jack smiles as his spirits lift. "Oh, sorry. I thought you were just trying to be polite when you said that."

"No, I was serious."

"My mistake," Jack says, getting his game back on. "In that case, why don't we set up a lunch or something next week?"

A quick, easy feeling descends over them just like it did the first time. Helen is pleased to feel this. She gets a big smile on her face. "Actually, you know it's almost lunchtime now, and I'm hungry. What about you?"

Jack shakes his head with a smile. He's feeling it too. "I could go for something to eat, sure."

"I know this great vegan place in Red Bank. We could go there!"

"Vegan?" Jack asks with a frown.

"Jack, this food is so good. Trust me, it's better than a steakhouse. If you don't like it, we can leave."

Jack thinks about this for a moment.

"It will be my treat," Helen adds, trying to close the deal.

Jack looks at her as he remembers their first encounter. "Uh, negative on that. Only if it is my treat."

Helen smiles, also remembering the issue. "Oh yeah, right. Okay, so we're on?"

Jack nods. "Yep. We're on."

"Sorry, guys," Mia says as she returns to the room. "My ex is up to his old tricks again. He can't even be bothered to pick up his son for football practice. Looks like we have to go."

"Okay," Helen says happily. "Well, you go ahead without me. Jack and I are going out for some lunch. Jack can drop me back home later, I think. Would that be okay, Jack?"

Jack nods warmly. "Yeah, sure, no problem."

Mia is taken aback. "How long was I out of the room? 30 seconds? And you guys set up a lunch date already?"

'Guess so," Helen smiles.

Mia nods her head knowingly. "So that is why you wanted to come with me today."

Helen smiles back at her sheepishly.

"Okay, Mia says with a slight edge of cynicism. "I could see Susan Sarandon going out for lunch with Tucker Carlson before I could see this. But hey, I don't want to stand between you and your soldier boy. You kids have fun."

The route to lunch takes Jack and Helen across a long bridge that separates Atlantic Highlands from the affluent area of

Rumson where Helen lives. It's a beautiful drive across the river where a line of big, expensive homes line the banks on the south side of the river.

"Isn't that your home there?" Jack asks, pointing toward the shore.

"Hardly a home," Helen replies, "but yes, that is my house."

Jack looks at Helen curiously. "Why do you say that?"

"Okay," Helen sighs with a certain resignation. "I guess it's best I get this out now. Do you want the long version of the story or the short version?"

"Whatever you are comfortable with," Jack says. "Or don't tell me at all. That's okay too."

Helen smiles and decides to go with the Cliff Notes version: "I was working as a hairstylist when I met Jeffrey, my ex-husband. He kind of swept me off my feet into the world of his very wealthy family. Suddenly, I went from a one-bedroom apartment to this humongous house his parents bought us as a wedding gift."

Jack is surprised by this. "Wow, that's some wedding present."

"Yeah," Helen nods, "but you know how the old song goes. They say a chair is still a chair even when there is no one sitting there. But a chair is not a house, and a house is not a home."

Jack isn't sure what she means by all this, but he senses that the marriage has gone bad. "I guess that means things didn't work out."

"Yeah, Jeffrey was a nice guy but a horrible husband. He didn't know what to do, so he stayed away most of the time. He was more comfortable at his parent's home and spent most of his time there."

"Mama's boy?" Jack asks rhetorically.

"Uh, yeah, slightly," Helen says sarcastically. "But to be fair, it wasn't all him. I had a lot of my own issues."

"Oh," Jack says, unsure if he should ask about the details.

"I was orphaned as a baby and never had a real home. It was always one place and then another, so I never grew roots anywhere. I never developed long-term relationships because I always waited for 'what's next.' I think I was like that in my marriage too. Jeffrey even said to me one day. 'You'll never belong to me because you will never belong to anyone. You'll always be an orphan at heart.' When he said that, I just felt so damaged."

Jack doesn't know what to say to all this. He suddenly feels a little uncomfortable. Helen senses his discomfort and stops her monologue. "I'm sorry, this is way too much, too soon."

Jack reaches over and puts a hand on her knee. "It's fine, don't worry. I get it. You know, military life is a lot like that. Always moving from one place to another. I was lucky that my family home was there to return to."

Helen looks at him with a new level of warmth in her eyes. "Yeah, that must make all the difference in the world. My house is just a shell of a place—a piece of the divorce settlement, nothing more."

"But what about your niece? Isn't she family to you?"

Alexia? She isn't a real niece. She's just a girl like me from the foster care world."

Jack thinks about this momentarily but then returns things to a more pleasant level. "Well, I know a good real estate agent if you are looking for one."

Helen likes Jack's well-timed sense of humor. She puts her hand on top of his. "Maybe we can look for a new place together?" Jack looks over at her, a bit surprised. Helen realizes her faux pas and shakes her head with embarrassment. "I mean, you know, different places, not the same place, of course."

Jack smiles and nods. "Hey, would you mind if we make a quick stop before we go to your vegan place? I just need to drop off this envelope."

Helen looks at the envelope on the dash. "Sure, no problem.

Hopefully, it is something mysterious and James Bond-like. Then you'll tell me you work for the CIA."

Jack laughs. "Well, sorry to disappoint you, but we are just going into the Latino section of town."

"Oh," Helen says curiously. "I don't think I have ever been there."

25

LUNCHTIME 911

The ride to Sofia's neighborhood is uneventful except for one rather aggressive tailgater in a giant pickup truck. Jack can feel his blood begin to boil but catches himself before slamming on the brakes. Instead, he pulls off to the shoulder and lets the truck pass. Helen looks around, wondering if they have reached their destination, but Jack sets her straight. "Just letting this truck go by."

"Oh," Helens says, catching on. "That was nice of you."

Jack smiles devilishly. "Don't be fooled. I'm in a special program called 'Road Rager's Anonymous.'"

"Really?"

"No, not really, but it's not a bad idea, now that I think about it. We'd have weekly meetings. 'Hi, I'm Jack, and I am a road rager!"

Helen smiles and goes along with the joke. She mimics how the group would respond. "Hi, Jack!"

They both share a giggle and silently recognize how much they enjoy each other's company.

After a few more turns, Jack's car passes into the barrio. Helen looks at it all with keen interest, almost like a tourist on safari. "I feel like I am in a foreign country," she says. "Like I need a passport."

Jack glances over at her. "Does it make you nervous?"

Helen isn't sure what she feels. "No, not really. It's just so big. It's like a little town of its own."

They turn onto Cherry Tree and stop in front of Sofia's house. The house looks very quiet. The chickens are in their coup, and the lawn looks like it has been freshly mowed. The front porch has a few toys on it, but other than that, it's very *"tranquilo."*

"Who's house is this?" Helen asks.

"This is the home of the woman and her daughter helping me clean my house. These papers are for the daughter—just some school stuff. I'll be back in a second. I'm just going to put them in the mailbox."

Helen is curious but holds back her questions as Jack leaves and heads toward the house. He walks as quietly as he can up the front steps, tiptoes over to the mailbox, and tries to lift the lid silently, but it squeaks. Jack curses under his breath and tries to place the envelope inside without making any more noise, but the front door suddenly swings open, and Ricki appears with a big smile. "Apple Pie!"

"Hey Ricki," Jack says quietly. "I just want to drop this off for Sofia. No need to disturb anybody."

Ricki turns back toward the inside of the house and yells. *"¡Apple pie está aquí!* Apple Pie is here!"

Jack feels like running, but he knows he's trapped now. A few seconds later, Sofia appears at the door. She seems surprised to see Jack. She starts to smile but then catches herself and puts on her angry face. *"¿Qué pasa?"* She asks cooly and deliberately in Spanish.

Angelica and Roberta follow Sofia to the porch, curious to see what the old Americano is up to. Jack is beet red with humiliation on his face. He holds up the envelope. "Uh, I was just dropping this off for you."

From the car, Helen watches the scene unfold. Ricki tries to take the envelope from Jack, but Roberta slaps his hand away. "What is it?" Sofia asks.

"There is a note inside that explains everything." Jack holds the envelope out.

Sofia slowly accepts it. "Okay, but what is it?"

"Just take it, okay? I don't want to talk about it in front of everyone. It's private."

"Private?" Sofia says with a strange look on her face.

Jack starts to get angry. "Ah, Christ. It's the damn GED papers I got for you, okay? I didn't want to throw them away."

Sofia studies Jack carefully. Secretly, she appreciates the gesture but hasn't forgiven him for the outburst at his house the last time they were together. "Thank you," she says for lack of anything else.

Jack hesitates for a minute, sensing Sofia's softer demeanor. He's not sure what to make of it and remains cautious. "You're welcome," is all he can muster. He then adds, "Well, then that's that."

Sofia is about to say something, but before she can get any words out, Ana screams from inside the house. "Mama!"

Clinging to the envelope, Sofia hurries into the house with everyone else, anxious to discover what's happening. Jack remains on the porch, peering through the open door. Within seconds, more panicked screams fill the air. Whatever the situation is, it is clearly an emergency. Compelled to investigate, Jack turns to Helen, who is still watching from the car. He raises a hand, silently requesting a few more minutes, before disappearing into the house. Inside, he can hear Sofia calling out Estella's name. Suddenly, she emerges from a room and sees Jack. "Help!" she cries out.

Jack races to the room and sees Estella lying lifeless on the floor. The family is trying to figure out if she is alive or not. Ana shakes Estella to see if she will wake up. "Mama! Mama!"

"What happened? Jack asks.

Sofia turns to Jack. "Mama says she was in another room when she heard my grandmother gasping for breath. Then she heard her falling."

Jack responds, "I'll call 911." He reaches into his pocket for his phone.

Arnell squats next to Estella, placing two fingers on her neck to check for a pulse. All eyes fall on him. After a few seconds, he turns back and shakes his head negatively. Ana shrieks. Angelica starts to cry. Jack suddenly kicks into gear. He hands the phone to Sofia and tells her, "Here, talk to 911." He then drops next to Estella and starts performing CPR like the well-trained military man with battlefield experience that he is. "She's probably had a heart attack."

Sofia waits for dispatch to answer the call, but then Ana stops her. Even in this emergency, she does not want to engage with the system. She tells Sofia to tell Jack how she wants to proceed.

Sofia ends the call and translates for Jack. "She wants us to take her to the hospital in your car."

Jack can't believe his ears. "This is no time to play with her life, call!"

"You don't understand," Sofia yells back at him. "It's dangerous for us. And they don't come fast!"

Arnell has already had enough of all this. He puts his arms under Estella, picks her up, and heads for the front door. There is little Jack can do but throw up his arms and follow with the rest of the family.

Helen becomes alarmed when she sees people heading for the car. As Arnell heads for the back of Jack's SUV, Jack races to the front door and opens it. "Sorry Helen, we have an emergency." He then pushes the button to unlock the rest of the car.

"What do you want me to do?" Helen asks.

"We have to get this woman to the hospital," Jack says as he heads toward the back of the car. "Jump in the driver's seat!"

Helen swings into action as Jack lowers one of the back seats, giving Arnell enough room to place Estella in the back of the car. Once this is done, Jack races around to the back of the vehicle. "Let me get in there," Jack commands. Arnell gets out of the way, allowing Jack to resume chest compressions. "Okay, let's go! To the hospital—Riverside Hospital!"

Helen quickly nods and starts the car. The rest of the family gets in wherever they can, and they are off. Sofia ends up next to Jack.

"Check to see if she has a pulse."

"How do I do that?"

"Put your finger on her neck."

"Like this?"

"Yeah. Just like that. Feel anything?"

"I think so. Yes. A little bump!"

Jack continues with the chest compressions. "Okay, now, blow into her mouth like I did back in the house."

Sofia looks down at her grandmother and repeats what she saw Jack do in the house. "Pinch the nose."

"Yes."

The car suddenly lurches forward. Sofia falls on Jack. Jack uses his torso to get her back up. She regains her balance and proceeds to do her part of the CPR.

Helen quickly gets them to the hospital and heads for the emergency room on the north side of the building. "Helen, don't go to the front door," Jack yells from the back. "Just pull up at the door the ambulances use!"

"Okay, got it," Helen replies as she spots the ambulances.

Jack pumps hard on Estella's chest and turns to Sofia. "When we get there, jump out and go through the big doors used by the paramedics. As soon as you get inside, start yelling as loud as you can, 'heart attack outside. Stat!'"

"Me?" Sofia questions, intimidated by the task.

"Yes. You can do it. Just make sure to say 'stat!' And make sure they bring a gurney. You know, one of those roller beds!"

Sofia nods her head. "Stat."

The car pulls up in front of some parked ambulances. Sofia jumps out of the car and runs for the EMT entrance. As she nears the doors, they open, and two paramedics exit from the building, rolling a gurney back to their truck.

When Sofia sees the paramedics, she yells, "Heart attack. Stat!"

The paramedics come to life. "Where?" one of them asks.

"In the car right there!" Sofia says, pointing to Jack's SUV. The paramedics rush for the car, and Arnell jumps out and races to open the back hatch.

Jack continues doing chest compressions as long as he can. Finally, one of the paramedics wheels the gurney in place. The other grabs a mic on his shirt. "Be advised, we have a code blue in the parking lot. Possible cardiac arrest. Older woman. Unconscious." He then turns to Jack. "Okay, sir, we can take it from here."

Jack stops doing the compressions so they can move Estella to the gurney.

"What happened?" The paramedic asks.

"Not sure," Jack responds. "I was outside the house. She just went down."

"How long has she been unconscious?"

"Five minutes tops. We started CPR within a minute or two."

"Awesome," the paramedic replies. "What is her name?"

"Estella," Sofia replies. "Estella Romero."

The paramedics quickly move Estella onto the gurney and race for the doors. The family follows them. Jack walks around to the passenger door and gets in. "Let's park and then we'll go in and join them." Helen nods and proceeds to the parking lot.

Inside the emergency room, more technicians join in to help. Estella is rolled into a room. When the group tries to follow, a nurse stops them. "Okay, guys, we'll take it from here. I need you to follow me." Sofia translates, and the group follows the nurse to the waiting room.

The family finds a line of open seats against a wall. Arnell and Roberta take the first two seats. Ricki sits next to Roberta, with Angelica on his other side. Next comes Ana, followed by Sofia. Ana is crying. Sofia finishes sending a text to Memo, then turns to console her mother as best she can. There is an assortment of other people in the room. Some are Latino, some white, and some Black. Sofia carefully looks around to see if anyone looks like a secret agent from ICE.

A few minutes later, Jack and Helen come in the front door of the emergency room. They see the group and take up seats next to Sofia and Ana. Ana reaches across Sofia and taps Jack on the leg. "Gracias," she says to Jack. "Gracias por todo." {"Thank you for everything."}

Jack looks back at her. He offers a slight smile and says, "De nada."

Sofia looks up at Jack curiously. It is the first time she has heard him truly speak Spanish. Jack sees her looking at him. "You did a good job in the car," he says to her. Sofia nods, then looks over at Helen. Helen just smiles at her but doesn't try to say anything. A door suddenly opens, and an emergency room doctor appears with a positive look. "You're the family with Estella Romero?"

Ana is the first to nod affirmatively. The doctor then pivots just a little bit back toward the door. "Can you follow me?"

The group looks at each other curiously. Sofia quickly stands and translates. "He wants us to go with him." The family isn't sure if this is good news or bad news. They all stand and follow the doctor through the door. Jack isn't sure if he and Helen should go. Ana grabs his arm and pulls him along. Jack motions Helen to follow.

The group files through the doorway, down a hallway past several rooms. Ana looks desperately in each room for Estella but doesn't see her. Finally, the doctor opens a conference room door and points everyone in. As they enter, Ana starts to become anxious. " Where is she? Are we going to see her?"

Roberta grabs Ana's hand. "We will ask as soon as we can."

Sofia isn't sure what to think about all this. She grabs her mother as they all look at the doctor. "Does everyone here speak English?" he asks.

Jack points at Sofia. "Just the kids."

"Okay," the doctor says to Sofia. "Can you translate for me then?"

Sofia nods, overcome by a deep sense of foreboding.

"Estella," the doctor says, "as you probably already know, suffered a heart attack. You guys did an amazing job getting her here so quickly."

Sofia translates quickly with a growing tremor in her voice.

The doctor pauses to let Sofia translate, then continues. "We did everything we could, but I'm sorry she did not make it."

Sofia suddenly breaks down. "No," she cries.

The doctor looks at her sympathetically. "I'm really sorry for your loss."

Ana doesn't need a translation to know what's happening. "No, Mama, no!" She quickly moves toward the doctor. Roberta and Arnell grab Ana as she sinks to the floor. Angelica sits in her seat and drops her head in tears. Ricki awkwardly tries to reach out for Sofia, but she pulls away from him. She bolts from her seat and runs out the door. Ricki and Angelica try to go after her, but Jack holds them back. "You kids stay here with your parents. We'll go get her."

Jack and Helen find Sofia standing next to a tree on the side of the hospital. She grabs the tree and collapses. She holds her head in her hands as she sobs. Helen nudges Jack. "Go. I will wait here."

Jack silently moves toward Sofia. Sofia wipes her nose, grabs her phone, and looks to see if Memo has texted her back. Nothing. She starts to call him but gives up when she sees Jack coming towards her. She hides her face in her knees.

"I'm really sorry," Jack says as he steps up next to her. "I know she meant a lot to you."

Sofia suddenly looks up at Jack with a mix of sorrow and anger. "She didn't want to die here!"

"What?" Jack asks, not sure what Sofia is talking about.

"She didn't want to die in this country. She wanted to go back home."

"Sorry," Jack says with better understanding. "I didn't know that."

"I promised I would help her get back there!"

Jack suddenly feels at a loss for words. The awkward sensation reminds him of the many times he wanted to say things to his daughter but could never get the words out. He can sense Sofia is waiting for him to say something. He grasps for the right words. "I'm sure you did your best to make that work for her."

The polite but empty words disappoint Sofia. She lets her head fall back on her knees. Jack stands there, angry at himself for being so inept. But what he just learned about Estella wanting to go back reminds him of something. "I had a grandfather that was a lot like your grandmother."

Sofia looks up.

"He was the first in our family to come here from the old

country. He made it very clear in his will that he wanted to be buried back in Ireland."

Sofia looks up at Jack. She wipes away a tear. "What's a will?"

Jack struggles with his back to sit on the ground next to Sofia. She lifts a hand to help him. "A will is like a letter you leave behind when you die. In the letter, you make your last wishes known, like who you want your money and things to go to."

"My Abbi couldn't do that. She didn't know how to write."

"Maybe she had someone write it up for her. Like your mom."

Sofia thinks. "Did your grandfather not like it here? Is that why he wanted to go back?"

"No, he loved this country. It's just that in his heart, Ireland was his real home. It's where he was born."

Sofia thinks about this for a moment. "Did you take him back before he died?"

"No, he died here. But we did honor his wishes. We made a trip to Ireland and took his ashes back to a cemetery in Dublin. He's next to where his parents are buried."

Sofia remains silent, thinking. Jack puts a hand on her shoulder. "I know you couldn't get your grandmother back to El Salvador before she died, but you could still honor her by taking her ashes back."

"No, we can't do that."

"Why not?"

"Because it's different for us."

"How's that?"

Sofia lowers her head. "We can't go there. We can't go anywhere or do anything without getting in trouble or deported. It's not like with you or your grandfather. This country loves you, but it hates us."

Jack is offended. "Not true at all. Everybody hated the Irish when we first came here. When my grandfather came here, he had to live in a basement with no electricity or water. And he got beat up all the time."

Sofia isn't moved. "I live in a basement!"

Jack realizes he has overstepped his bounds. "Look, all I am trying to say is, your grandmother deserves a medal of honor for what she did. Do you know what that is? The Medal of Honor?"

"No."

"It's the highest military award for valor. It's for people who do great things, like sacrificing their lives for others. And that's what your Abbi did. She sacrificed it all for you. So you should do your best to honor her by getting her ashes back to where she wanted to be. And if you can't do that, honor her by making something of yourself that would make her know it was all worthwhile."

"I don't think that is possible for me," Sofia says. She then looks down at her stomach. "Maybe my baby, but not me."

Jack reels at her silly, immature attitude. "If my grandfather thought like that, he would have never escaped the slums of New York, started his own business, and built the house I live in."

Sofia turns and looks at Jack carefully. She had never thought of him as being part of an immigrant family before. "Your grandfather was the first in your family to move here?"

"The very first."

Sofia studies Jack carefully. She feels a new sense of connection to him, but now she is the one who is at a loss for words. Before she can figure out how to express what she is feeling, Memo appears. "Sofia," he yells. Sofia stands and reaches out for him. Memo grabs her. "I come so fast I had like no time to text you. I'm sorry. *Lo siento.* I'm sorry."

As Memo holds Sofia and tries to rock her with some

comfort, Jack decides it is time to stand up. "Hey, sorry. Can you guys give me a hand here?"

"Oh, hello, Mr. Jack," Memo smiles. Both he and Sofia turn to help Jack get up. Not far away, Helen watches intently. Once Jack is up, Memo suggests they all return to the hospital and rejoin the rest of the family, but Jack urges them to go without him. "I've got to get my friend home," he says, pointing to Helen. "You guys go ahead."

Memo glances over at Helen and smiles. "Oh, hello, Missus Helen."

"Hello, Memo," Helen says with a slight wave.

Sofia looks at Memo with a curious look on her face. Memo smiles. "This is Missus Helen—she bought the three benches." Sofia then turns back to Helen and manages a slight smile through her tears. Helen nods.

Before they part ways, Sofia turns to Jack, struggling to find the right words. She hesitates momentarily and thinks about hugging Jack but can't find the courage. With a heavy heart, Sofia turns away, her steps carrying her with Memo toward the waiting room. Yet, an inexplicable force seems to pull her back. She halts and slowly pivots. The defiant look that had always adorned her eyes is replaced by tenderness. Without uttering a single word, she closes the distance between them. Her arms reach out and envelop Jack in a warm, comforting hug. As the embrace lingers, Jack feels a surge of emotions welling up within him as well. He reciprocates Sofia's hug with his arms tightening around her.

~

The sun is just about to set when Jack finally gets Helen back to her house. He pulls up to the front of her house and stops but does not shut off the motor. "Well, sorry we never made it to lunch."

Helen turns in her seat to face Jack more squarely. "I have to say, I don't think I have ever met a person quite like you."

Jack is caught off guard a bit. "Is that a bad thing?"

"No, no," Helen assures him. "That's a good thing. You can be tough but sensitive too—like you were with that young girl, Sofia. Is that her name, Sofia?"

Jack is a little embarrassed. He doesn't like being known as sensitive. He doesn't know what to say other than, "Yeah, Sofia."

"I can tell she really loves you."

Jack has to chuckle. "She spends most of her time being angry with me."

"How did you get so involved with this family anyway?"

Jack thinks about it momentarily, then realizes it is difficult to explain. "Long story."

"Well then, why don't you come in? We'll cook something to eat, and you can tell me the whole thing."

Jack thinks about this for a moment. He still doesn't understand why this beautiful woman would give him the time of day. "You sure?"

Helen lets out a breath that carries an edge of frustration. "What do I have to do? Put a disco ball on my head?"

Jack thinks. Helen waits. He turns the car off and sharply opens his door. Helen smiles. She stays in her seat until Jack comes around and opens the car door for her.

Inside, Jack is once again amazed by the expansiveness of the place. Helen takes Jack's coat and tells him, "Make yourself at home." Jack looks around, not sure where to go to make himself at home. Finally, Helen picks up on his discomfort. "Come, let me show you around."

Helen takes Jack through the various parts of the house. It is all finely put together with everything it takes to make a fabulous home. "I've done everything I can to make the place homey, but somehow it never quite gets there." Look, there are Memo's benches. You see them out there?"

Jack takes a look and smiles. "They're good."

"Yes, I love them," Helen says. She thinks momentarily, then asks, "So what makes a home a home to you, Jack?"

The question catches Jack off guard. He stumbles to find an answer. "I don't think it is just one thing. It's a lot of things."

"Like what?"

"Well, like the smell of food, for one. When I smell the foods I grew up around, that feels like home. I know it sounds stupid, but—"

"Not stupid at all," Helen says. "Tell me one dish that really does it for you. The one that makes you feel at home."

Jack doesn't hesitate. "Shepherd's pie."

"Shepherd's pie!" Helen laughs.

"Sorry," Jack says, embarrassed.

Helen gently touches his shoulder. "Don't be sorry. If that is what you like, that is what you like."

Jack feels strange. "I don't think I've ever told anyone that before."

Helen is pleased. "Well, you know what? In celebration of Jack revealing his secret love of shepherd's pie for the first time, I say we celebrate and make ourselves a big fat shepherd's pie for dinner! You game?"

Jack smiles. He is enjoying this. "Game!"

They turn and head toward the kitchen. Helen grabs Jack's arm. "You know how to make it, right?"

"I think I can accomplish that mission. Do you have any lamb?"

"Lamb?" Helen asks, confused. "I thought shepherd's pie was made with beef?"

"Aye, no, Darl'n," Jack says with his mock Irish accent. "Real Irish pie is made with lamb. Only those twatty Brits use beef."

Helen laughs. "You really are Irish."

"Aye, and what's your background?" Jack asks.

"English."

26

EL DESTINO

If Sofia and the rest of her family thought they would have time to grieve the loss of their beloved Estella, they were sorely wrong. No sooner did they get home than the hospital was on the phone asking about final arrangements. The days that followed were a logistical whirlwind that left little room for the raw emotions they were grappling with, forcing them to compartmentalize their sorrow in order to function. And if that wasn't bad enough, the family also had to deal with the local myths about what happens to the bodies of undocumented immigrants if they are left at the hospital too long. These rumors claimed that if a deceased loved one is not picked up quickly, the hospital will cremate the body and put the ashes in an unmarked mass grave.

A lack of English made it impossible for Ana to take care of all the demands, so it all fell on the shoulders of Sofia. But Sofia was dealing with her own issues, like finding a place to live and getting the prenatal care Memo was insistent about. In the midst of making funeral arrangements for her grandmother, she finds herself in the waiting room of Dr. Carlos Castro, a hispanic obstetrician that Memo found. As in the hospital, she is constantly on the lookout for undercover ICE agents lurking about.

"I'm telling you once more again, it's just a *estúpido* myth," Memo tells Sofia quietly as they sit in the waiting room. "Stupid peoples make shit just to scare people."

"Okay, okay, *te creo*. I believe you," Sofia says as she leans against Memo and scrolls through her phone. "Can we just stop talking about it now?"

Memo looks down at her phone and sees that she is looking at web pages about repatriating a dead person's ashes to their home country. "Why are you looking at that for?"

"I convinced my mom to send Abbi's ashes back to El Salvador. I just want to see how you do it and how much it costs."

"You yourself want to return ashes?"

"No, just send them and put them where she wants to be buried with the rest of her family."

Memo looks curious. "Who are you going to send them to?"

"I don't know, "Sofia responds. "Maybe Juan or Arnell have some family that can help us."

"I knew this crazy *loco* guy who was hit by a car and killed. His *familia* sent his whole body back."

"That would be too expensive for us. His family must have had a lot of money."

"Look there," Memo says, pointing to the phone. "It says the only legal way to ship ashes is the US post office."

" Is that true?" Sofia frowns.

" That's what it say," Memo says with a sad face. "That's so cold more than ice to just go to the post office with her ashes. Your Abbi, she deserves more better than that."

Sofia scans the information, gives up, and leans back on Memo's shoulder. "I know. It would be a lot better if we could take them back ourselves."

A woman dressed in scrubs at the front counter holds up a clipboard with some forms. "Sofia?"

Sofia looks up. "Yes."

The nurse extends the clipboard toward her. "Can you follow me?"

Sofia and Memo are escorted into the doctor's office. That's where the older, fatherly Dr. Castro sits behind his desk. Normally, patients are taken directly to an examination room, but Dr. Castro is old fashioned and likes to interview pregnant couples before he takes them on. He doesn't stand up. Instead he waves toward the chairs in front of his desk. Then, once they are seated, he silently sizes them up for a moment.

"So you are Sofia," he says with a knowing smile after finding her name on the form. Then turning to Memo, he asks, "And you?"

"I am Guillermo Jose Jesus Gonzales, but the people just call me Memo. *Yo soy el padre.* I am the father."

Dr. Castro nods his head with amusement. "Okay, well, that is good to know," he says while jotting Memo's name down on the corner of the form. He then puts the documents down and looks at the young couple. "And, uh, are we married?"

The question makes them a bit uncomfortable. They both squirm a bit as Memo waves a hand. "Uh, no, not right now. But I asked her more times than Moses is old. I mean, it's just that she has many things in her boat house happening."

Dr. Castro, of course, has heard this all a thousand times before. "Okay," he says slowly, waiting to see if Sofia wants to add anything. When she doesn't, he says, "Then let me ask you, was this a planned pregnancy?"

Both Sofia and Memo fidget again. They look at each other, then back at Dr. Castro with guilty faces.

"It wasn't really no planned," Memo finally says. "It more was like destiny."

Dr. Castro's eyebrows rise as he tilts his head with interest.

"Destiny. Now that is a new one. I haven't heard that one before. How does that work?"

Memo thinks for a minute, then looks Dr. Castro in the eye. "Doctor, the first time I saw this girl, I could see that everything I do in my life till then was all on the road to that moment. I no plan it, but I knew it was big windy destiny."

Sofia slaps Memo on the leg to let him know she wants him to stop, but it does make her smile.

Dr. Castro makes a note of this. "Is there some medical reason you need an ultrasound at eight weeks?"

Both Sofia and Memo look confused. Memo asks, "Is that not the right time?"

"Most women wait until the second trimester, around 14 weeks. But some, who have special conditions like to come in earlier. I've done them as early as six weeks."

"Oh," Memo says with a slightly embarrassed look. "No medical problems. We just listen to people on YouTube."

Dr. Castro smiles. "No worries, just want to know if there are any clinical issues. So let's just go ahead and look at young 'Destino' and make sure everything is okay."

Dr. Castro leads Memo and Sofia into a small room with a simple exam table and ultrasound setup. There is a computer console with a monitor screen. Attached to the setup is a hand-held transducer that resembles a microphone. "Okay, Sofia," Dr. Castro says as he puts one hand on the examination table. "If you will just lie down here on your back. And Guillermo, I'm sorry, but you must stand over here."

"No problem," Memo says as Sofia gets into position.

Dr. Castro fires up the computer and grabs the transducer. "You've probably seen pictures of the fancy examination rooms with big chairs and wall-mounted monitors for the whole family to watch, but don't worry, the results here are just as good."

Sofia and Memo look at each other, unaware they are at a

low-budget facility. Memo just shrugs. "We are happy like bees, Doctor. No worries."

"Have you ever had an ultrasound before, Sofia?" Dr. Castro asks.

Sofia shakes her head no, but asks, "Does it hurt?"

Dr. Castro giggles. "No, not in the least one tiny bit. Let's pull up your shirt here so we can see your tummy. Yes, that's it. Now, I will put a little ultrasound gel on the transducer here. It may feel a little bit cool, but it helps us get a better image of your baby."

Sofia nods as Dr. Castro lubes up the transducer and holds it above her stomach. "Okay, ¿estás lista? Are you ready to meet your new baby?"

Sofia looks at Memo. Memo smiles at her with pride. She then looks back at the doctor and nods her permission silently. Dr. Castro gently places the transducer on her stomach, then pushes down just a bit as the computer screen comes to life with strange black and white shapes.

"Okay," Dr. Castro says with a soft fatherly voice. "This lets look at the basic anatomical structures—especially the head and heart—to make sure everything is okay."

Sofia suddenly gets concerned. "This won't hurt the baby, will it?"

"No, no. Nothing. We won't be able to tell the sex yet but look there; you see that? That is your baby's heart beating. Can you see that?"

Sofia suddenly gets a big smile on her face. She reaches out for Memo's hand. Memo beams with pride as he takes Sofia's hand. "There you are, big Destino!" he shouts.

Dr. Castro moves the transducer for a few more quick checks, snaps a few pictures, and then records a video clip.

"Is everything okay?" Sofia asks.

Dr. Castro returns the transducer to its stirrup and then

turns to the young couple with a warm smile. "*Felicidades*. Your baby is healthy and doing very well. No complications."

Sofia looks up at Memo with a big smile. Memo leans down and hugs her. "Welcome to our new life. It's going to be beautiful! You, me, and Destino!"

"Or Destin-a," Sofia says.

27

EL MEMORIAL

few days later, the morning of Estella's memorial mass dawns, and the household bustles with quiet but meaningful activity that carries the deep weight of the day. Faces are washed and scrutinized in mirrors. Dress clothes are retrieved, and shoes are laced up. In the heart of the kitchen, Estella's ashes rest upon the table, cradled within a new, polished wooden urn. The container, a testament to Arnell's craftsmanship, bears Estella's image on its front, her presence lingering in the room.

Outside, the weather mirrors the gravity of the occasion. Dark clouds gather, and the wind picks up, heralding the approach of a Nor'easter, one of the region's notorious storms. Gusts of wind rattle the window panes. Sofia consults the weather report on her phone and is greeted by a big red warning, declaring the imminent arrival of a dangerous storm.

Ricki appears and pulls on Sofia. "Is Tío Jack coming? Is he?"

"Oh, now he is your Uncle Jack?"

"Did you call him? Did you?"

"Yes, I called him, and he said he would come."

Ricki gets a big smile and runs off to tell Angelica.

Just minutes before the family heads out the door, Ana's phone lights up with a call. Ana doesn't recognize the incoming number but thinks it might be the church and picks it up. "Diga," she says, then adds, "Hello?"

"Is this Ana?" A man with a deep voice asks in English.

"Moment," Ana says and hands the phone to Sofia. "It might be the church."

Sofia grabs the phone quickly. "Yes, hello?"

"Hello," the man with a deep voice says. "My name is Lou Caprissi. I'm a member of the Gulfstream Health Club and got your number from Juan."

"Yes," Sofia responds curiously.

"I am calling because I am looking for some help to clean my house."

Sofia rolls her eyes. "Um, we are just on our way to church. Can you call back later?"

"I'm sorry," Lou says. "Bad timing?"

Ana pesters Sofia to find out who is on the phone. "Can you hold on one second?" Sofia asks.

"Sure."

Sofia places her hand over the phone's microphone and then tells her mother it is a man looking for cleaning services for his house. Ana, always desperate for work, especially now with the extra expenses of the funeral, doesn't want to lose the gig. " Who is he?" Ana asks.

" He says he is from the club and got the number from Juan." She then lifts the phone again. "What is your name, again?"

"Lou. Lou Caprissi."

Juan, who is now next to Ana, nods assuringly. Yes, he knows the man, and it is okay. Ana then nods affirmatively to Sofia, and Sofia speaks into the phone. "Okay, she can do that for you. When would you like to do this?"

"Next week would be best," Lou says, "but I am flexible."

Sofia discusses the options with her mother, and both parties agree to Saturday. Lou then asks, "Okay, so what is your address?"

Sofia hesitates for a moment. Something about the way he is asking does not sit right with her.

Lou continues. "I'm only asking because I understand I need to come by and pick her up. So I need the address for that."

Sofia goes against her instincts and gives Big Lou the address. "23 Cherry Tree Ave."

"Okay, great. And her name is Ana? Right?"

"Yes," Sofia responds.

"Are you Sofia, her daughter?"

"Yes," Sofia says, growing more suspicious.

"I'm also a friend of Jack from the club. He mentioned you guys to me and said you are outstanding."

"Oh, I see."

"Sofia," Lou says in a friendly manner, would you mind telling me your mom's last name?"

"Why do you need that?"

"It's just for my contacts on my phone. I've got a whole bunch of Anas in here. That's a very popular name with us Italians too. It will keep me from calling the wrong Ana. Know what I mean?"

Going against her better instincts, Sofia goes along with the request. "It's Rivera. Ana Rivera," she says impatiently.

"Rivera," Lou says, confirming the name. "Ana Rivera - that's a beautiful name. I like that. Is that your last name too?"

"Yes," Sofia says quickly. "But really. I'm sorry, we have to go now."

"Okay, sorry," Lou wraps up. "I'll see you very soon. Looking forward to it. And congratulations on your pregnancy."

"Okay, thanks. Bye," Sofia says suspiciously and hands the

phone back to her mother. "Okay, he's good for nine on Saturday morning. But how does he know I'm pregnant?"

Ana is perplexed by Sofia's statement. "What?"

"He said, "Congratulations on your pregnancy."

Ana decides she doesn't want to think about it anymore. "Juan or Mr. Jack probably told him. "Does my lipstick look okay?"

A local police cruiser slowly passes the Holy Family Church as Jack pulls into the parking lot with Helen. "This must be the place," he says.

"I'm glad we brought an umbrella," Helen says, looking at the dark skies.

"Yeah, not looking good."

At the front of the church, Jack and Helen step up to the parvis where the entire Rivera family warmly greets them. Ricki runs out and grabs Jack with a big smile on his face. Jack hugs him, then turns to the rest of the family. Juan simply offers a warm handshake, as do Arnell and Memo. "Hello, Mr. Jack," Memo says.

Ana greets Helen with a hug, as do Roberta and Sofia. Ana and Roberta then politely hug Jack, leaving Sofia to greet Jack last. Jack extends a hand to Sofia, thinking she may no longer be in the mood to hug him, but Sofia just moves forward, bypassing Jack's hand to give him a solid hug. Jack hugs her back with a warm smile. Ricki claps loudly with approval. "Again! Again!" He demands.

"Ricki, *cálmate*," Roberta says as she places a hand on his shoulder.

Ricki refuses to calm himself. "*¡De nuevo!* Again!"

Everyone senses Ricki is about to erupt volcanically. Roberta wisely doesn't try to stop him again. Instead, she turns to Sofia with a helpless look. Sofia gives in. "Okay," she says to Ricki. "You ready?"

Ricki jumps."¡Sí, Sí!"

Sofia turns to Jack. Jack smiles and opens his arms to a big long embrace. Ricki claps with joy, then turns and hugs Angelica. The action is strangely contagious, and the whole group starts giving each other hugs.

Watching all this inside their parked car, Robert Mathews and his wife Sandra are spellbound. "Well, if that isn't stranger than fiction, I don't know what is," Robert says.

"Is that the infamous Jack?" Sandra asks.

"That be the man, in living color."

"And is that Sofia he is hugging?"

"The one and only."

"I thought you said they were like fire and ice?"

"I think I need to reconsider my atheism. This is a miracle."

"Who is the older woman Jack is with? Is that his wife?"

"No, he's not married. I think she might be the one he met online."

"He's into online dating?"

"Yeah, I guess the ole boy's still got something going on."

"She's beautiful."

Inside the church, Father Vinny appears at the altar with his attendants and looks out to check the level of attendance. The pews are mostly empty except for the Rivera family and the out-of-place Anglos, who sit amongst them, all bunched up close to the altar. The wooden box holding Estella's ashes sits on a cloth-draped table in front of the altar.

Father Vinny reads from the Bible up at the main altar for a moment. He then proceeds to a small lectern off to the side, closer to the attendees. He looks at some notes already on the podium, then looks up at the crowd and speaks Spanish with a thick Italian accent.

"Estella Romero, a mother and grandmother devoted to her family, was one of the newer members of our church here, but she made herself well known in the short time she was with us. No sooner did we know her name than she was letting us know how we should change things around here to make it more like her church back home, which she claims was perfect in every way."

There are a few giggles from the pews. But Jack seems frustrated. He looks to Robert as if to say, "How long do we have to stand here without understanding a damn word of what is happening." Robert leans closer to Jack as if he is going to translate, but Father Vinny senses the problem and switches to English for a moment. "I'm explaining how Estella became such a well-known person at Holy Family." Jack nods appreciatively, but then Father Vinny switch es back to Spanish.

"One of my best memories of her came after Sunday mass during the summer. The bright sun was at my back, making my cassock almost see-through. Estella grabbed me by the arm and said, 'That was a nice service, but back home, priests would never wear their golf shorts under their robes.'"

Everyone has a good laugh at the story except Jack and Helen. Robert leans in and tells Jack, "Estella busted the father here for wearing golf shorts under his robe during a mass."

Jack smiles, then leans toward Robert. "You sure he isn't Irish?"

Robert leans in and whispers a running translation as Father Vinny continues. "Estella was very much a woman of tradition," And her love for her home country of El Salvador was never-ending. She always longed to return there to end her days, but that was not God's will. Estella ended her earthly life here in New Jersey, surrounded by her loving family. In those final days, she found peace knowing our only real home in this life is in the company of the people we love and those who love us. And that is only temporary because our real home is where Estella is now, with God almighty. Amen."

"Amen," the audience repeats.

"Now, one thing Estella's family desires is for her remains to be placed in the family cemetery in El Salvador. And that, I'm happy to announce, is what will happen. For that, we can thank Guillermo Jose Jesus Gonzales for a generous contribution allowing one person to carry Estella back to El Salvador."

There is a soft gasp among the family members as they all turn to Memo. Memo enjoys his little surprise with a smile.

"Guillermo doesn't think the ashes should just be sent through the mail," Father Vinny continues. "He wants them hand-carried there. I volunteered to be the one to escort the ashes to Santa Marta, but it is Guillermo's wish that Estella's granddaughter, Sofia, be the one to do that as soon as her status makes that possible."

Sofia and her entire family gasp again. Robert, who is intrigued by this new development, continues to whisper into Jack's ear. "They're taking Estella's ashes back to El Salvador." Jack reacts with a little smile, remembering he suggested it to Sofia outside the hospital.

Sofia turns and looks at Memo without smiling. "Memo, what did you do?"

"Sofia, I know how bad you feel. Like a loyal kiddy cat, you promise Estella you take her back to where she once belonged. I say to myself; I just want to help my future wife make good, like fresh French bread, on that promise."

"But how am I going to do that? You know I have no papers."

"Hey, it takes a little while, but I don't think Estella is in a big, mountain-size hurry."

Sofia looks around at the rest of her family. They all seem pleasantly surprised and thankful for the gesture. Sofia turns back to Memo as she suddenly gets an angry look. "Did you say 'future wife?'"

Memo shrugs sheepishly. "Well, you know..."

"No, I don't know."

Memo looks around and then takes a knee. "Sofia..."

Sofia grabs him by the arm and tries to pull him up. "No, don't do this here. Not now!"

Memo resists her tug. "No, I am doing this right here and right now. Sofia, love of my life, will you marry me?"

Sofia gets tears in her eyes. "Stop."

"I will not stop now or ever. You are everything to me. So please just say yes."

Sofia looks around at her family. She even notices Jack watching her. She can tell there is not a single person in the room who objects. Ana herself stares at her daughter, silently approving. Sofia then turns back to Memo as she wipes the tears away. She holds her hands out and cups his face. "You are crazy, but you are everything to me too. Yes."

"Yes?" Memo asks.

Yes! Yes, Yes! I will marry you. I will be your future wife."

Suddenly, the group erupts in applause as Memo rises to his feet and takes Sofia into his arms.

Father Vinny crosses himself.

Jack, Helen, Robert, and Sandra are the first to emerge from the church after the memorial. "Well, that has to be one of the most unique marriage proposals I've ever seen," Helen says with a quirky smile.

"So sweet," Sandra adds with her own smile.

"So young," Jack says with an edge in his voice.

Before they go much farther, Memo and Sofia call to them

from behind. "Jack, can you wait a minute? My mom has something she wants to give you," Sofia says.

Everyone stops. Helen turns to Sofia and goes to hug her. "I'm sorry for your loss, but that was so beautiful. And congratulations!" Sofia accepts her hug with a warm embrace. When she lets go, she looks at Jack to see his reaction. Jack stares back at her for a moment. In his head, he thinks she is still way too young to get married. But he can also see this is the happiest she has ever been. He just smiles. "It's good to see you so happy. Congratulations."

Sofia also gets a round of congratulations from Robert and Sandra as Helen hugs Memo. "She's a lucky girl. You're a real catch."

"How are my furnitures doing? Memo asks. Do you like them?"

"They're brilliant," Helen says. "Everyone who comes to the house talks about them. I may have a big lead for you. The CEO of New Jersey Transit called me about them. He might want to make a big order for his train stations."

Memo's enthusiasm can't be stopped. "Very good! Hey, Helen, if you want to be my sales guru, let me know. I earn you lots of commissions!"

"Memo, stop," Sofia says, placing a hand over Memo's mouth. "Sorry," she says to Jack and Helen. "He never stops."

"Well," Jack says. "Whatever he's doing, he seems to be doing it right."

Robert then extends a hand to Memo. "I've heard about this furniture you make. Sounds great. We will definitely check it out."

"Sure, sure," Memo says as Ana and the rest of the family enter the parking lot with Juan holding Estella's ashes. Ana has a small gift-wrapped package she extends to Jack while speaking to him in Spanish.

Sofia helps Jack get a handle on what is happening. "She

says this is just a small gift to thank you for all your help—especially with Estella."

"Not necessary," Jack says, extending his hand to accept the gift. "But thank you. And thank you for all your help with my house."

Sofia translates back to her mother. Ana smiles and speaks to the group in Spanish. Sofia Translates. "She wants to know if you want to come over for some tacos and apple pie?"

"And apple pie?" Jack asks with a look of surprise.

"You made Ricki a big lover of it," Sofia says with an ironic smile. "He won't eat unless he can also have some apple pie."

Robert, Sandra, Jack, and Helen look at each other, unsure what to do, so Jack decides. "Sure, that would be great. Everybody good with that?"

Ana seems pleased. Then, before they all part, she grabs Jack by the arm and thanks him for something.

Robert suddenly gets a strange look on his face and turns to Jack. "Did you recommend her services to somebody?"

"No," Jack says curiously. Not that I remember."

Robert turns to Ana and asks her who said they were recommended to her?

Ana looks to Sofia for the name of the man who called. Sofia thinks for a second. "Lou? I think his name was Lou."

Jack suddenly gets an alarmed look on his face. "Lou Caprissi?"

"Yes, that is the one," Sofia says.

Jack and Robert share a concerned look. "What exactly did he say?" Jack asks Sofia.

"He just said he wants help to clean his house. So he's coming to pick us up next Saturday."

Jack turns to Robert. "Do you know anything about this?"

"No," it's the first I have heard of it.

Jack looks around the parking lot to see if he can spot

anything suspicious. "What the hell is he up to?" he asks himself.

The whole group can see the concern on Jack's face. Sofia speaks up for everyone. "Is there a problem?"

"Yeah, I am afraid so," Jack says, thinking through the situation.

"What's wrong?" Sofia asks.

Jack ignores the question. "How did he get in touch with you?"

"He called on my mom's phone."

"How did he get her number?"

"Juan gave it to him at the club," Sofia answers.

Jack grows more serious. "Look, do me a favor. Do not get involved with this man in any way until I can figure out what is going on." Sofia translates and a look of fear overcomes the group. Jack senses the fear he has raised. "It could be nothing, but let me just make sure. Okay?"

The group agrees, but they remain confused and nervous. Sofia feels a sense of validation. "I knew there was something wrong with all the questions he was asking."

"What kind of questions?" Jack asks.

"He wanted to know our last names and things like that," Sofia replies.

"Did you give it to him?" Jack asks.

"Yes."

Jack turns to Robert and Sandra. "Okay, you guys just go with them to the reception. I'll meet you over there after I figure out what is going on."

"You need some help?" Robert asks.

"No, you guys just go over to their house. I'll call you soon as I can."

"Yeah, okay," Robert says.

"Thanks," Jack says. "Nice meeting you, Sandra."

"Good to meet you too, Jack," Sandra smiles.

Back in the car, Jack pulls out of the parking lot, thinking over the situation. "Helen, it's probably better I take you home. This could get ugly."

"It's that serious?"

"Yeah, I'm afraid it is."

"Jack," Helen says. "If you need to call this guy right now, go ahead. I won't be insulted."

Jack glances over at her. "It's not going to be pretty."

Helen raises her eyebrows with a bit of a grunt. "Trust me, I am no stranger to ugly conversations. It's fine. Just do what you need to do."

Jack briefly thinks about it, then pushes the phone button on his steering wheel. "Call Lou Caprissi."

"Hey, this is Lou," the recorded voice booms over the speakers in Jack's car. "Sorry I missed your call."

As soon as he hears the voicemail beep, Jack erupts in anger like a true Marine. "You better not be up to what I think you are up to. You call me, or I will come over to your goddamn house. Call me!"

Jack clicks off the call as he heads for Helen's house. Helen remains silent and asks no questions. Jack thinks for a second, then hits the phone button again. "Call the Gulfstream Health Club."

"Gulfstream, this is Nancy. Can I help you?"

"Hello, Nancy, this is Jack O'Mally. I'm a member of the club."

"Yes?"

"I'm the guy with the walking sticks."

"Oh yeah, sure. How are you?"

"I'm good. Listen, do me a favor. You know Lou Caprissi?"

"Not sure who you mean. Sorry."

"The big Italian guy who always comes in with his son Bobby—the kid with one eye that is a little off."

"Yes, I know Bobby. Sure."

"Can you tell me if they are in the club right now? I've got a bit of an emergency."

"Sure, what did you say their last name was? I'll look and see if they are checked in."

"Caprissi."

"Caprissi," Nancy says as she types the name into the club's computer system. "Yes, they both checked in about 30 minutes ago. Do you want me to page them?"

"No, that's okay. I'll just come over and talk to them in person. Thanks for your help."

"Sure thing. Anything else?"

"No, thanks. That will do it."

A few minutes later, Jack turns into Helen's driveway and approaches the front door. "Don't get out," Helen says as she opens the passenger door. "It sounds like you need to move."

"Sorry," Jack says.

"It's okay. I'm here if you need me. Call me?"

"Will do," Jack says, then meets her halfway in a small kiss.

"Be careful."

"I will."

As Jack drives off, Helen feels a raindrop on her face. She looks up to see a black wall of clouds on the horizon. A gust of wind chases her inside.

28

SHOWDOWN

The Gulfstream Club is not busy when Jack shows up. He passes the front desk without scanning his membership card.

"Hey, sorry," young Nancy says from behind the front desk. "Can you scan in for me, please?"

"Sorry," Jack says without looking at Nancy. "I don't have my card right now. I'll get you next time."

"But sir..."

Jack doesn't answer her and continues with angry determination. Nancy picks up the desk phone and calls her manager. "Mrs. Whitney, I just had a guy refuse to scan in."

Jack charges straight into the men's locker room, yanks open the steam room door, and steps in with all his clothes on. The steam generator is operating full blast when he enters, and the visibility is almost zero. "Lou, you in here?"

"Right here," Lou says from his usual perch, bare-chested with only a towel around his waist. Sitting just below him is Bobby.

Jack has to get right on top of him to see him. "What the hell are you up to, son of a bitch?"

"Whoa," Lou says with alarm. "What are you all steamed up about?"

"You called Ana and Sofia?"

"Yeah, what's it to you?"

"What for? Why were you calling them?"

"I'm looking for somebody to clean my house."

"Bullshit. What are you doing?"

"Jackie Boy, do me a favor. Go take off your clothes, grab a towel, and come back with a little more respect."

"Respect?" Jack laughs. He turns and leaves the room, goes to a shelf stacked high with white towels, and grabs one. He rolls it up, takes it over to the sink, and wets the thin end to make a whip, then barges back into the steam room. "One more time," he threatens Lou. "What the hell are you up to?"

"What the hell?" Bobby yells. He starts to stand up, but Jack quickly turns and snaps the towel at him. It cracks across his arm. "Ow! Shit!"

"Sit down!"

Bobby sits down, holding his arm. Jack turns back to Lou. He holds the towel up and stares at him, waiting.

"What are you, ten years old? This is freak'n ridiculous," Lou says.

Jack snaps the towel at Lou. It hits his stomach with a loud snap. Lou responds by lunging at Jack, slamming him against the tile wall. Jack uses the wall to push Lou off, then grabs him wrestling style and pulls him to the floor. Jack tries to pin Lou, but Bobby suddenly grabs him in a bear hug from the back and picks him up. Jack screams in pain. "My back! My back!" Bobby refuses to let go as Jack wriggles in pain.

"Let him go," Lou says from the floor confidently. Bobby lets go and Jack falls onto the lowest bench in the room. He can't do much else other than moan with agony.

Bobby helps Lou up off the floor. Lou gets a mean look on his face and turns to Jack. "Turns out your friends over at 23

Cherry Tree Avenue have a deportation order hanging over their heads. They're fugitives."

"What the hell have you done?" Jack asks as the pain in his back subsides.

"I did what you should have done a long time ago. I turned over their information to our pal Tony at ICE. And thanks to my information, he found them in the system."

"You goddamn idiot," Jack growls. "You have no clue what you are doing."

"Oh, like you do?" Lou laughs. "You let that little bitch get under your skin. Just admit it."

"Go to hell!" Jack yells.

"Tony already turned their names and address over to the enforcement guys."

"What are they going to do?"

"What do you think they are going to do? They'll pick them up and put them on a bus back to Tacoville!"

Jack slowly shakes his head. His anger overcomes his pain, and he lunges at Lou. But just as they hit the floor, the door swings open, and three giant-size trainers dressed in club uniforms come in.

"Hey, hey! Break it up!"

It takes some effort, but eventually, the trainers separate the combatants. Jack and Lou are restrained by the trainers but still face each other. Lou just shakes his head. "All you Micks are the same. Two French fries short of a happy meal."

Jack rushes home and finds the card given to him by Tony. He calls Tony in a rush and gets lucky. Tony picks up. "Hey, this is Jack O'Mally. I was just calling to see what is going on with that information Lou gave you?"

"Yeah, I already turned it over to ERO."

"Is there any way you can rescind it?"

"Not really. Why?"

Jack tries to think quickly, "Uh, there are some complications."

"Like what?"

Jack doesn't know what to say. "There was a death in the family, and there may be some complications with a pregnancy. You don't deport people needing medical attention, do you?"

"Jack, the process is out of my hands now. But trust me—they will be given every consideration made possible under the policies I helped create. They are generous and fair policies. It's better you just trust the system at this point."

"God damn," Jack says. "That's it?"

"Jack, it's the law. We have a country, and this country has immigration laws that must be followed—otherwise, we would just have chaos."

"Yeah, but I can vouch for these people. They're good people!"

"I know, but the truth is they have broken the law. Just being good doesn't mean you are above the law."

"Tony, I need a favor here."

"I'm sorry, Jack. Just let the process work, and whatever you do, don't interfere. You'll only get yourself in trouble and hurt their chances of a favorable judgment."

"What does that mean, favorable judgment?"

"Their case will be reviewed before the actual deportation takes place. So if you want to help, do it then, not now. It's the only way."

"How do I do that?"

"As soon as they are taken into custody, I will get the case number and a phone number for you to call. You can ask to present information supporting them at that point."

Jack realizes Tony is not going to budge. "So, is there any way to find out when your guys are going to do this?"

"A solid lead like this will most likely be acted on immediately. They don't want to wait and lose them to a tip-off."

"You sure?"

"ERO works 24/7, so yeah," Tony says with pride. "It's probably in the process now."

"God damn," Jack says sadly.

"Hey Jack, I gotta say, Lou is right. This is a hell of an idea you came up with. I think it's going to turn into something, so thanks for that. But one more time, don't interfere. You with me?"

"I understand, "Jack says in defeat.

"I've got your number here on my phone. I will call you as soon as I have anything."

With that, Tony hangs up, and Jack is left standing in the middle of his man cave with a stunned look. He walks over to the window and looks out over the backyard as the first hard rain of the Nor'easter starts to fall. Up in the sky, some Canada geese fly over, honking as if they are mocking Jack. He turns, picks up his phone again, and calls Robert.

"Well, I think the best thing to do is get in touch with an immigration lawyer," Robert says over the phone

"How do we do that?" Jack asks.

"Sandra has some pretty good contacts in that area. I'll ask her. When is this going to happen?"

"I think it is going down now," Jack says. "That's the problem."

"Holy crap, really? You want me to tell them?"

"I was told not to interfere."

"Who told you not to interfere?"

"Tony, the guy from the ICE office."

"Holy crap. This is serious."

Jack turns back to the window without responding. The sky is darker. The wind is more potent. Jack thinks through his options.

"Jack, you still there?"

"Yeah," Jack says.

"What do you want to do?"

Jack seems to make up his mind. "Get Sandra going on that immigration lawyer. I'll call you back in a few minutes."

"Got it."

As soon as they hang up, Jack calls Helen.

"Everything alright?" She asks.

"Far from it. I don't want to drag you into this, but I need a favor."

29

TACOS AND APPLE PIE

Dark unmarked government cars arrive at the Rivera house at about 6:30 in the evening as the storm picks up momentum. Usually, ERO agents like to make their visits early in the morning, but in this case, it was decided to go during the storm in hopes that it would keep the family in their home.

The six agents assigned to the mission don't approach with screeching tires and guns drawn. They just pull up quietly in front of the house, get out of their vehicles, and calmly walk toward the front door. Two are dressed like plain clothes detectives, while the other four are openly armed and wearing bulletproof vests with "Police" inscribed on the front and back.

As the agents quietly approach the house, they hear music inside. Happy grins pass from one agent to the next. The two in plain clothes take a position at the front door. The two in tactical gear step to the side, out of sight from the front door. The other two quietly move to opposite sides of the house and head toward the back.

"You got the pictures?" One of the plainclothes asks the other.

"Yeah, right here," The second one says, pulling out a small vinyl sleeve with a batch of headshots.

The chief objective of an ERO operation is to gain entry to the house. To do it without asking permission, they need a signed warrant from a judge. But on most occasions, they don't have time or can't find a sympathetic judge, so they use "alternative" methods to gain entry. One popular technique is to show up at the front door and tell the occupants they are looking for someone who has been breaking into local homes. "Would you mind if we step in to show you a few pictures of suspects to see if you recognize anyone?" Once inside, they can start looking around and asking the occupants to identify themselves. If the agents come up with a name on their list, arrests can be made.

One officer heading toward the back of the house passes a window. The music is louder, and he can hear voices but can't see inside. He grabs the microphone on his lapel and whispers into it. "Sounds like the party is toward the back of the house."

"Okay, roger that," one of the agents at the front door responds. "Let me know when you are in position at the back."

Once everyone is in position, the lead agent knocks loudly on the front door. The officers wait a few seconds, then knock again. When no one responds, one of the men radios to the back. "No answer in the front. Be ready for a back door departure."

The two officers at the back step out from their hiding place and approach the back door. When they do, they find the back door standing wide open. They alert the agents in front, then proceed slowly toward the door. "Police," the lead agent says as he knocks on the door frame. "*¿Alguien en casa?* Anybody home?" They listen for a response but get nothing, even though they can still hear voices. They try again as some agents from the front of the house arrive. "Police," the agent shouts. When there is no response, he looks toward his superior, who nods to proceed.

Inside, the agents slowly find the room where the music is coming from, but the only people they find there are Father Vinny and a small mix of white and Hispanic people. Sofia and the rest of the Rivera family are not present. Father Vinny holds up his hands to show them he is not a threat. The other people in the room follow suit. "We are not armed," Father Vinny says with as much authority as he can muster.

"Who are you?" one of the plainclothes officers asks.

"I'm Father Giovanni Fontana, pastor of Holy Family Church. The rest of us are church staff and friends of the deceased."

The ICE team glances at each other, feeling the onset of failure. "Deceased? Who died?" The lead agent asks.

"Estella Romero, an elderly woman who lived here. We held a memorial for her earlier today."

"Anybody with the last name Rivera here?"

"I don't believe so," Father Vinny says with an innocent look.

With another exchange of uneasy glances, the ICE agents lower their weapons. The lead officer, now looking slightly embarrassed, tries one last time. "Would you be willing to show us some identification?"

"I'm sorry," Father Vinny says, with calm authority. "Are you from the Red Bank Police?"

"We're from Homeland Security."

"ICE?"

"Yes."

Father Vinny doesn't blink. "Do you have a signed warrant from a judge to enter this house?"

"No, but the back door was open."

"That is true," Father Vinny responds. "But I don't believe

that gives you the right to come in here without the occupants' consent."

"Okay," The lead officer responds. "Understood. We just wanted to make sure everyone was safe. It's unusual to see a back door open in this kind of neighborhood."

Father Vinny shows a hint of a smile. "Well, as you can see, we are all perfectly okay. Is there anything else?"

One of the other agents looks around the room. "Any of you know Sofia Rivera? We just have a couple of questions. No big deal."

No one raises a hand. Father Vinny just smiles. "Sorry, nobody here by that name."

"Okay, sorry to bother you, folks," the lead officer says, trying not to show his disappointment and frustration. He turns to his team and motions them all out of the house. "Here, take my card. If you see Sofia or her family, ask them to call me. I can help."

Father Vinny takes the card. "Why don't you go out through the front? It'll be easier for you."

Once outside, the ICE team show their disappointment. "God damn Tony," one of the officers curses as they head back to the cars. "He sent us out here on a wild goose chase."

"Somebody tipped them off," another says with anger in his voice.

"No shit, Sherlock."

～

On the other side of the river, bright flashes of lightning fill the night sky over Jack's house. In his driveway, Helen's big Range Rover SUV is parked just behind Jack's Cadillac. Robert and Sandra's car and Arnell's old SUV are on the street. Inside the kitchen, Ana holds the wooden urn with Estella's ashes in her arms as she stands with Sofia, Memo, and the entire Rivera family on one side of the center island. On the other side are Jack, Helen, Robert, and Sandra. Between them are trays of tacos and pupusas that were taken when they all rushed out of the Rivera home.

Everyone looks confused and nervous. Jack is apprehensive but resolute in his decision to rescue the family and bring them to his house. Finally, after a few awkward moments of silence, he steps forward to speak. "Sofia, can you translate for me?"

Sofia nods her head but doesn't smile. She is very anxious about what is going on.

"I'm sorry to ruin this important day for you, but as I said at the house, we just learned the authorities were headed to your home to enforce a deportation order for you guys. And we thought it best to get you out of there until we can get a better handle on things."

As Sofia translates, fear quickly grips the rest of the family. Ana can't help but think what it would be like, after all they have struggled for, to end up back on the streets of San Salvador with no home to go to. Juan wonders what he would do. He has already been granted asylum and has a work permit, but would he let Ana be sent back without going with her? Memo has the same problem, only his situation is even more complicated with the baby. He, too, has a work permit, but he wouldn't be permitted to remain with Sofia if she were apprehended. He wouldn't even be allowed to accompany her back to El Salvador. He would have to go there and find her. Arnell and Roberta both know their entire family is under a deportation order. But how does that work with kids who have special needs like Ricki?

"How do you know all this?" Sofia asks Jack.

Jack studies the room for a moment, glances over at Robert, then turns back to the group. "Because it is partly my fault."

Sofia translates, but it only adds to the fear and confusion.

Robert then turns to Jack and asks, "Do you want me to help you explain?"

"No, I want to tell them myself," Jack says, trying to man up. But just before he can speak, Sandra's phone lights up with an incoming call. "It's the lawyer," Sandra tells her husband. "I'll take it in the other room."

Once Sandra is gone, Jack takes a deep breath. "About a year ago, I had this idea to set up a 'Neighborhood Watch' program to report illegal aliens."

Sofia tries to translate, but it doesn't work. "What is a Neighborhood Watch?"

"It's like a police force," Jack says.

Sofia turns to the group. *"Es como la policía,"*

The shock and horror quickly register across the Rivera family. *"¿Policía? ¿Jack es policía?"* Ana asks.

"My mom wants to know if you are a policeman."

"No, I'm not a policeman," Jack says with growing frustration.

Robert can't hold himself back any longer. " Jack is not a policeman or a bad guy," he says in Spanish. "He is a good guy."

"What are you telling them?" Jack asks.

"Hold on a sec," Robert says with a hand lifted. "Let me explain something to you," Robert continues in his limited Spanish. "Did you know Jack's grandfather built this house? Do you know Jack was born in this house? This home means everything to him, but there is a For Sale sign outside. Did you happen to see it when you came in? Do you know why it is there? It is there because Jack wouldn't give your names to ICE."

The family looks at each other, even more confused. "We don't understand," Sofia says.

"Look, Jack needs money if he wants to stay in his home. A man was going to pay Jack a lot of money to tell ICE who you are and where you live. But Jack said no. He'd rather lose his family home than do that to you."

"Oh wow," Memo says with a surprised look. "But why did Jack tell us he was going to start a group to report illegals?"

"Once upon a time, he had an idea to do that," Robert says authoritatively, but he changed his mind. I think you guys showed him it was a bad idea."

"Then who is the man who called us, the man called Lou?" Sofia asks.

"He was the guy who was going to give Jack the money. When Jack said no, Lou had to call you to get your names and address."

"Ah," Sofia nods as she turns back to the family and explains.

Ana nods. She understands. But understanding and believing are two different things.

"Please don't be frightened," Robert says. You have nothing to fear from Jack. "He is not here to hurt you. He is here to help you."

The Rivera family waits to see if Robert will say anything else, but Robert ends it there. The only one who says anything is Jack. "Would somebody tell me what the hell is going on?"

Memo steps up just a bit. "Mr. Jack, he is saying you have made a big defense of us." What he said was, you choose to sell your house instead of telling ICE about us."

Jack shoots a glance at Robert, then back at Sofia. "Well, it's a little more complicated than that."

"But that is basically it," Robert says. "There is a For Sale sign out there. You did that instead of giving them up. I was there. I saw it."

"Okay, okay. I guess you could see it that way," Jack says, giving in to Robert's version of the story.

Once again, an awkward silence descends upon the room. The Rivera family turn to each other, looking for someone to lead the way, but no one seems to have a clue what to do. Sofia looks at her mother, but Ana is as helpless as the rest. Sofia then turns to Memo. He just smiles. She then slowly turns to Jack. Jack stares at her apprehensively. After a long, decisive moment, Sofia finally makes up her mind. A soft but sincere smile comes to her face. "Thank you, Jack. *Gracias.*"

Upon hearing and seeing this, the rest of the family speaks in a chorus of thanks in both English and Spanish. *"¡Sí, Gracias!"* "Thank you!" *"Gracias, gracias, gracias!"*

Sandra comes back into the room, holding her phone up. "I've got the lawyer on speaker. This is Alberto Reis," Sandra says, "an immigration lawyer I work with occasionally."

"Hola, mucho gusto," Alberto says from the phone speaker. The group responds meekly and listens intently. Then, Alberto gets right to the point. He asks to know why they have a deportation order. Did they not go to their asylum hearing?

"No, we missed it," Arnell responds.

"Why did you not go?" Alberto asks.

" No, we went," Arnell replies. "But when we got there, they said we missed it."

"Did you go on the correct date?" Alberto asks. "The one that was on your discharge paperwork?"

Arnell nods. "Yes, the date on the paper and the hour. But they changed it."

"They changed it for earlier or later?"

"Earlier. Like a week earlier."

"Did they notify you?"

Arnell checks around the room to see if anyone knows anything about a notice. When it is clear they don't, he turns back to the phone in Sandra's hand. "No."

Alberto thinks for a moment. "Do you still have the paperwork with the original date on it?"

"Yes."

"Okay," Roberto says. "This is something that they like to

do. Don't ask me why. It messes up a lot of people. But here is the deal. If I can get that paperwork to a judge, I could probably get the case reopened."

Nobody is quite sure what this means. "Will that cancel the deportation order?" Sandra asks.

"Yes, once the case is reopened, the deportation order will be halted pending the outcome of the new hearing."

Sofia quickly translates the good news to the group. A collective sigh of relief fills the room. "Does that mean we can go home?" Sofia asks.

"I wouldn't do that until I get the case reopened."

Sofia frowns. "How long will that take?"

"Once I get the paperwork from you, a couple of days, maybe a week. In the meantime, stay where you are. That order is still in effect."

As the information gets translated, all eyes turn toward Jack to see how he will respond. Jack holds back his decision for a moment. He looks around the room at the strange collection of people. It makes him think about a recipe that a big Guyanese cook used to serve at the Marine base in Florida. She called it "mix-up-rice" because it included just about everything in the kitchen with a big batch of rice. Jack always liked the name of that dish. He liked using it to describe military shipments filled with odd collections of items. Instead of calling it "consolidated cargo," he would just say, "That one is mix-up-rice." After a glance at Helen, Jack turns to the group. "Looks like my house is going to be 'mix-up-rice' for a few days." When nobody seems to get his joke, he adds, *"Mi casa, su casa."*

The group smiles with relief until Jack holds up a finger. "I only have one request. Can we please do our best to speak English?"

Memo giggles and turns to translate, but just as he does this, a sudden massive gust of wind from outside is followed by a loud crack and a house-shaking crash. The lights sputter and then go out.

"*Aiyeeeeee,*" comes the collective shock of losing light.

"What happened?" Helen asks fearfully.

"Damn it," Jack snarls as he reaches for some small flashlights in a drawer. "I think a tree hit the house." He hands the first flashlight to Sofia, then another to Memo. He then takes a third and heads for the back door.

Outside, the wind howls like a hurricane through the trees. "We're lucky the leaves have already dropped," Jack yells to Arnell, Juan, and Memo as they follow him to the side of the house. "These trees can't handle this kind of wind when they have leaves. We would have lost more!"

When they arrive at the corner of the house, they find a large spruce has fallen across the main electrical connection and taken out a corner of the roof. The resulting sparks from the severed cable have caused a fire under the awning and it looks like it is gaining traction.

"Oh shit!!" Jack yells. "Fire!"

Memo shines his flashlight into the flames. "Oh no!"

"*¡Fuego!*" Arnell declares.

Jack turns to Memo desperately. "Quick. In the pottery studio over there! There is a fire extinguisher on the floor by the door! Get it!"

Memo runs off to the pottery studio, leaving Jack and Arnell to watch helplessly as the fire grows. Arnell grabs some snow off the ground and throws it at the flames, but it does little to slow things down.

Memo returns with the fire extinguisher and hands it to Jack, who quickly pulls out the safety pin, points the hose at the fire, and pushes down on the handle. A cloud of white extinguishing agent fills the air but it doesn't rise high enough to reach the fire. "We're too low," Jack yells looking around in desperation.

Memo grasps for ideas. "Do you have a *escalera*—how you say? Ladder?"

"Yeah," Jack yells over the howl of the wind. "But it's all the way around the front, in the garage. We don't have time. This wind is fanning the flames."

"Here, give to me!" Memo yells. Jack hands him the red canister, and Memo tries to get the nozzle up closer to the fire, but they are still too low.

Finally, Arnell reaches out for the bottle. He hands it back to Jack and then shouts at Memo to help lift Jack.

Memo quickly gets the idea and stoops to grab Jack just below the knees. Arnell does the same thing, and within seconds they have Jack hoisted up. Once again, Jack presses the handle on the extinguisher. This time, the retardant reaches the flames, and the fire is slowly extinguished. Jack empties the bottle to make sure the fire is completely out. Once he is done, Memo and Arnell lower him back to the ground.

"Whoa," Jack sighs with relief. "That was a close one."

"*Mierda* man. That was scary as anything," Memo agrees.

The men all stare at each other for a moment, and then Jack extends a hand to Arnell. "Thank you. Good idea. *Gracias.*

Arnell nods, accepting Jack's gratitude.

Inside the kitchen, Helen and Roberta have found some candles, which have lit the room enough for a small dinner party. "How was it?" she asks Jack as the men come back into the kitchen.

"Bad," Jack replies. "The tree hit the electrical line and started a fire."

"Oh my god," Helen replies with a look of fear. "Were you able to put it out?"

"It's out, but that whole section of the roof is destroyed. It looks like we will be off the grid for a while. We'll fire up the generator when it stops raining."

"We could go to my house if you want?"

Jack considers it for a moment and then decides against it. "We'll be alright here for the night. There's no sense going out in this again."

"Okay," Helen says. "But it is there if you change your mind."

"You want to go home?" Jack asks.

"Not really."

"You sure?"

"Sure."

"*Tío* Jack," Ricki says. "*Tío* Jack, I want apple pie."

The group giggles a bit.

"*Tío*, what does that mean?" Jack asks the group.

"He's calling you uncle," Sofia says.

The group giggles a bit more. Jack lets it go. "Yeah, sure, 'Tío Jack' has some apple pie." He turns, opens the door to the fridge, and removes a silver tin. As soon as he places it on the island, Ricki grabs a piece and starts putting it on top of a chicken taco.

"Ricki, no!" Roberta commands. But Ricki doesn't listen to her. Instead, he takes the taco topped with apple pie and stuffs a big bite in his mouth. He chews it and gets a big smile on his face. He likes the way it tastes. "Oh well," Roberta says with a giggle. "It all goes to the same place anyway."

"I try it," Memo says. He makes himself a taco pie combo and is surprised by how good it is. "Wow! It's very good! Ricki has an excellent idea! You guys, make sure you taste this!"

Slowly, the others get into the groove and join the taco and apple pie sampling. Even Robert and Sandra join in. Finally, laughter starts to fill the room. Sofia strikes up some music from her phone, and the party is on.

Jack and Helen stand by the sink, watching the action. Jack suddenly becomes serious. "Well, I guess this means I'll have to take the house back off the market."

"Really?" Helen asks.

"Yeah," Jack says with a sigh. "Who wants a home with a tree going through the roof?"

Helen gets his message. "What are you going to do?"

"I don't know—call the insurance agent to see if I am covered."

"Mia will not be happy about this one."

"Guess not."

"Look, if you need some help in the meantime—"

Jack lifts a hand to stop Helen. "Ep!"

"Sorry, I just—"

"This old home has been through some real ups and downs, but somehow, we always come through. Somehow, I think it is going to be alright."

Helen smiles and nods as Sofia shows up with two plates of food. "You are the only ones who haven't tried it."

Helen accepts a plate, but Jack hesitates as he scrutinizes the food on the plate. "Tacos and apple pie?"

"Yeah, tacos and apple pie," Sofia says.

Jack gives in and takes the plate. He scoops up the taco and cautiously prepares to take a bite. "Wait," Helen laughs as she reaches for her phone. "I want to get a picture." She quickly gets the device into photo mode and points it toward Jack. "Okay, go ahead." Jack places the food concoction in his mouth and lets his taste buds take over. By the second chew, his eyes widen a bit, and a grin grows on his face. Helen snaps a photo as everyone laughs.

30

INDEPENDENCE DAY

Nearly six months later, on a glorious, sunny 4th of July, Jack's daughter, Beth, makes a surprising appearance at her father's house. Driving a shiny mid-size rental car, she arrives with her husband, PuzzleMe, and their son, Keiren. Beth looks very much like her pictures in Jack's man cave. In-person, however, she has an eye-catching radiance about her, with long brown hair and an Irish twinkle in her eye. But at the same time, her hard times are on display with evidence of small wrinkles around her eyes. By contrast, PuzzleMe is tall and lean but clearly a sensitive soul and one hundred percent an artist, complete with bold jewelry, braids, and baggy clothes. On the one hand, he can look a bit hard-edged, but on the other, he has a warm, infectious smile that can fill any arena with good vibes.

With a nervous look, Beth removes an envelope from her purse containing a check for fifty thousand dollars made out to Jack. She then heads to the front door with her family, prepared to inform Jack that they finished PuzzleMe's album, which was picked up by a prominent New York hip-hop label. They had to come to New York to sign the contracts, so she thought, why not? Why not pay the old man his money in person and have the satisfaction of seeing his face when she tells him, "Thanks for having so little faith in us." But as they near the front door, they hear the sounds of a lively party drifting from the backyard. The front door is wide open, so they don't knock. They just walk in. The first people they encounter are Ricki and Angelica, playing video games on a big TV.

"Is my dad here?" Beth asks with a confused look on her face.

"Huh?" Ricki replies.

Beth turns to PuzzleMe with a shocked look on her face. "Oh, my god. He must have moved out." She then turns back to Ricki and Angelica. "I'm so sorry. My father, Jack, used to live here. I didn't know he had moved. The door was open and...."

"Tío Jack?" Ricki asks.

"Jack! Yes! Do you know him?"

Before Ricki or Angelica can answer, Roberta rushes into the room. "What are you doing? Let's go! The ceremony is starting!"

Ricki and Angelica put down their game controllers and start for the back door with Roberta, but Angelica hesitates and motions to Beth. "He is in the back," she says sweetly. "I will show you."

As Beth and PuzzleMe soon discover, the backyard is filled with a "mix-up rice" group of people attending a wedding ceremony for Sofia and Memo. Not only is the entire Rivera family there, but also Robert Mathews and his wife, Jack's Neighborhood Watch buddies, Vlad the Russian, Fitzy the Financial advisor, Mia, Father Vinny, Dr. Castro, Helen's niece and her wife, and of course Helen, who sits right next to the man himself, "Tío Jack."

"Dad?" Beth asks with a perplexed look as the wedding processional begins.

Jack is shocked and surprised to see Beth but doesn't want to disturb the ceremony. He motions for her and PuzzleMe to sit next to him. He then turns to Helen and whispers, "My daughter Beth and her family." Helen smiles at Beth to say hello and then turns to watch Sofia being led down the aisle in a radiant white dress by both Arnell and Juan.

"What is going on here?" Beth whispers to her father.

"Long story. What are you doing here?"

"We sold the record. We stopped by to drop off a check for you."

"You didn't want to just drop it in the mail?" Jack asks.

"No, I wanted to hand it to you personally."

Jack frowns. "Can you wait until after the ceremony to get your revenge?"

"Guess we will have to."

Jack then leans closer to Beth. "Stay for the reception. They brought in a Salvadoran band from Virginia."

Beth stares at her father to see if he is being sarcastic, but he has a strange, happy smile that she has never seen before. "Okay," she says cautiously.

As the sun begins its descent, casting long shadows across the lawn, the bride and groom turn to each other with gleaming smiles. Memo holds their baby boy "Destino" in his arms, looking as proud as any young father can be. As their vows are exchanged, the air hums with unspoken emotion.

"I do," Sofia says with a soft, confident happiness in her voice.

"I do bigger than Mountain Everest," Memo says in his own unique way.

Everyone giggles, then erupts in applause when the young couple kiss for the first time in the union of marriage.

∾

Following the ceremony, laughter and the clinking of glasses fill the air as guests mingle, a merry soundtrack to the celebration. As promised, a Salvadoran band from Virginia adds their unique sound to the festivities, and the opening rounds of a 4th of July fireworks show from the marina below begin to fill the night sky. Beth isn't sure she can trust what is going on at her old family house, but Jack assures her it is all real. "I finally found the right strategy to save the place," he says.

"Yeah, and what's that?" Beth asks.

"You're looking at it," Jack says, pointing to all the hubbub.

"I don't get it," Beth replies suspiciously.

Jack returns her doubtful look with a wise grin. He knows there is no way he can explain everything. There is no way to let her know how this Salvadoran family came to *his* rescue in the end. There is no way to tell her how Ana and Sofia made the place look fresh again. Or how Arnell, Juan, and Memo fixed his roof for free even after he got a big fat check from the insurance company for the storm damage. Nor could he explain how it came to be that Sofia and Memo now live in the guest house and actually pay rent on it, as well as the pottery shop, which Memo uses as his bench production facility. There is no point going into all that or how Sofia became an influencer on YouTube as the "Bird Nerd" after the aviary was finally finished. Yes, the Rivera family has an ongoing struggle to be granted asylum, but things are looking better for everyone.

"Beth girl, " Jack finally says. "You were right—our unity is our diversity. I gave up on Blue Bayou."

"Wow," Beth says with a slightly shocked look on her face. "I can't believe I am hearing this from you."

Helen, standing next to Jack, can't help herself. She leans in toward Beth. "I know, isn't it great?"

Beth still looks a little perplexed. "I think it is going to take me some time to absorb all this. But, oh, Dad, this is my husband, PuzzleMe, who I don't think you have ever met."

Jack looks across Beth to see PuzzleMe. PuzzleMe extends a hand to Jack with a big smile. Jack looks over at the hip-hop artist with a blank look but then smiles, accepting the handshake. "It's been a long time coming, but I'm glad we finally get to meet."

"For sure, for sure. Straight up." PuzzleMe responds with a look of relief.

Beth then takes baby Keiren from PuzzleMe and presents him to Jack. "And this is your grandson, Dad. This is Keiren."

Jack looks down, holding back any hint that his heart has quickly filled with sparks of joy and pride. But as the dark-haired little guy looks back at him with a happy face, Jack can't help but smile at the connection he feels. "Well, look at you," Jack says, poking Keiren softly. "You look like trouble," he jokes.

Just as Keiren giggles at Jack, a thunderous clap of multi-phase fireworks from the Marina fills the night sky with a rainbow of colors. It is a majestic and awe-inspiring sight of white, red, and blue sparkles accompanied by a symphony of loud, piercing whistles that add an extra layer of excitement to the mesmerizing display.

"Look, Destino," Memo cries as he holds his baby son up in the air. "Fireworks. Beautiful."

After another round of explosions in the sky, Beth looks around the scene and then turns back to her dad. "J.J. would have loved to see this."

Jack, surprised by the statement, turns to Beth. "You think so?"

"I know so," she says.

Jack cautiously reaches out to put his arm around his daughter. She accepts it and responds guardedly by putting her own hand on her dad's shoulder.

Sofia, standing in front of Jack next to her husband and child, turns back and sees Jack arm in arm with his daughter.

She smiles at Jack, and Jack smiles back at her. For the moment, everything is great.

END

ACKNOWLEDGMENTS

I'm almost embarrassed to say I don't have too many thank you's for this book. From the beginning, it was just a tale that kept building in my head, and one day, I just started parking by the bay and writing in the passenger seat of my car for an hour or two in the mornings. I never really discussed the book with anyone because I wasn't sure I could describe it- or pull it off. So, in terms of writing, I want to thank the Seastreak Ferry of Highlands, New Jersey, for its excellent free parking lot by the water and all the people who park there at night and drink. The little liquor bottles they tossed out allowed me a clean-up activity when I was blocked. I also want to thank my Apple Macbook Air for its portability and long battery life. This also goes for my phone carrier, allowing me a good hotspot to stay connected to Google Docs. Docs was brilliant and never let me down. Some days, I was actually writing on my phone, and the ability to just jump into the doc from different devices was thrilling. I also want to thank the township of Atlantic High-lands for being such an interesting place.

When it comes to people, I really want to thank, first and foremost, the people of Central America who were so kind to me when I lived there as a teenager and worked there as an adult. I also want to thank all the Salvadorans who live near me and allowed me to peek into their lives and culture. One huge thanks also goes out to Steven Dudley for his book MS-13, which was a major motivator for me. Also, to Homer for the

Odyssey. For unknown reasons, some of his story strategies got into my book. Another shout-out goes to Thomas Anthony Musca for his entrepreneurial spirit and cement furniture designs that were a source of inspiration.

Once there was a draft to read, my two sisters, Suzanne and Katherine, bravely took on the role of alpha readers and navigated their way through an indecipherable mosh pit of words. Their dedication and truthfulness opened the path to the final version of this book. Another thanks goes out to Debbie Diaz who actually took the time to read the manuscript twice and provided good cultural sensitivity guidance. And a big shout-out goes to my good friends Brant Reiter and Jason Orans who also took an early look and provided invaluable feedback.

After another draft, I moved on to beta readers. Here, I want to thank Fiverr for setting up a fast and easy way to get your book read without leaning on your busy friends and family. At Fiverr, I want to thank Dannie Ray for offering excellent insights and encouragement. I also want to thank Brian Wallace for his hard work as a beta reader and line editor. For proofing the Spanish, special thanks go out to Debora Arditi and Ana Sofia Lara Martínez for making it real.

AND FINALLY, a big hug to the love of my life, my lovely wife Caroline, who put up with all my hours sequestered away in self-imposed solitary confinement. I'm a lucky, lucky guy. Te amo!

ABOUT THE AUTHOR

This English/German American boy had some crazy parents who retired early and moved to Central America with their teenage son (me!). It was Costa Rica, to be exact. My father loved the whole region, and we traveled extensively throughout the area, from Guatemala to Panama. This is where I went to school, where I lost my virginity, smoked a lot of pot, and learned to ride a horse, thanks to a local farmer. My friends were a mix of kids from all over the world and many locals. It was a beautiful part of my life, but it came to a screeching halt when I graduated from High School and moved back to the States to go to college.

The summer of my high school graduation, my parents and I packed up our little Toyota Corona with the Costa Rican plates and drove up the Pan American highway back to the motherland. But no sooner did we enter Texas than something odd happened to me. What I thought would look familiar looked foreign and strange. All the big cars and trucks that surrounded us on the interstate highway intimidated me and made me feel small and poor. It was very disorienting and alienating like I was a stranger in my own country. I could not define it, nor did I talk about it. Only later did I learn that I was stricken by something called "reverse culture shock."

According to many psychologists, reverse culture shock can occur when a person returns to their home culture after living in a foreign country for an extended period of time. It can be a difficult and confusing experience, and it made my early days of college life rather strange. I didn't join the swim team or pledge to a fraternity. Instead, I started hanging out with a group of Cuban refugees and thought a lot about the culture and people I left behind.

I don't think I ever fully recovered from my reverse culture shock, but I did manage to get a BA in English and an MFA from the School of Theater, Film, and Television at UCLA. During my graduate studies, I started working as a news cameraman for CBS in Nicaragua and El Salvador during the Iran/Contra days. I also produced and directed a feature documentary (Saviors of the Forest) in Ecuador with my good friends Terry Schwartz and Todd Darling. It was nominated for a Grand Jury Award at the Sundance Film Festival. In addition to this, I researched, wrote, and packaged a real-life drama in the rain forests of Brazil with partners Marcheline Bertrand, Javier Moro, and Caito Martins. The resulting script was sold to Ridley Scott and developed into a major motion picture project, but unfortunately it never made it in front of the cameras.

After graduating from UCLA, I met my soul mate, Caroline, who captured my heart. On a trip to Tahiti, we got engaged, then came home and persuaded 40 friends and family to go back to Tahiti with us for a week-long wedding party. Following that adventure, we moved to NYC, where I was hired by the New York Times to work in their documentary division, 212 Films. After that, I became a freelance video journalist for ABC News, CNN, Discovery Channel, and National Geographic Television. For National Geographic, I specialized in assignments in South America, specifically the Amazon region of Brazil. I also started a YouTube channel called BillsChannel, which started out as a wildlife channel and peaked at 2.6 million subscribers. After moving back to California for 6 years and producing independent documentaries, I returned to the

East Coast again with Caroline. We took up residence in the New Jersey Township of Atlantic Highlands just South of New York City. It was in Atlantic Highlands that I started to see the things that inspired me to write Great Again. This is my first novel.